CRATCH

Mike Gutowski

Cratch is a work of fiction. Names, characters, places and incidents are the products of the author's imagination or are used fictitiously. Any resemblance to actual events, locales or persons, living or dead, is entirely coincidental.

For permission requests, contact the publisher, at:

Email: dadx3g@msn.com
Twitter: @dadx3gMike

Printed in the United States of America

Publisher's Cataloging-in-Publication data
Gutowski, Mike.
Cratch / Mike Gutowski;

ISBN 978-0-578-42892-5
eBook ISBN 978-0-578-42894-9

1. Dark Fantasy. 2. Science Fiction-apocalyptic and post-apocalyptic; aliens / UFOs. 3. Horror; supernatural fiction

First Edition
Revised

Dedicaticn:

To "Muffin" McCoy, on a long ago promise.

"Reality is merely an illusion, albeit a very
persistent one."

Albert Einstein

Imagination

Is

The

Chasm

Between

Real

World

And

Dream

land.

Contents

Prologue

Neapolitan ice cream. Good stuff. I eat it now as I contemplate a three-part question: Is life a blessing, curse, or existential coagulation of reasoned thoughts? Perhaps all three, like the ice cream. To which flavor vanilla, strawberry or chocolate does each part of the question attach, I wonder. The story I am about to tell, and I trust you are reading, tries to answer the question that seems to have no answer for one, for some, or for all. If in your life, you can solve the riddle, please let the world know, please.

After the accident, he spent much of his usable time in the light of the dark, of choice, but more so by necessity. I am Brother Henry. My assignment to live and work in Balmoral allowed me to first-hand understand the blessings and curses of many families. I have composed the story of this cursed man and his family, some from observation, some from interviews of those who have known him or have known of him, and still much from his spoken narrative. I have passed the information, including my research notes, on to the Church of the Holy See in the hope it may help in dealings over trials and tribulations which have come and have yet to come. Hopefully my written words will help purge him of deeds which have blackened his soul.

He can't use a pen or pencil because his hands are wracked by a curse. The curse allowed him to dig through cement and even steel. It allowed him to see all and yet feel nothing. It forced him to eat table scraps while he watched residents enjoy the fruits of fine chefs in fancy restaurants.

A curse works like a gun. It is not effective unless the trigger is pulled. The Slavs knew this fact when necessity to inflict such vicious and vengeful destruction upon a transgressor victim arose.

A curse works like a disease. It is insidious, slowly working a way into the host's life, ruining it at opportune times.

"He" is Tihomir Goralski. This story is his and that of his family as they lived wracked, burdened by one of the Slavic Curses. Perhaps knowing it will help others, afflicted in the same manner as he and his family, navigate the tortuous journey of such a life.

Onionhead was a Slavic folk tale about a curse where an apparition appeared each generation to take over the soul of the first born of the cursed family. One book spoke of this apparition. A copy was rumored to be housed in the bowels of the Balmoral city library yet finding it has confounded me to this day. My hope was to determine the elements needed to activate the curse; then to reverse or extinguish the malediction.

The door to Onionhead's realm was opened by this mysterious, potent Slavic curse; hurled at a Goralski clan member many years ago in the old country. The curse summoned a demon named Likho who entered the human world through a floating door or rift which connected both worlds human and demon. This type of demon spiritually attached to a Slavic family. The curse killed the first-born, but not until the first-born achieved a level of moderate happiness; and at least not until the first-born lived to about age thirty-five.

The Goralski clan latently discovered some means of protection, at least enough to fend off some of the emotional entrapments of the curse. Cats could help dull some of the curse effects but not break it completely. The cat protections couldn't be found by reading any of the curse books, many of them lost, locked away or hidden now. The Goralski clan was likely the first to discover the feline protection;

or perhaps they rediscovered a long-ago forgotten protection, learned through generations of trial and error. The sad result of the curse was the only known way to break it remained a mystery, otherwise, the family line must end to extinguish it. Such a result had not yet been succumbed to by this family. They have survived the curse longer than other cursed families, by hundreds of years.

Liszt's "Liebestraum No. 3" plays on my radio. And so, we begin.

PART FIRST - ONIONHEAD

1

Balmoral was a city aspired to become an urban success story. Years ago, city leaders determined to attract more business and industry to the area. The plan was working. The residents were happy. As economic conditions changed for the worse in the broader social sphere, political winds shifted. The city elders determined attraction of government funds a more expedient path to political success and power entrenchment as a counter measure to hard times. The difficulty, for the individual resident in the private sector, when adaptation to shifting economic winds blew wrong: increased government funds tended to morph citizens into sheep. The sheep, of necessity more so than desire, paid lip service to the politicians in power to shield from the economic and societal wolves hovering all around. Some citizens determined lip service to be a small price to pay for comfort. Others resisted the temptation to speak out and found comfort in silence and conformity. The city still flourished enough for a viable culture to form. There was no other way found by humans to achieve a balance such as this one and yet maintain a semblance of real community.

The politicians liked sheep. Sheep voted reliably. Private sector residents were free to make up their own minds; measure accountability differently, less reliably for the needs of the current politicians in power. An insidious corollary to this system: rewards can be garnered through increased incompetence. For instance, Balmoral was number one in STDs. The drug addiction problem, for good measure, insured the employment of numerous residents in the social services and penal systems. More safety personnel, like firefighters and police were needed, because the public funded residents were encouraged to become needy and helpless. The private residents learned to sit in the back seat of this political vehicle. They

were expected to buckle up and shut up; and get out
and push further through taxation increases when the
vehicle ran into a ditch. Yet the private residents
still lived admirably, comfortably enough; self-
massaged in their sentimental mindset by the thought
this city still promised a future. They had yet to
give up on it.

Tihomir's family did not give up on it. There existed
a collective sense, even among the public sector,
this city was intended for much more. This city had
a reputation for resistance to the norm in years past.
It gifted to the Nation a National Anthem still
butchered in song today by all manner of celebrities
at public events. The descendants still held onto the
anthem as a means of remembering a reason for
existence as a community.

Balmoral was an urban neighborhood of red brick
rowhouses capped by flat, asphalt and gray pebbled
rooftops. Abutted by concrete sidewalks, traffic
signal intersections and orange fire hydrants
sprouted from nearly every other street corner. A
square in a few portions of the sidewalk in each block
held upright a tree. Sometimes the roots popped up
and through the concrete sidewalk; cracked it.

Taverns had sprung at nearly every other intersection
corner to provide a sullen solace to residents who
toiled at a day driven by dusty winds, noisy machines,
random gunshot sounds, police sirens. A "little"
street corner store which doubled as a butcher shop,
candy store, newspaper distributer, populated a
nearby corner in Tihomir's neighborhood.

Stray cats warned of and warded off petty demons,
human and otherwise, seen and unseen. Barking dogs in
chain-link fenced yards doubled as sentry and
defender of the human inhabitants. Rats and German
cockroaches created a nuisance sub-culture in too
many places, yet served as cleaners of the inedible,
unusable detritus of the population. Alleys, carpeted

by cement slabs, ran like solid rivers between the
rowhouses; behind and in front of and around, so they
became an unofficial avenue of mischief and grief
when they were not allowing foot traffic or Arab-like
(pony-led carts carrying top soil, fruits,
vegetables) merchant business conducted gracefully;
like a Shakespeare scene, among a chorus of
neighborhood housewives.

"Shee-aat!" Tihomir shouted from his second floor
rowhouse room. He looked around to see if anyone had
heard him spout a curse word. At age thirteen, such
things still worried him. Safe. He looked down at the
bastard book he hated, cradled in his hands like a
moldy lunch sandwich. It was taking too long to read.
He bent the right page tip inward; formed a pyramid-
sided corner. He threw the book down to the bottom
part of his bed. Required reading for school fatigued
him. He preferred comic books and his own choices of
science fiction and fantasy at the library. The
tossed book embedded just under the comforter surface
like a fossil into rock.

He snatched at his pea coat. Cat's paw pulled threads
randomly sprouted from it. His sister's cat had
apparently invaded his room once again. The aroma of
golumpki boiling in a large pot on the downstairs
kitchen stove top yanked him back momentarily, but he
managed to break free of the sumptuous culinary
Polish meal temptress.

Tihomir ran out of the skinny, red brick rowhouse he
had called home since birth; down the snow-white,
concrete sidewalk. Dusk rapidly descended; closed
like a theatre stage curtain. Half running, half
skipping, in eager anticipation to see his friend
Zeke a few doors down, he bounded up the white marble
steps, leaped two of the three at one time, then near
fell into the vestibule through the scratched-up
storm door; further shredded his oversized, bargain
basement coat just below the right elbow at the usual
shredded place. It was mid-autumn, but in these

neighborhoods, you only had one coat which serviced two seasons. So, he was too hot or too cold most of the time.

Now mired in sweat, his vision darted around the first floor living room, aching for a glimpse of his friend, to frantically advise there were thirty minutes more of free time until his mom finished cooking supper. A sweat drop crept down his forehead and slipped into the tear duct area of his right eye; created a slow burn. Thirty more minutes, almost a rally cry, equaled one television show; a lot of free time at age thirteen. But Zeke was not visible in the quickly darkening room. It seemed three times as dark in the house as outside.

Tihomir suddenly heard the finger snap click of the sidewalk streetlight turn on, but the light still wasn't very bright; just dim, dimmer than usual. Darned streetlight was about to go out. He was apprehensive about shouting Zeke's name because he had barged in unannounced. He didn't want to spook his friend who was easily turned moody. A slight stir of shoes across the second-level floor sounded. Zeke must be upstairs, he thought. As Zeke's dad was not yet home from work and his mom not yet back from the corner store, some precious hide and seek time was at hand. Tihomir wondered if Zeke's somewhat plump but curvaceous older sister would be home from school soon. Tihomir yearned to catch a glimpse of her beauty to sustain him for another day.

The stairs to the second floor were high and narrow, almost mountain steepness it seemed; much like his own house. He took each step, one at a time, trying not to beat out a hymn on the oak surface. His thighs started to slow burn as he neared the top. He was familiar with the landing on the second floor. Despite near pitch-blackness he knew where the door to each of three rooms outlined the narrow hallway. The skylight above, cloudy as the cataracts of an old man, allowed a certain measure of near liquid beams dotted in dust particles to pierce small in width yet tall in height area.

He ignored the door to his immediate left; it was usually closed, and it was the parent's bedroom. The bathroom was the first door at the top of the landing, usually all the way opened. The partial view of the nearest claw foot of the bathtub startled him at first, but he quickly put two and two together and realized it was still just the tub and not a monster about to spring upon him.

He caught his breath as he shook off the thought of a claw-footed bogeyman bear-hugging him, and leaned forward, slowly, to push open with his right shoulder the three quarters closed door to Zeke's cave, in the room adjacent to the bathroom. Tihomir's first step into the room found what was left of the throw rug.

"Hey buddy," he whispered into the suddenly rancid smelling dark air.

"Zeke?"

All was quiet. His eyes still adjusting to the darkness of the entire house, he surveyed the room. From previous visits he knew Zeke's bed was flush against the short far wall at a right angle to the only wall holding a window. No motion was detected.

"Zeke?"

No sound. The rancid smell went beyond his nose and started to itch his eyes. Then he detected a slight jiggle motion at the upper corner of a whitish-beige blanket on the bed. He could make out a hump under the blanket, at the corner of the wall, which he at first thought was more than one balled up pillow. He was about to take another step into the room when he was startled to hear a moving sound behind him, like the wind suddenly making tree limbs groan. As adrenalin shot into his limbs, he whirled to his left.

The blackness was shattered by a floating, whitish, round ball trailing a gray sheet that flew towards his face. The ball showed a face which, rounded to double the size of a pinky ball, had two rows of shark-like teeth. The apparition flew towards his face. Instantly his mind jolted him with the thought, "This is a face with no skin!"

There was one eye set in a skull socket like a plugged golf ball. Then Tihomir finally heard a human voice he recognized.

Zeke shouted "RUN!"

The plugged eye, shark-toothed skull head kept coming at him. Tihomir's eyes watered from the smell of an onion type stench. The skull was supported by the body of what appeared to be a smallish in build man caped in a greenish black cloak.

"AAAHHHH!"

A weird moaning sound shot out of the skull's mouth. The apparent apparition was now so visible it could be plucked like a potato out of the ground. The mouth was so wide open it could take a bite the way of a snake.

The door behind Tihomir moved, then pushed forward into his upper back as he instinctively backed away. The phantom onion head's target, Tihomir, backed just enough to escape loss of face flesh. Then blackness, then cloudiness, then Tihomir's hands clumsily and simultaneously rubbed his eyes and probed his own face tissue to determine if it still existed as he marked his self-analysis. He was relieved to conclude what he determined was still in the affirmative, that is, he still had a face. Zeke's voice then broke into the moment.

"Nice joke, huh?"

"Joke? You jerk."

"Yea. I used fishing wire and glow sticks. I know how much you love fearing the dark."

"Your room smells like crap."

"Rotten potato peels. I used potatoes to help construct the face. Just another added effect to throw off your senses."

Zeke's older sister blew in through the front door of the vestibule below. The sound of her footsteps clomped upwards through the gray wall-papered silo of the narrow steps. The only light on the stairway beamed down from the skylight above the second-floor landing.

Tihomir shook himself as he tried to escape the dirt of his cowardice. He brushed back his hair and sucked in air to expand his chest; a lame attempt also to expand his sinewy biceps. Zeke's sister looked sideways at Zeke and Tihomir as she glided by them. She quickly turned to comment on the disheveled scene in Zeke's room. Looking at the crudely constructed ghost Zeke had fastened to the fish wire, which now hovered near the edge of the darkness in Zeke's room, she complemented him as only an older sister could manage.

"Who's that, another one of your freaky friends?"

Zeke frowned at her. Tihomir was agog in a gaze of holy light only experienced by boys in love on the cusp of puberty. Tihomir's whole being was energized yet weak. The sound of her voice enveloped him; massaged his body. Then a slam of the door at the end of the cramped hallway meant Tihomir would not see her again for another day; a seeming eternity. Zeke shook his head sideways.

"Her cruelty is only surpassed by her stench."

"What?" Tihomir was still in a daze. "I think she smells great."

"You would. Well, I was gonna show you the new comic books I picked up at the little store today. Seeing as you nearly peed yourself a bit ago, I think my work is done. Anyway, looks like it will take a while for you to escape from that mental web my sister just spun around your weak-ass."

"Yeah. I better get home. See ya tomorrow, early. Can't wait to do some exploring."

Tihomir slowly walked home. His feet barely touched the ground. His insides glowed.

"She called me freaky. Cool."

2

The neighborhood was not unlike many such urban machinations. Average yet comely existence was the essence of the human experience. Small, bright patches of humane moments made it partially bearable, after the evisceration of all but the soul had been inflicted upon the inhabitants. Joy and tears, happiness and dreadful grief stalked all in the area, readied to pounce at any time, sometimes simultaneously. Allowance of time or inclination didn't lead to extravagant elegance.

In such neighborhoods, families had their demons, but none born more insidious than the Onionhead curse. The Goralski family, in a past century, had been cursed by a gypsy mom distressed over the attempted courtship of her eligible daughter by a Goralski male forebear. The curse was hurled to strike a first-born child. The first-born shall not live past the thirty-fifth birthday--that being about the time much emotional attachment to family and friends had been attained. The future, pulled out from under the first-born by the Onionhead demon, truncated the efforts of the cursed and family in the noble effort to reach the full potential of shared efforts, happiness and success. On the thirty-fifth birthday the demon Onionhead came to claim the cursed one from this life. The corollary—-the cursed human could not die until the moment of birth thirty-five years hence.

The Onionhead Curse, the 11th Curse in the Slavic Book of Curses, had been suffered by the Goralski's for all of twenty generations. There was no known cure. Have you ever wondered why cats have nine lives? Cats were not a crucible for a cure, but they were aware of the Onionhead demon, so they stayed close to the curse's victim to help ward off the ill effects of Onionhead if possible. The cats served as protectors. When cats crouched and hissed at night, seemingly at nothing, there WAS something there.

Tihomir reached home, more specifically at the front door, where an upside-down horseshoe was screwed into the red brick above the front exterior door. He looked at the horseshoe and wished for good luck, as he often did before entering. His dad was working late again. His mom worked not far down the street at a bakery. She was home. Various pots simmered on the kitchen stove located at the back of the house. The pots, some bigger than wash buckets, were embodied by sumptuous dinner product: balled up ground beef the size of baseballs; cabbage leaves which enveloped the beef. The aroma of simmering golumpki invaded every room of the two-story rowhouse. Tihomir's favorite meal beckoned. His mom had already set out a plate of the treasured meal which included sauerkraut and sliced beets. The aroma entranced him. The precious golumpki would taste even better the next day and after as leftovers. He scooted into a chair at the kitchen table. Duke, his white Spitz, dutifully lay at his feet awaiting jewels of food about to fall from Tihomir's lap. His mom attempted to tune into Tihomir's impending intrigues.

"Any adventures planned for this weekend?"

Tihomir winced. "No, not really."

"Your favorite show is on TV tonight," his mom reminded.

"I know. Gotta go to sleep early though. Zeke and I are getting up early."

"Oh?" His mom continued to ooze of her usual, smothering curiosity. Her house dress was suddenly blown sideways by a wind invading the kitchen window screen. The dress clung to a hint of chubbiness against her left side.

"Looks like we might have a storm tonight."

Tihomir pretended to not hear her observation. A

storm would not stop him from the early morning
pursuit. Still, he winced. A storm would delay plans
to explore the sewer pipe at the park down by the
Herring Run drainage area. He gobbled down the
treasured golumpki meal. Duke lapped up the scraps
intentionally dropped by Tihomir onto the linoleum
floor.

"Night Mom." Tihomir zipped from the table, Duke in
tow on an invisible line.

"Ahem," mom murmured.

Tihomir abruptly stopped, turned around, bent and
kissed mom on the right side of the forehead.

"Love you Mom."

"Good night Tihomir."

3

A black cat, green-eyed, scraggly and wiry haired, the kind of cat that likes to move things nightly; the kind that stares while sitting motionless as a statue looking into space; or perhaps sees things only cats can see; sat as sentry atop the edge of a rooftop at the corner house of Tihomir's rowhouse block. The sun peeked above the false horizon created by miles and miles of rowhouse rooftops of Balmoral; planted there some one hundred plus years ago.

Balmoral was a place where life wasn't sugar-coated. It was the place where a nineteenth century author died in a gutter outside of a tavern, under mysterious circumstances; and the place where curses still lived, brought to the neighborhood by the many emigrated ethnic groups, generations ago. Usually, what you saw was what was there: no dark, unmasked or unopened fold of existence lurked. Still, in some neighborhoods, resistance to stark reality maintained a resting place. A city of many pubs and taverns allowed for a quick respite from the harshness of the cement and mortar jungle; served as an easy, smooth escape from stone-cold reality; and muddled the puzzle of life enough to give citizens a reason for one more day to figure out their long-term plight.

The city was never a paradise, yet jewels of beauty were gradually mined by the citizenry and government. After the 1904 fire gutted the downtown area, the only building that survived primarily intact was the Library. In 1968 there were the race riots after a civil rights leader was assassinated. In 1981 there was Onionhead. The former cataclysms were chronicled and mourned. Onionhead was not mentioned by newspapers in detail but alluded to in short, back pages' articles, around Halloween time, as a mythical demon nuisance. In each instance of tragedy, the citizens nobly recovered and continued onward.

Tihomir Goralski was one of many who played a

character in the continuing saga of Balmoral families. He was the first-born of a first-born. He suffered from short term memory loss, but for unknown reasons to him, he could always remember "C" is for cat as a young child.

He had never liked cats much since when he was little. He saw how Una, his grandma's cat, scratched up the furniture and clawed up threads from the rugs. One day, in the basement of her house, Una viciously attacked him. The cat jumped out from beneath an array of old kitchen table chairs, scratched on Tihomir's legs and would not let go. Eventually Tihomir was able to shake off the cat, but not before long cuts were inflicted upon his shins.

Tihomir, deep in a sleep nurtured by digestion of golumpki and sauerkraut, was just reaching the climax of another dream about Zeke's sister. In this one, she was a warrior princess. She had just won a glorious battle and was seated around a campfire. He was watching her, from a place he could not discern, perhaps from behind a tree on the edge of the gathering of other female warriors. They were seated on long, crudely chopped tree trunks. Zeke's sister leaned over to stoke the fire with a thin tree branch, as she leaned forward, her warrior skirt raised up against the back of thick, taught thighs. He squinted to see closer, at the ridgeline of her skirt. He felt an energy inside himself about to burst on the anticipation he might see under the skirt and discover the mystery there which yet eluded him. His body tensed, and he felt an incredibly pleasing sensation in his groin area. Then a chorus of thunder arose, then a flash and crash of lightening shook his very being. He could not breath. His chest felt heavy. He tried to move but he was pinned. Then he felt a rough rubbing on his face. It was slimy. He tried to focus on the edge of the warrior princess' skirt, but the view was fading away. Suddenly, a loud sound invaded his brain.

"Ruff!"

Tihomir's upper body sprung up in bed as Duke fell back.

"Darn, Duke!"

It was morning, but still dark outside. It was the morning time that preceded morning, when the stars were still visible. Tihomir glanced outside the window near his bed. He saw a cat on the neighbor's shed.

"Don't worry Duke, just a cat greeting the morning."

Tihomir rolled out of bed and nearly hit his head on the floor. He had packed his stuff the night before, just needed to brush his teeth and get a snack. He dragged himself to the bathroom, he listened first, once he perched in front of the mirror. The outside was nearly silent, except for the milk truck delivery sounds of engine revs and clanking glass bottles, and some bird chirps. The truck was still a few blocks away judging by the sound of it.

He looked in the mirror, brushed off the loose dog hair which had meshed into his. Duke was a white Spitz. His hairs were almost pointy at times. A finger comb would do for now. He half asleep fumbled for the toothbrush; squeezed a knotty glob of some toothpaste onto it from the half-full tube. The sting of the paste irritated that repressive ulcer which bubbled up from time to time inside his lower lip. The brushing done; he grabbed some clothes from the bottom of his bed which he had spread the night before. Khaki shorts were marked by many pockets, as he couldn't have too many of those; what with all the implements needed for this journey.

A pen knife, thermos of water, binoculars, the tools of the young adventurer adorned his pockets. The indicated excursion implements bulged his shorts as

he pulled them up onto his thighs. A t-shirt, somewhat
scraggly from the unfolded dump of laundry into his
chest of drawers, briefly mugged him as he pulled it
onto his head and downward. Duke was back asleep on
Tihomir's bed, so he was unable to make it. He will
hear about it later, Tihomir thought.

He walked to the front of his room, to check outside
the front window. He looked down. Dad's car wasn't
back yet from his night shift at the police station.

As Tihomir continued preparations for the trip he
recalled some stories dad told him about. When dad
first met mom. Dad learned mom was a cat lover. Mom
gave dad a Persian-like, Maine coon cat kitten; just
a runt from a litter. The cat would jump on dad's
chest quite frequently in the early morning hours of
the Balmoral day. The cat became mom and dad's
protector. Then dad told Tihomir about the fabled
Onionhead curse when Tihomir was about 7 years old.
Cats were the only creature on earth capable of the
speed, sense and instinct to slow Onionhead. Cats
sensed Onionhead's transformation from the spirit
world dimension into earth's dimension. Dad came to
believe cats were known to help protect the host from
the demon. For centuries, cats had temporarily foiled
the demon thirst for firstborn blood, but eventually,
Onionhead always won.

Duke knew something was wrong. He was in the back
yard as Tihomir continued preparations for the
drainage pipe exploration at the Herring Run stream
near the Parkside park. Duke started to circle around
in the yard. He sniffed. His tail hanged low. His
ears were pressed against the side of his head.
Tihomir, upstairs in his bedroom, peeked out the
window into the back yard to see if Duke had completed
his morning duty. Zeke was due over any moment.
Tihomir noticed Duke's actions and started down the
stairs to the first floor. Once there, he quickly
moved through the dining room, then the summer

kitchen where mom stood hunched over and emptied the washing machine clothes into the dryer. "Morning mom." Tihomir then opened the screen door and stepped onto the cement stoop. He looked down to his right because he could hear Duke make a slow growl sound in a low, dark space under the summer kitchen.

Tihomir's mom, screamed from the summer kitchen, "Duke! Get out from under there!" Tihomir heard mom heave for a second wind scold, "before you get bit by a rat!" Tihomir knew his mom didn't want Duke to drag a rat into the house, only for her to have to chase it back outside with a broom. "Maybe we need more cats in the neighborhood," Tihomir wondered, but then he immediately dismissed the thought. "I'm out with Zeke, Mom, be back in a few hours."

4

The Herring Run stream split a grassy park dotted by baseball fields in the summer and soccer fields in autumn. A thick, long line of trees served as a natural border on each side. Tihomir and Zeke walked along the banks of the Run and scoured the narrow sand and stone beach for rocks, coins, frogs, turtles and whatever else might mysteriously appear. The sound of the rippling water gurgled at the edge of the sand. Zeke picked up a smooth, flat, black stone and skipped it across the water's surface. "Beat that." Tihomir had counted three stone hops before Zeke's stone disappeared. Tihomir made his attempt and accomplished only two skips. They continued the hike along the water's edge and arrived at a point where a large, concrete pipe gaped at them from across the stream. The pipe was burrowed into the bank of the Run on the opposite side of them but there were larger stones and rocks that served as a breach at the water's surface. The rocks acted like a bridge access from their side and on over to the pipe. The anticipated day's adventure had finally advertised itself.

They hunched forward along the rock and mud path and made the way up to the opening of the rainfall drainpipe. Their sneakers collected pebble, mud and leaf detritus strewn along the path. The pipe beckoned their entry simply through majestic, immobile silence. What could be found inside the pipe and at the other end of it taunted adolescent imagination. "Pretty dark inside there, even in this daylight." Zeke's observation wasn't lost on Tihomir's mind. "I brought a flashlight," Tihomir noted. "Click," the light bit into the darkness. Their footsteps were short at first like the footfalls of a rodent testing a prowl upon the concrete back alleys of their neighborhood, and just as quiet.

The long, main portion of the tunnel, fairly straight, was abutted by smaller in circumference tunnels on each side. "Let's stay in the main part so we don't get lost," Tihomir suggested. Zeke was in front. "Sure, okay." After about 200 feet, Tihomir had been counting his steps, they noticed a dim light at a not so distant part of the tunnel ceiling. Zeke blurted, "Looks like a sewer grate opening up ahead." It was much further along than they anticipated. Tihomir looked behind, "I can barely see the light from the entrance any longer." Then a sudden noise disturbed their attention. "Hear that?" Zeke stopped. The splash sounds of moved water echoed from the connected tunnels. Tihomir asked, in a somewhat nervous tone, "What's splashing the water?" The humidity of the tunnel environs caused their shirts to become sticky. Tihomir lost track of his steps. He glanced behind and saw no sign of the point where they had entered. Then they heard female, raised in tone voices coming from the lit end of the tunnel. Zeke started to jog towards the light ahead, but his sneaker's impacts betrayed the squishy texture of mud. They reached the light from above. Zeke whispered, "It may be my sister's high school Field Hockey team practice." The entry point for the light was a sewer grate. Something, a ball perhaps, skittered across the metal grate. Then two cleats scraped across the grate. The light dimmed, but they could make out two shapely, bare legs, except for green, short socks, extended from the cleated shoes. Tihomir's heart began pounding as he squinted. He resisted the temptation to hold the flashlight upward as they would be exposed below. The female athlete above bent over and picked up a soccer ball. The bending raised her athletic skirt enough to expose a sliver of her underwear stretched taught against her bottom. Then a shadow emerged as the Sun, seemingly on cue, distracted their view. The athlete was gone.

They stayed, silent, and listened to the female athletic activity; and they greedily anticipated a second glance upward to spy one of the athletes. The water splash sounds at the other end of the tunnel increased in volume. Tihomir shined the flashlight and began to fear the water level rising. It was now about half a foot higher. "We better get out of here." Zeke didn't want to leave just yet. Tihomir started back towards the direction of entry. His sneakers and socks, now wetted heavy, weighed him down a bit. Zeke began to follow. Tihomir couldn't resist shining the flashlight into one of the adjacent tunnels and froze when he saw rats climbing along the sides. "We have company." Tihomir started to run and then noticed the tunnel walls seemed to be moving. The flashlight beam reflected the smooth finish of roaches scattered randomly along the tunnel sides. The measure of his heart pounds almost reached the same rate as his vision of the female athlete's underwear line. Finally, the open end of the tunnel beckoned a respite. The echo of Zeke's water-logged sneakers now banged hard into the muddy stream of the tunnel bottom. They made it back onto the bank of the Run. Tihomir looked up at the sky. Storm clouds where moving towards them from the north. A low, rolling thunder rippled in the distance. "I guess we should call it a day before the storm comes."

On the walk home, Tihomir noticed his grandmother leave the storefront of the local psychic medium. The medium was well known in the neighborhood. Zeke couldn't help himself and blurted out, "Your Busia made her monthly visit again." Tihomir had hoped Zeke didn't see her. Tihomir whispered, "It helps her try to understand things, strange things, you know?" Zeke shook his head sideways, "What's to understand?" Tihomir quickly chimed in and tried to end the conversation with, "Life." Zeke laughed, "Plenty of time for that, when we're old." Tihomir tried to get Zeke to admit their neighborhood masked some odd trappings. "That joke you played on me with the onion head and white sheet, you know what I mean. We both hear things at night," Tihomir noted. Zeke didn't want to give in just yet. According to him, the footsteps they would sometimes hear on the rooftop was a squirrel; the loud cat screeches during the rain was just another cat fight; the whistling sound they sometimes heard late on a Sunday from the steeple at the Church about two blocks over was just the wind. "You never read," said Tihomir. Zeke joked, "Why read about ghosts, demons and UFO's when there is Playboy magazine, and Mad magazine." Tihomir then exaggerated, "Oops, I forgot about Playboy." They both laughed. "Mad magazine isn't so bad," Tihomir summed up. Tihomir didn't tell Zeke about the intention to someday soon obtain a consult with the psychic medium.

When Tihomir got home, he noticed the quiet, which was only interrupted by his imagined taste of some kielbasa strips dipped in mustard. "Mom, I'm home!" he shouted. He didn't hear a stir of sound. He started to walk to the back of the house when he heard the front storm door rattle. He turned around and noticed his Busia coming up the vestibule step. She was in her usual old, near-tattered dress. She hadn't purchased a new dress in years, even during the holidays when mom especially encouraged such. Busia's shoulders were stooped, as if the weight of the world were upon her, all the time. She was stocky in build. "Hey, Busia, where's Mom?" Busia frowned, "What, no how's Busia?" Tihomir laughed. "Sorry, Busia." Then he walked over and gave her a hug. "Your Mom got a phone call and out she went a little while ago. I imagine she will be back soon." Busia somewhat waddled towards the kitchen.

"Let's sit down for a snack, just a bit." Tihomir agreed. Busia seemed to know things before they happened. On days when she sensed something unusual or somber was about to happen, her facial expressions became dower. On this day, she seemed to force a smile, at least a hint of one. Smiles were a good mask for intense emotions. Tihomir sat down at the kitchen table. Still, it was too quiet. He didn't hear Duke's paw scratches on the upstairs, wooden floor. Duke should have been down here by his side by now. "Duke!" He prodded. Still quiet. Busia brought over a plate of kielbasa and a bowl of mustard and a butter knife. Tihomir picked up the knife and started to push it into the long roll of kielbasa. The knife clicked onto the porcelain plate. Each click freed a cookie sized, round disk of kielbasa from the long sausage roll. He carefully dipped the disk into the mustard bowl, then plunged the disk into his mouth. "Mmm," was the only sound Tihomir could make. Busia asked, "Where's your Duke?" Tihomir didn't answer as his mind was still on his sight of when Busia left from the psychic's office.

Tihomir tried to think of a way to start a conversation about the psychic. As his thought trailed off the meaning of the question, Busia said, "I went to see that psychic, Sophie, today. I have been feeling strange things lately." It wasn't unusual for Busia to say she felt strange things, but she didn't usually say it to Tihomir.

Tihomir heard the front door open. It was his mom coming in. "Mom, where's Duke?" His mom looked sad. "T, we have to talk."

Mom sat down at the kitchen table next to Tihomir. Busia looked more solemn than ever. "T, after you left this morning, I went down to the back yard and called for Duke to come in. I didn't hear him anymore. I walked down to the back of the summer kitchen. I saw him lying on his side near the space below the summer kitchen, where the rat had been hiding. Pieces of the rat were scattered around his snout. I think he attacked and ate part of the rat." Tihomir wasn't sure what to think. Mom continued, "Duke didn't wake up when I called to him again. His breathing was slow and rough. I pulled a towel off the back clothesline and wrapped him in it and took him down to the Vet's office two blocks over. Not long after, the Vet came to me and said Duke had died." Tihomir was beside himself. "What happened?" Mom spoke somewhat matter of fact now, "The Vet thinks the rat may have eaten some poison. The Vet was somewhat shocked that Duke could even catch the rat, but the rat may have been slowed down by the poison." Tihomir's mom leaned over and hugged him. Tihomir tried not to cry but a jutted drip of a tear betrayed his effort.

"Let me talk with him for a bit," Busia said. Tihomir's mom left the room but not before she gave to Busia a knowing glance. "Let me tell you a story." Busia folded her hands into a single fist, leaned forward, stretched her arms, took a deep breath, then sighed. Busia indicated there is much to understand about Tihomir's family, especially for the first-born of the family.

"Many, many years ago, when both sides of the family lived in the old country, there was a dispute amongst a gypsy clan and a young man on your father's side. I see by your eyes you wonder how long ago. Centuries, centuries ago it was. The young man had fallen in love with a young woman of the gypsy clan. Her clan had been on the move for a while and finally settled on the outskirts of a town where your ancestor, the young man, lived. The mother of the young woman found out about the romance. Her clan was very possessive of family encounters with folks outside their clan. When the young man, stubborn and bitten by love, refused to give up on the romance, the gypsy mom cursed him. The young man didn't tell his family right away about the curse because he was afraid his family would take retribution against the gypsy young woman and her mother. Eventually, the young man and a woman from his village married. A family name was given to the son, the first-born of the young man's family.

The son was bestowed the name Tihomir. The curse did
not involve a simple, short-time burden as the young
man's family learned over the next few generations:
the first-born of each generation died at or around
age thirty-five. The young man, when he was old and
on his death bed, told a family member about the curse
hurled against him. His son had died mysteriously at
about the age of thirty-five. The family went to the
nearest Church for help. The Church Elder determined
the curse incantation invoked the possession of Likho
of Slavic demon mythology, but we call it Onionhead."
Tihomir wondered why "Onionhead" for a name. Busia
interpreted his facial expression and answered,
"because of its facial appearance".

Busia wasn't sure if Tihomir, at this point, was bored
or transfixed. Tihomir remained silent. He verbalized
his confusion as, "I thought that tale was a myth."
Then, after further thought, he burst out "I am the
first-born!"

5

A cat peered at him from around the corner of a rowhouse. Tihomir still mourned Duke. Tihomir picked up a stone and tossed it near the cat, not to strike it, but to get it to move because Tihomir didn't want to see it now. The cat hid behind the corner of the house. As Tihomir approached, he heard some low sounds. As he walked beyond the end of the house, he saw the cat brushing up against a litter of small, puffy kittens. One of them stumbled over towards him and looked up. The kitten's eyes captured his heart, tugged at it, stuck a claw in it. He leaned down and picked up the black and white fur ball, petted it; enjoyed the warm feeling the softness evoked. He clung it to his chest, walked back to the house, up the staircase, and watched the kitten explore his room for a long time. He called it "Sand" because it reminded him of an ice cream sandwich. For the immediate future, caring for Sand helped him get through to the time of what was to come.

There were onions growing wherever those born of Slavic descent settled in Tihomir's neighborhood. Cooking the onions seemed to be a way to keep Onionhead and other demons at bay. The onions seemed to cry out during pot boiling on the summer kitchen stove.

Families in Balmoral had moved many times to get away from the demons. Settling into a larger group of Slavs meant more onions in force for use in chasing away demon influences. To help empower the strength of the feasts of kielbasa, golumpki, sauerkraut, red beets and more, a local Priest would come to each house at Easter to bless the food settings at the feast table.

After one of these feast table blessings, Tihomir's dad told him about an evening when his dad was a young teenager. He found himself chased by a wild group of neighborhood teenagers from the next neighborhood over. He didn't see it coming at first as he was

walking home from a soccer team practice. He had
strayed to a corner store to check out the comic books
rack and the baseball card and candy counter of the
little store. The teenagers from the adjacent
neighborhood were somewhat older than him, and a few
of them larger in height and width. He knew he could
run fast, if needed, as he was the fastest runner in
his own neighborhood. After buying the simple
pleasures of baseball cards and comic books, he left
the front of the store energized by the joy he would
consume from opening each precious card pack and the
turn of each page of the comic books. As he turned
the corner which marked the boundary of the two
neighborhoods, he encountered about five of the older
teens. They tried to grab his cards and books,
knocking the cards out of his left hand. His father
said he felt a jolt of energy engulf him, as if
lightning bolts had shot through his veins. He
grabbed the largest teen who had emerged from the
shadows of the evening and swung him around into the
brick exterior of a building. The other teens in the
gang were stunned. For a few moments there was silence
after Tihomir's dad turned around to fend off the
remainder of the gang, but the gang ran not without
the baseball cards and all but one of the comic books.
Tihomir's dad chased them, and caught each one, and
beat them using his fists, until each card pack and
comic book was surrendered. He still couldn't explain
how he caught each one as they had scattered in
different directions. It was as if he could still see
them; smell them when they were not there in front
of him; where they had gone; where they were hiding.
He wasn't sure what happened to the first, largest
teen who was thrown into the brick wall. He never saw
any of them again. He listened to the radio, read the
newspapers for the next few days. No stories could
he find. He didn't tell his parents or friends about
the incident. He could not figure out how he did it.
He remembered his father had died a few months before
and he was still very distressed about it.

6

Western Poland border, Gorale, 1460 AD

Anthony Goralski, a first-born, one day from age thirty-five, finished the last move of the shovel and patted the dirt on his young daughter's grave. He somberly looked over at the two other graves he had just completed; that of his spouse and youngest son. The oldest of his tiny clan of children, Melvin, was away at his uncle's farm.

Anthony visually surveyed the scene at the village center. He knew this town would not become rebuilt. Easy prey for the group of Tatar warriors who had combed the depths of this black oak forest would have to become another place. Here would continue to rot, decay, and become overgrown by the black oaks.

The types of arrows imbedded into the bodies of his neighbors and kin were the damning evidence of the deed. The warriors had ransacked the small town of Anthony's birth, killed all who had not fled, and taken any implements or supplies to replenish the warriors for more attacks. Many villagers had fled or were missing, but some, like his family, had been murdered. Anthony heard the horrific news as he returned from a trade trip at a nearby village. Many houses in the village were burned which included the one Anthony and his family had constructed a generation ago. The only task left was to avenge the loss of family. His duty now was to vanquish the Tatar invaders, but not just vanquish them. Signs of their demise must become a warning to Tatar clans: stay away, don't come back, ever.

He started the walk into the black forest. After a long while, as the sun was descending below the shadow of the trees, he came upon the Tatar encampment. There were seven of them, scattered in a semi-circle around a low fire. The fire served only for warmth at this point. Suddenly, Anthony felt a sharp pain in the back of his head, and all went fuzzy and dark. When he awoke, he was seated, bound to a tree. Between his legs, at his groin area, blood had pooled at the point where his groin should be. They had castrated him while he was unconscious. Slivers of his skin were missing from each forearm and each thigh. A few of the Tatar warriors were sitting around the fire, chewing the fried skin. Some of them had already finished the meal and were sleeping. The fire pit was low in light now, almost down to the embers. Anthony knew he would die tomorrow, but not before he allowed Onionhead to help him get revenge for the death of his kin.

All the warriors were sleeping now. Anthony crept over to each one; first, gagged each in succession with a tree branch to crush the tongue and break the wind-pipe; then, as each tried to crawl away, Anthony used the warrior's own arrows by pushing the tip into the heaving throat; then he found a knife and gutted them. He leaned against the trunk of a tree, seated. He knew he would see his murdered family members again soon. As morning started to stray rays of light into the forest surroundings, his head lowered, chin to chest, his breath composed the morose music of the death rattle.

7

Central Poland, Warsaw, 1882 AD

Frank Goralski started another day in a series of never-ending days, at work, for the Russian Cossacks police force. He wasn't a Cossack. At his age of seventeen, he had already serviced the horses and tended to the weapons and other tools and equipment of the regiment for three years. It was a decent job for the time, but the job served a dual purpose. Poland was a divided country, governed by Austrians, Prussians and Russians. There was officially no longer a Polish country, and there had not been for a long time. The Poles never became accustomed to occupation of their native land. They retained their culture, religion and life routines, except not to only tend to their own needs, but to also service their occupiers needs, wants and desires. The Goralski family worked to chip away at their subjugation, as had many families across the Polish lands. Resistance to the foreign occupation had ebbed and flowed. The temperament for action had become extremely high, yet the Poles were able to keep secrets and feign agreement to their plight. The Goralski's were blessed with a first-born son, Frank, and his many sisters. On one terrible night, the curse of the first-born was unknowingly unleashed by one of the Cossacks.

The Cossacks enjoyed the Prussian beer at a local pub on a regular basis. Sometimes they invited Frank into the pub with them as a bonus for his fine work. The food and drink, excessively good for the evening, spurred one of the Cossack's to make a boast about taking one of the neighborhood women for his own pleasure. Some at the table encouraged him on, playfully, but some remained silent and looked nervous. The nervous looked at Frank. They knew that Frank's family lived in the neighborhood. Frank pretended not to notice the issue. The boaster reached over and slapped Frank on the shoulder, then

the boaster put on his cap, tightened his belt, and
left the pub. Frank looked at each of the remaining
Cossacks, in silence. He excused himself and they
understood why.

Frank quickly walked the several blocks to the small
house where his family lived in a part of town crowded
by Polish and Russian families. On his mind was one
thing: his sisters. He reached the house, hurried up
the steps, opened the front docr, only to hear
whispers and sobs. His Busia was there. Frank knew
something was wrong. Busia told him what had
happened. A Cossack had accosted Frank's sister as
she was returning from her job as a seamstress. Some
of the neighbors found out about it and quickly got
the word to Frank's father. The father went out
looking for his daughter but had not yet returned.
Frank was the first-born of a first-born. His father
had lived longer than all the first-born before him.
His father did not know the Cossacks the way Frank
knew them. Frank feared the brethren of the drunk
Cossack who left the pub early may corner his father
and make an example of him.

Suddenly an energy struck Frank he did not know. He
felt as if his blood was boiling. His muscles
stretched and hardened throughout his body. He knew
something was sorely wrong. He started running up and
down the streets, into the dimly lit, narrow alleys
between the houses and narrow streets. He started to
feel the sense of closeness to his targets. He reached
a point several blocks from his house. The pub was
across the street. He ran into the pub after slamming
open the heavy front door, almost knocking it off the
iron hinges. The pub was near empty except for the
barkeep and a man seated in the far corner, his upper
body slumped over onto the table. Frank looked at the
man who was slumped over. He reached the table after
slipping among shards and pieces of a wooden chair
splintered across the floor. A chair leg jutted out
of the back of the hunched over man. Frank sniffed
the air, looked down at the man, then leaned to turn

over the body. Before he completed the turn, a
sickness enveloped his body, mind and soul. He felt
weak, then strong, then weak again. He looked at the
man's face, his father's face, eyes still half open,
a slight grin lined the corners of his lips. He was
dead. Frank started to cry. He crouched down, sat
next to his father and hugged him tightly. He could
smell the odor of the Cossacks on his father. Below
the table, was another body, the body of one of the
Cossacks from the group Frank helped service in his
job. The Onionhead demon had begun to inhabit and
infest Frank's body during the search for his father
and sister. His father must have been killed during
that time. Frank could hear male laughter in the alley
behind the pub. He looked at the barkeep. The
barkeep's face was white with fear. Frank stood,
slowly walked to the rear door of the pub, and opened
the back door into the alley.

Three Cossacks stood around a scene which Frank could
not make out. Frank could smell the scent of semen
among the men. They turned around and came at him as
wild boar would chase prey. Before they reached him,
he could see another of them crushing against his
sister who was bloody on the upper part of her dress,
a look of shock on her face, as she lay on her back
in the middle of the alley. Her body shuddered. The
sight of her shudder sent Frank into an instant rage.
He could not really relate, later, exactly what
happened. He just remembered that the three Cossacks
who rushed him were no longer standing. Each was
slumped onto the cobblestones and dirt in the alley.
The drunk Cossack was still pounding his penis into
the sister's loins. Frank remembered he kicked the
Cossack in the side. The Cossack was so drunk, he
could only list over onto his back. Frank picked him
up with one hand and raised him off his feet, then
crushed his neck with one tightened grasp. The
Cossack dropped to the alley brick floor, limp, dead.
Frank bent down, lifted his sister, and carried her
home. The curtains of many neighborhood windows
dashed and swirled as Frank walked past them,

carrying his sister. He finally reached home, entered, and lay her onto the couch in the first room to be tended by the women of the house. Busia came over to him and looked him in the eyes for a long while. He was still in a daze. He tried to speak, but Busia interrupted, "Don't say anything...I know."

Frank's family urged him to flee, take a freighter to America and escape the Cossacks and perhaps end the Onionhead curse by using distance as an ally. He was reluctant. He feared for the retribution he knew would be launched by the Cossacks upon his family and friends. His Busia urged him to go and not look back. Frank promised to send money he earned back to his home to help his family, so they could escape to America. He promised he would help as many of them as possible. He secretly boarded a freighter headed for Balmoral City on the east coast of America.

8

Tihomir was looking forward to his class field trip to Calvert Cliffs. Millions of years ago an asteroid or comet had fallen to earth and crashed into the eastern coast of America. A resulting tidal wave surge from the Atlantic Ocean filled the created void over the course of many years to form what is now called the Chesapeake Bay. Parts of the meteor were found at Calvert Cliffs. During the field trip, Tihomir felt parts of tiny pebbles and stone chips strike his lower leg area while walking among his classmates at the site. It was as if the tiny pieces became attracted to his body while he was walking the area. Some of the stones and dirt began to stick to Tihomir's leg to the point where it felt like pins or needles sticking into his leg. They worked their way down his leg, into his shoe. He scratched and scratched but he could not dislodge the tiny invaders.

A nearby scientist and guide for the class at the site, Doctor Zygmunt Zeis, noticed Tihomir's discomfort. "Are you okay, son?" Tihomir tried to brush off the dirt, but it stuck harder. He sat down on the dirt and stone area of the ground. Some blood started to ooze from his left leg. He started to wince in pain. The scientist had a magnet in his tool kit. He noticed the dirt and stone move towards his kit. He pulled out the magnet and the stones and dirt moved from Tihomir's leg and onto the magnet, leaving tiny bloody holes, like dots, on Tihomir's leg. The scientist opened a first aid kit and started to administer aid.

When Tihomir reached home, he became imprisoned in his room, to the bed specifically, under the covers tucked around him by his mom. Mom said wait until dad gets home and tell him what happened.

When dad returned home from work, Tihomir could hear
his mom telling dad what happened, as she had heard
it from the school nurse.

Dad came up the stairs still dressed in his police
clothes. He arrived at Tihomir's room and looked at
Tihomir. Tihomir remained silent. He didn't want his
dad worried about him. His dad asked "Tihomir, what
happened?"

"I fell. I hurt my foot...or I thought I did."

"Are you hurt or not?"

Tihomir thought for a second. He felt a need to tell
his dad what happened. His dad, a respected police
officer, would know the answer to all Tihomir's
questions, he thought.

"I fell. My foot stung, worse than that bee sting
last year. Way worse. A scientist man helped me. I
think he was a geologist or archeologist or something
like that."

Dad looked at him. Dad's thought processes were
evident in his eyes, boring into Tihomir's brain.

"I checked my shoe. It had a hole in it, a very thin
hole. I looked at the ground where I had stepped, and
my eyes started to water up. But there wasn't anything
sharp on the ground, just a plant. It had a funny
smell. It made my eyes water up, like an onion does
to you."

"You hurt so much you cried? Let's see the foot."

Tihomir stuck his leg out from under the bed covers.
Dad looked; he didn't find anything except what
looked like a healed skin area which bore a thin
strand of a scar.

"Dad, what was it?"

Tihomir's dad showed surprise in his face, "How do you feel now?"

"Okay, I guess. But it really hurt. I thought I had stepped on a nail or something. I saw a hole in my shoe. The scientist guy took off my shoe, and blood gushed out from the bottom of my foot."

"Did they take you to the hospital?"

"No. The scientist guy, I remember, he said his name was Ziggy, started to put gauze on the bottom of my foot, but by then the bleeding had stopped, and then when he was done, I looked at it and I didn't even find a cut, just a line in the skin where there was blood. The scientist guy looked kind of shocked."

Tihomir's dad then told Tihomir a story about when his dad was a little boy, he witnessed his mom breathe life into a neighbor's baby who had stopped breathing. "Your Busia promised me to swear to never tell anyone about that." Tihomir then said, "That sounds like mouth-to-mouth resuscitation. We learned about it in school." Tihomir's dad acknowledged, "Yes...yes, that's what it was, but no one had heard of it yet. She was worried people would think she was a witch if they knew what happened."

Tihomir's dad shared some more information. "When I was a bit younger than you, I tried to jump off a roof wearing a towel like a cape around my neck because I thought I could be like Superman. Busia found out what I was doing, and she ran outside and shouted at me "Tihomir what are you doing. You can't fly." Thinking I was smart, I shouted, "Superman does it this way on the radio." Your Busia told me the radio was sometimes make-believe. Tihomir asked, "Did you jump?" Tihomir's dad said "No", but he added probably would have if a group of crows hadn't flown by and scared him back into the house through the window.

Tihomir stood on the flat roof, black gravel stones laid out like a beach before him. "Okay, son, we have to take all of these stones down to the back yard. Scoop them into the buckets and carry them down." His dad's white t-shirt was ripped in places, at the neck in front, on the sleeve on the left, and some holes pocked the stomach and back areas. They were standing on the roof, two stories up, and the yard looked like a postage stamp below.

Tihomir scooped the stones with his bare hands, scraped each hand with every scoop, on his fat pads and near his outer wrist bones. The buckets were ungodly heavy, so that he could only lift them waist high. He then tied a rope to one end and lowered one bucket, then the next into the crawl space and further down into the closet landing. Then he lowered himself down into the space, lifted a bucket with each hand, walked into the bedroom; then into the hallway; then down a flight of stairs to the first floor; then into the dining room walked some more; then into the kitchen; then down the cement stoop of three steps to the back yard and dumped the stones from each bucket into a pile. He then went back the way he came, up to the roof, and repeated this pattern about fifty times, until all the small, black stones lay in a pile in the back yard.

His dad began tarring over the old roof surface to cover seams that had opened due to weathering. Tihomir sat in the closet below to await further instructions. He wondered about what he overheard at the dinner table the evening previous when Busia and his mom were talking in the summer kitchen. Their soft-toned conversation indicated to him there was a book at the main library that may contain information about the family curse.

On a Saturday morning, early, Tihomir visited the main library in Balmoral to search for the Slavic Book of Curses. He arrived so early; the doors were still locked. He sat on the top step of the wide, concrete block steps which beckoned to passersby. There was little citizen foot traffic currently for a Saturday morning. He strained to hear whether anyone was yet inside the library. Several pigeons stared down at him from the high above eaves at the edge of the roof top. He noted bird droppings farther out along the cobblestone walkway in front of the steps. Finally, a loud bang, and a hard click warned of a turned lock. A solemn welcome commenced from the staid librarian who poked her gray-haired head out of the doorway. He had seen her many times during the school year, as one of his favorite trips resulted in a visit to the library, the most noble task he could imagine. She didn't smile this time, likely due to a hangover earned the evening before at the tavern around the corner. Tihomir believed she may have lived at the library, but he wasn't sure. The librarian made her steady way to behind the main desk, where she usually conducted the business at hand, like a maestro at the opera house symphony. He asked the librarian about the "Slavic Book of Curses". She peered down at him over the edge of thick eyeglasses after scrunching up her nose. He was led down a long spiral staircase to a dark hallway abutted by high bookshelves on each side. He asked the librarian where he should go next. She told him if he walked along, someone would help him find what he needed if it was necessary. Tihomir was confused by this instruction, but he was eager to taste the discovery of the knowledge which he had craved for so long.

He found a room, in the special reading section. It housed many old manuscripts and books. It was not forbidden to enter, just monitored by a curmudgeon of an old man who seemed too old to still exist. No one watched this section. The old man merely pointed further down the hallway. The ceiling became lower the farther Tihomir walked. He found a black door pocked on one side by multiple adorned knobs. He looked back to ask the old man a question. The old man was still there. The old man raised his left hand and turned it as if he was using one of the doorknobs. Tihomir looked at the doorknobs again, closer this time. The old man murmured, "As long as the lights are on...but when the lights go off then it is time to leave."

The door, unassuming in nature, like a janitorial closet door, was ajar, suddenly. Tihomir heard a sound, moved closer, noticed an exceptionally fine light emanate from it, along the edges near the hinged part of the door frame. His curiosity moved him closer. As he reached for the door handle a black cat suddenly brushed against his legs and tripped him into the door. The thick, heavy door didn't move forward much.

"What the ...?"

He put his hands out to push against the door but there seemed to be resistance to the effort from the other side of it. Finally, it gave way, perhaps due to a break of the grime in the door hinge joints, perhaps due to a sudden welcome for the guest. Suddenly the only light in the room, entering from the hallway, was supported by a click sound which stimulated electricity. The room became rife in shadows cast by light emanating from the random sconces anchored along the walls. If this room was the place to search, the time to start the journey had begun. He didn't know how the book would appear, whether hardcover or soft; many pages or an incantation rich few.

He walked among the tall library shelves. The smell of old parchment perfumed the room's air. A heightened sense of purpose intoxicated him. He found a black book, somewhat thread-bare at the edges of the spine. The book title was faded and unreadable. Tihomir read a section about "Curse Elements". It revealed to him:

"Words or incantation; the curse can be written down and placed in a holy place, close to the gods so they can hear or see it and apply it to the subject; an object involved, such as a doll, or writing the victim's name on an object like a bowl, then the bowl is thrown down and broken."

Another section of the book referenced chronic wounds which would draw blood as a sign of a curse. Tihomir recalled it seemed every year since he was little, he had an injury that drew blood such as falling in flip flops on the concrete alley, dripping blood everywhere; or caused blood to be drawn, at the hospital for a tonsillectomy; fractured ribs after getting bulled over by a larger player during a basketball game; a cut below his left eye while tripping into the corner of the backyard concrete steps; a cat scratching his legs. He also remembered his dad recently underwent left knee surgery. He started to wonder if Onionhead needed this blood every year to grow strong enough to apply the final curse.

He placed the old book back onto the shelf and continued searching. The lights flickered briefly but he was able to keep walking forward by putting his right hand onto the path of books stacked on the shelves to his right side. Then when the lights came back on, he felt a brief, heated sting into is right hand palm area from static electricity. He pulled back his hand and squinted to see the cause of the pain. A red, hard cover book poked out from the edge of the shelf. The book was thick. He needed two hands to remove it from the shelf. The book was newer in condition than many of the other books on the shelf, as if it had rarely been opened. It had no title. He turned the cover and noted many symbols and signs drawn into the outer edges of the pages. There were also handwritten notes, perhaps in pencil, in the margins of some of the text, but not written in English. He found a part in the book about Witchcraft and Curses. He read about The Evil Eye and Hexes. None of the references related to generational curses, except one: Menstrual Power. A single drop of a woman's menstruation blood combined with other select ingredients, then administered during a curse incantation, could create a powerful spell which deactivated the victim's energy. The curse, near unbreakable, could last long into future family generations of the cursed subject. Some protective measures involved planting certain botanicals on one's property. Tihomir guessed planting onions and eating them in food dishes served as a means of defense. The lights in the room went out. He felt his way back to the door and entered the hallway. He didn't find any cure for the curse. He began the trek back to home.

Police Officer Goralski, Tihomir's dad, drove on duty his assigned vehicle. The Officer thought he hit something on one of those Highlandville neighborhood streets in the city, lined on each side by red brick rowhouses topped by flat gravel roofs and bordered by marble front steps (usually three) which sprung from the concrete sidewalk at street level. He stopped in the middle of the street, shifted the transmission into "Park" gear, and turned on the vehicle emergency lights. Patrons of the tavern at the corner could be heard debating the latest sports controversy projected from the television inside.

Officer Goralski exited the vehicle to get a good look at the front bumper area. The engine was still humming as Officer Goralski looked down at the front-end area where he saw nothing of consequence. He then lay down on his back to peer under the vehicle when a dark, smallish figure appeared in the driver's

seat, according to a somewhat inebriated witness
smoking a cigarette while standing on the sidewalk
outside the tavern. The police car then moved
forward, over top of Officer Goralski, which pinned
him and suffocated him to death. This evening marked
his thirty-fifth and last birthday.

9

After the funeral, in his grief, Tihomir sought solace from Busia. The solace was not forthcoming. Busia told him about his father, and the ravages of the curse. Tihomir learned his father had been injured many times on his job as a police officer, yet there are no hospital records of his injuries. He had been shot, stabbed, assaulted by a gang from Pigtown, knocked out of his police vehicle when it was t-boned by another police car that ran a stop sign. The Onionhead curse was unrelenting in the creation of suffering for the cursed one. Busia tried to find a cure for the curse or a means to extinguish it. No such means was found. There was a book called "Slavic Book of Curses" she heard about, but she could not find it, nor could her family cr friends find it here or in the old country. She said there are some curses, so evil, they are not written down, but they don't die, they are merely passed down from generation to generation of the family who discovered the machinations and materials to create such poison of the soul. Even the Baba Yaga of many of those generations was consulted to no avail. "Don't lose hope", Busia counselled. The first-born of each generation inherited the curse, yet also carried the burden of extinguishing it. "I will be here for you."

An old Polish woman from the neighborhood stood in a church, talked with a priest, about Tihomir and the curse. This priest eventually alerted the office of The Holy See in Rome about Tihomir's existence, important in the few decades ahead which remained for the world as it was presently known.

Tihomir's life radically changed. His high school and college years passed quickly but not absent the repetitive, self-healing injuries and cursory relationships which allowed him to fit in and lose himself in the crowd. Those times are another story not necessary to know here. He lost touch with his mom and Busia as tensions in the family increased.

His friends became few until they were none due to
his inability to communicate his dilemma. He hid his
reality behind a veil he could not allow to be
pierced. He tried to stay out of trouble, but trouble
found him like flies found stink and death. He moved
out on his own to face his inevitable future. He found
a job after college as an insurance investigator. The
job allowed him to travel all over the city where he
learned much about the culture and issues facing many
of the communities. He became a lost soul in this
city where it was near impossible to become lost.

End Onionhead

PART SECOND - ZONER

1

Every day itched a search for something to do. During the search, an avoidance of the prevailing authority's will or wrath, whether parent, spouse, boss, friend or government source, morphed into an ever-present danger lurking nearby. Everyone worked towards a moment or more of solace; a place or state of protection from the prevailing officialdom. Tihomir Goralski's early adulthood story began, like all stories began, subjected to these mores.

His first work duty, in exchange for a small increase in weekly pay, was to pick up that day's mail; deliver it before all others arrived at work; except for one sleepy-eyed male boss and one buxom female secretary who assisted in opening and categorizing the tasks presented by the client letters received. He was driving, making sure the sack of mail in the back of his old, beige Chevette wasn't spilling over in the back, under the rear hatch. Traffic on a city street, in the bowels of Balmoral, amidst rowhouses, still lit streetlamps, traffic lights and telephone poles and their wiry appendages decorated the view. Six in the morning, before much of the rest of the city had stirred itself to assigned tasks, he proceeded onward. The sky still bore signs of the pre-dawn gray about to be pierced by a hot sun.

The drive through the city streets included his effort to find on the radio knob a station that worked, as most didn't work because the radio went on the fritz when the Chevette reached 7,000 miles, a mystery the dealership could never resolve. He entered the suburbs, where the trees became more dominant in appearance and where the rowhouses gave way to patches of semi-detached and single homes. The traffic lights were farther apart from each other. A strip mall exerted itself upon the roadway side at one interval due to legally passed zoning ordinances in some cases and spawned by the political graft that allowed collaborators to overcome the residential solitude. For every mall storefront there was a local politician living high on the hog. He stopped at a traffic light just down the street from the office building where he worked as an insurance investigator, in the suburb of Townsend.

BOOM!

The back of the Chevette was caved in by a faded green Chevy Nova. Tihomir's head banged back against the headrest pad. After the stars in his brain cleared, he looked in the rear-view mirror. A gray-haired head he could see sticking to the underside of the Nova's windshield on the driver's side. The Chevette slowly drifted across the traffic intersection, against the still red traffic light. A Dunkin' Donuts delivery truck swerved, nearly t-boned the Chevette, then scraped the median sidewalk and kept going. The thought of a chocolate crème-filled donut temporarily alleviated Tihomir's anxiety. He was able to pull over to the curb on his right. He overlapped his unbuttoned G-Man styled overcoat across his upper body, then exited after a hard push against the driver's door and lurched back to check on the Nova. He could see an older looking male in the driver's seat. Tihomir recognized him as the chemist who worked in a small building, Melki Medical Labs, just across the street from where Tihomir worked. Tihomir had been to the building a few weeks ago to drop off paint chip samples he took from the interior walls of a rowhouse for a lead paint poison case he had been investigating in the city. The chemist was dressed in a dingy gray and frayed looking lab coat which clung to his pear-shaped upper frame like a candy wrapper, as if he had not removed it in days. A name tag pinned to the left chest area of the lab coat read "Dr. Zygmunt Zeis". The Doc raised his head, looked dazed. Smoke seeped from under the hood out of the front of the Nova.

"Doc, you okay?"

The Doc rolled down his window. He stammered out a response.

"Oh, it's you. I have the test results ready for you on those paint chips."

"Thanks, Doc, but are you okay?"

"Yes, yes. Sorry, too much on my mind lately."

"Stay in the car," Tihomir responded.

Tihomir looked around and down the street in both directions. No vehicles were moving. The streetlights had just clicked off. He looked around at the nearby houses. He could see some lights were on, but nobody seemed to be outside yet. He walked behind the Nova, then pushed it across the two-lane road, onto the other side and along the street.

"Doc, turn the steering wheel to the left."

Tihomir then pushed the Nova onto the parking lot at Melki Medical Labs. He then walked back to the front of the Nova to pop the hood, but Doc stopped him.

"That's okay. I can call someone to take care of that."

The Doc started to get out of the driver's side.

"Doc, turn off the ignition."

Doc did so. As he stood outside the Nova, he started to tip. Tihomir held him upright and walked alongside him until both negotiated the steps down to the side door, the only door that ever seemed to be in use.

"How did you do that, push the car like that?" Doc asked.

"That's what I do, Doc. That's what I do."

"Bad weather coming, bad weather." Doc added.

Tihomir looked up into a clear blue sky as the Sun exerted dominance over the great expanse of it. Still, there was an icy chill in the air, which foreboded something wicked this way was to come. Tihomir walked back to his car. The back-end damage didn't look as bad as he had initially thought. He started it, backed up, crossed the street and parked on the lot in front of his work building. He reached back from inside the passenger compartment and pulled out the mail bag. At least the mail hadn't flown everywhere.

He entered the lobby carrying the mail bag over his shoulder, saluted the elevator doors, pressed the "up" arrow button, the doors rolled open, he entered, enjoyed the stomach tickle from the sudden upward surge, a bell sound echoed, the doors slid open, he walked to the large window in the second-floor landing and looked over at the Melki Medical building. "Damn, I forgot to pick up the paint chips report." He turned around and entered the large door into the sprawling office area inhabited by long, rectangular tables, plastic chairs, chunky green desks in the secretarial area, dropped the mail bag at the mail processing desk, plopped his coat onto the long table across the aisle at his work area, sat in one of the plastic chairs at the mail table, opened the center drawer of the mail area desk, slid out a letter opener, and started separating the papers into categories based on investigation type: locate; surveillance; assets check; worker's compensation check; background check; insurance application check; disability status.

The empty rows of desks in the middle of the room would soon become occupied by other investigators. Separate desks formed a long column next to the large windows, which allowed a view to the rear parking lot and awaited the arrival of managers who supervised the investigator groups. The mail secretary had arrived as evidenced by the door squeak at the room entrance. She removed her dark, blue winter coat and hung it over a chair at the boundary between the mail table and the file cabinets sentried along most of the interior walls. She picked up a few of the pile stacks Tihomir had created, then she turned towards the filing cabinets, which exposed the form fit of the light brown dress pressed against her skin, to look for blank folders stacked on the cabinet top. As she reached upward to pick up some folders, her taught dress rose from the hem just below the back of appealingly thick thighs. The dress hem moved halfway upward of her thighs and tightened further around the curvy line of a most plump and pleasant-in-appearance derriere, highlighted by the upward tilt of her bare right heel from the surface of a too high shoe tip from sole to floor. Tihomir unsuccessfully attempted to avoid a side glance. The secretary's delicate right hand then clutched a blue magic marker. She commenced to address a label with the name of the client, subject matter of the investigation, and date of receipt to identify the folder, then stuck the label on the file folder, turned back around to face the mail table and placed it on the desk. The dress was made of an untimely thin material, given the impending weather situation Doc anticipated. The dress betrayed the lines of a thong when the secretary stretched one way or another in the slightest manner. A ruffled white blouse which seemed to serve as a hammock for a generous dose of two, taught breasts distracted attention from the waist down assets. None the less, Tihomir toiled towards conclusion of envelope edge severance and categorization of the specific contents.

A somewhat portly well-suited man, a manager, nicknamed secretly by his underlings as "Walrus", entered from another door not visible to the general employee populace, tugged on his thick, brown moustache as he ambled over to Tihomir and asked him if he could stay until everyone left, to lock up, due to the predicted, impending heavy accumulation snow storm. Tihomir snapped his gaze from the direction of the thong print exposure on the secretary's butt area. He squelched a wince, "Sure."

Tihomir's co-workers entered, and as more arrived over the next two hours, talk of the storm, which had begun to slowly mass and accumulate, became front and center. He had plenty of paperwork to do in files scattered across his desk. An ashtray at one corner of his work desk held smoked cigarette butts. An in-progress butt dangled on the edge of the clear glass edge, about three-quarters consumed. His desk mate had noticed, as was his nature, the rear bumper and body panel damage to the Chevette. "No worries," Tihomir mumbled.

He took a break, walked out of the office door and along the second-floor landing of the office hallway. The building interior looked prettier when the lights were low. He reflected in a way that identified his current station in life. His simple theory of existence had evolved into "Life sucks, then you die." Of Slavic heritage (his head somewhat crooked in the back, especially seen from above, behind and side views, and slightly below average height; mesomorph body type), he was in a relationship with a tall, slim, blonde young woman who worked for a subsidiary company across the hallway. The first time ever he saw her face, he became entranced by a physical beauty he had never known. He knew now she was getting tired of him, his too much alcohol drinking, his too much cigarette smoking. She then came out to the landing from her office across the hall. The company she worked for had released everyone to go home. He soaked in the pleasant aroma of her incredible, natural scent. "See you tomorrow." He watched her slowly walk away, imagined wishing her well, imagined giving her the best of his love. He turned and went back into his office area to work at his desk, checked directions for the places he must visit for inspections, but lost track of the time.

He got up to stretch and looked out the room window. The snow had laid as a thick carpet of nuisance upon the parking lot. Then the "Walrus" came into the main area and announced everyone should leave now. Of course, Tihomir knew he wasn't included in that group. The bubble butt secretary immediately stood and headed for the coat rack. Others too scrambled to gather their paperwork and exit. After a short while, everyone was gone. The silence of the room enhanced his loneliness. A dull buzz from the sentry rows of fluorescent lights hovered above his head. The tick of a wall clock on one of the room columns sounded like a hammer hitting a nail. He walked back to his desk and continued working on his paperwork. His work concentration blotted out the regimental din of the fluorescents and their accomplice, the column clock. After a good while he had to stand up again to stretch. He walked along the back windows to make sure everyone had exited successfully, saw no vehicles, but now about a foot of snow accumulation. He had stayed too long. Now he stood completely alone, resigned to the fact he would have to find a vinyl lobby couch to sleep on until sunrise cold melt the legions of snow.

Now he had too much time to think. His girlfriend's face, a face of hope and grace, reminded him of his disparate failures. He hadn't, couldn't confide to her his secret, the curse. He came to realize he would have to reject her friendship, and later love, but he wasn't able to muster the courage to release her from what could only be the misery of his destiny. She had rescued him from his self-pity, over-drinking binges on too many occasions already, for his liking. He didn't want to reject her, yet he knew her love could not save him, and further his inability to express his love would only make things worse for her in the long run. He felt it was unfair to her for him to continue such a relationship. He never considered a serious relationship as an escape from his fate, yet he allowed himself to become captured by her beauty and charm. A false hope never failed meaning

for him. Falling out of love was an evil corollary
to falling in love in the first place. He had showed
her his many physical scars, at his shabby apartment
a while back, and he talked down about himself to
break the bond that had been forming between them.
He imagined she could do better than his destiny.
What made it worse was she had helped dig his car out
of a snowstorm a month ago when he was stuck on the
same parking lot, the one he peered down upon. He
couldn't imagine what she saw in him. He decided it
was time to take a nap on the lounge couch.

During the nap, he dreamed about his grandfather whom
everyone called Dziadek. Tihomir was a child again.
He sat at the edge of a green cloth couch adorned in
leaf and tree patterns. Every so often in the design
of the cloth, a woman in a long dress, wearing a wide
brimmed hat, smiled holding a closed umbrella over
her shoulder like a soldier standing at attention in
formation. Dziadek didn't talk much, but in this
dream, he told the story of Tihomir's father at the
time he was born. Busia was in the hospital delivery
room with the doctor and nurses. The doctor came out
into the hallway and told Dziadek that there were
complications, and Dziadek had to decide whether the
doctor should try to save Busia or the baby struggling
to see the light of day. Dziadek and Busia had been
trying to have a child for a while. He didn't
hesitate, "Save them both." Tihomir had many
questions, but the dream scene faded.

Tihomir awoke and walked out to the landing again.
The curtain of evening had opened. At the window he
looked down at his car. The snow had covered up to
the tire's tops, the wheel wells almost shrouded. All
around was in cinder block deep snow cover. He
realized he was going nowhere while employed as a
marginally competent insurance investigator, and he
was going nowhere in his car tonight. He would have
plenty of time to abhor thoughts of his
procrastinating, daydreaming, tragic-comic loser
life for an evening; to dream about tomorrow; waste

away in between. He had plenty of time to allow his opinionated rants about global cooling mania, city politicians micro-managing his life (root beer, poured from a keg, was now subject to the liquor tax; smoking was outlawed in all public places controlled by the government), and an over-reaching central government constantly trying to squeeze more money from his pay (to cover for massive income redistribution because the government knows better who should have the money) and control over his life. He zoned in and out of reality both literally and figuratively.

He called himself Zoner, to himself only. His mind wandered way too much for someone alone. He lacked self-confidence, so when he was talking to someone, perhaps as a device to mask this introverted nature, he could only see part of the other person's face, or he saw their wrinkled shoes, or their too round chin, or something to their right or left of their face; misplaced hair of the head; grimy jewelry around the neck or wrists; pretentious makeup against the face; with only a partial face in the picture as he could not bear to take it all in at one look. He continuously left unfinished business wherever he went. For some, they found ways to make life suck a little bit less before they died. For him, he soaked in as much misery as possible, so he could mentally vomit it back out, to refresh the demon inside him by making it heave, go breathless, gag, rattle the misery back out.

The snow kept falling, silently, dancing a slow jig; hordes of it as far as his eyes could see. A hushed mauling of the landscape ensued, methodically, as if ants marching to the disabled prey. His parked car, down below, perched surrounded, imbedded in the bleached nightmare. His head hurt from imagination pounding. He tried to shut it off; if he could only find the button, he would punch it hard. He squinted through the virulent swarm of snowflakes, looked across the street, over the top of the one story, small building below, where he hoped to see the lights turned on, if they still were turned on, at Angelina's Bar, a hangout for him and others of the Townsend wasteland; to pass time, forget regrets; emotionally consume jukebox music; trade fairy tales of past glories and tragic stories of a life half-lived, at best, and at worst, drink sorrows away; zone out, at least for one night.

He suddenly realized he didn't know anything about the little building he had just glanced over, Doc's work building, in order to glimpse his drinking destination. He considered the intended destination trek as a walk in two feet of snow for which no obstacle existed to forestall a good drunk fest. He could smoke a few unfiltered Camel cigarettes along the way. The taste of a Guinness dark stout draft beer was well worth the effort. Still, his imagination was clogged by a curiosity about the small building. He had never paid any attention to it until now. There was the hint of a light turned on inside. Someone may be there, but who?

His imagination was interrupted by the engine sound of a delivery truck plowing down the road, spraying snow away. The driver seemed to be on a mission, or perhaps the driver had just left Angelina's. The vehicle tried to stop and slid a one eighty half circle in the middle of the street, right in front of the entrance to the small building. The engine revved hard, sounded like a banshee, then the truck waggled forward side to side and was stopped by the cement stairwell jutting from the edge of the small building. The driver stumbled out and face planted into the snow. For a minute he didn't move. Then as if inspired, he flung the snow away from his body as if creating a snow angel. He exerted tremendous effort to get topside of the snow and remain straightened on his legs as he stood up. He lurched to the back of the truck, pushed up the back door. All was quiet outside, like in a church on Sunday during the moments before the Priest comes out to begin the ceremony, such was the effect of the snowfall upon the landscape.

The delivery man displayed every indication of the result of the warped temptations of Angelina's Bar, yet carried onward. He removed a white, taped box from the cargo area, carried it with both arms as if a wedding cake, then attempted to take the first step down the stairwell. Tihomir could see the disaster happening before that step. As expected, the delivery man slipped backwards and slid down the snow pocked steps as if a child sliding down a playground slide. The white box remained clasped in both arms. The delivery man's cap remained on his head, a miracle, until he came to rest at the bottom of the stairwell, box still clasped like a new-born in swaddling clothes. "This guy is brilliant if not a drunk fool, in respect to his duty," Tihomir thought.

The door to the stairwell area slowly opened. Doc Zeis reached out with both arms to clasp the box package, disappeared, then could be seen again at the doorway. He signed the delivery slip the driver had pulled from his jacket pocket. Then the delivery man finally sobered, perhaps relieved by completion of his mission, marched up the stairs, closed hard the rear door of the truck in an echoing slam, then hopped into the driver's side, revved the engine and waited for the wheels to catch pavement after blowing out all of the snowfall, backed into the empty street, sped to the corner, and turned left into the direction of Angelina's Bar. Tihomir believed he had just witnessed a mastery of delivery skills, a mastery of drinking while driving, only achieved as there were no other vehicles or persons on the road given the weather conditions, except the delivery driver would have to explain the damage to the front end of the truck's bumper. Tihomir looked back at the bottom of the stairwell. The door was closed and there was not a sign of Doc.

Tihomir remained standing at the second-floor landing

to consider whether he should take a closer look at the small building across the street. The weather told him no. His better senses told him no. There was no point. Just a box delivered. It was too cold. The wind started picking up to blow the snow sideways. He wondered why Doc was still at his office. The night descended in a desperate rage to consume the snow-covered landscape, but the streetlights sabotaged the effort to enhance the glow from the ground all along the wide swath of the snowfall blanket.

Since Doc was still in the building, Tihomir decided to make a visit. He walked down the stairs, instead of using the elevator, in order to get some exercise. He viewed the distance from the glass doors in front of him at the entrance. Before starting the adventure, he let his imagination loose first. His imagination captured a view from the back of a rat's head in the foreground, in the background he could see across the covered asphalt street, lined by cement sidewalks on each side, then across a lined parking lot, and he pinpointed a focal point to the left side of the entrance to the "secret" government office building. He was liking his interpretation, until the part where the snow had hidden the sidewalks and asphalt, meaning his dress shoes and socks would become locked onto by the snow at every step.

His imagination could see a few other rats had found a way into the lab building on the right side where the snow had not accumulated to any degree because the wind was blocked by the building. A congregation of three rats seemed to communicate about what had been found inside. Given the visibility of rats at the building exterior, in the middle of a snowstorm, there must have been a significant nest of rodents around, behind, or under the building; or perhaps in the wall or the area above the ceiling. The building only had one floor and basement. Doc must have been able to hear the rats squeak and move in the evenings. Perhaps the sounds were comfort to the Doc. The rats' paw prints would betray their point of entry.

Tihomir imagined he was a crow as he flew to the metal-barred basement window and looked in upon the contents he might find in the basement of the lab: many boxes, crates, shelves lined with containers marked by stickers of sequential numbers. A deformed rat lay in a corner of the basement, lighted only by the moonlight shining in from the metal-barred basement window. The bars' shadows further deformed the appearance of the rat's body.

The crow heard a noise from above, at the roof line, then saw Doc Zeis' face as it looked out from a sole, hazy windowpane. Some roaches worked their way, upside down, along the partially sloped eave of the roof. An unmarked black van pulled in front of the building to snap Tihomir out of his daydream. He patted his overcoat to make sure he was out of his imagined state of mind. "That's odd," he thought. Another delivery in this weather seemed to reek of desperation or significant deliberation, but which instance he didn't know. He became ever more certain he must find out. He buttoned up his overcoat. He could use the paint chip test results as a ruse to trudge through the storm to visit Doc, to learn more about his "business".

Two delivery men exited the van. They wore one piece, body length gray flannels, red gloves and black caps which didn't betray any identification, like the mystery van. The delivery men went down the staircase to the basement, one of them cradling a black container the size of a thermos. Tihomir took his chance, pushed open the glass doors, moved hurriedly across the parking lot, almost slipping onto his car as he passed it, then continued the adventure across the street. The lone, nearby streetlight flickered like a single candle on a birthday cake. He walked around the basement staircase to the other side, nearest the door, in the hope he could hear any conversation. Fortunately, the basement door was partially left open, stuck by the amount of snow which had fallen into the entrance way when the door was previously opened.

He could hear Doc Zeis' voice, "Is this the one?" A delivery fellow said, "I don't know Doc, officially, I don't know ... read this." Tihomir could see a bit inside the opened door area as he leaned over the metal railing. The Doc held in his right hand an uncrumpled paper invoice with numbers and letters on it while the delivery man still held onto the shoebox-sized black box. Doc moved the paper up to his lips and used them to hold the paper. He pulled eyeglasses out of his lower right lab coat pocket with his right hand and placed the stems neatly upon his ears and the bridge low upon his nose. The left hand remained for an unknown reason hidden in his lower left coat pocket. He then pulled from his lips the invoice and rubbed it along his lab coat to flatten it. "It's here!" Doc shouted in an intoxicated tone. Tihomir couldn't tell if Doc was intoxicated by the box or something else. The delivery men nudged open the basement door as the wind blew snow upon them, pushed the box against Doc's chest, then Doc cradled it in his right arm. The delivery men quickly ascended the stairs as if they were late for something or running away.

Tihomir bent down in a crouch. The storm was now unbearable. After the delivery truck left, he alternately walked and slid down the steps and shouted, before reaching the bottom, to the Doc as the Doc was trying to close the door. "Let me get that Doc." Tihomir kicked away chunks of the snow. Doc seemed surprised, then remembered Tihomir and said, "Oh, good to see you. Feeling better?" Tihomir's feet and hands were freezing and his face was burning from the cold. Parts of his hair were pocked with ice crystals. He was able to clear the doorway, then leaned his back against the door until it closed with a click near the door handle. "Got anything warm to drink, Doc?" The Doc nodded, "Call me Ziggy. Have a seat." The only seat was a metal folding chair at a small square table. The crumbs and spills on the tabletop indicated it was primarily used for food consumption. Tihomir sat down, unbuttoned his coat. The cement floor was spared the adornment of carpet.

Doc Ziggy went over to a small refrigerator in the corner of the room. He opened it and asked, "Pabst Blue Ribbon or Schlitz?" Tihomir frowned. "That's as warm as it gets around here," Doc laughed. He pulled out one can of each. He gave the Schlitz to Tihomir. For a basement, the room was warm, particularly given the cinder block walls, unpainted, echoing a somewhat Spartan existence as well as the spritz sound from the pull of the beer can tabs. They each took a long chug of their respective cans of a winter's night medicine. Tihomir looked at the expiration date on his Schlitz can. "This thing expired six months ago." The Doc passed it off as many things are expired yet people still use them. The Doc's tone plucked a nerve with Tihomir, ringing out of him the concern of his own ultimate demise at about age thirty-five.

The room wasn't engineered for comfort of the body. It was the inspiration for Doc's experiments, yet relatively warm given the appearance. Tihomir noticed Doc started to open the black box, spraying plastic bubbles to reveal a silver thermos container. "No, it isn't hot anything," Doc chimed. Doc was having trouble screwing open the top of the thermos. He used his left hand to make the turns. "Does that hurt, using that hand?" Doc shrugged, "Only when I use it." Tihomir was noticeably curious about the thermos contents, and Doc's left hand. "One of my experiments, on the government dime," Doc offered. Tihomir wondered if Doc meant the contents of the thermos or his left hand. The basement room was only lit in the part they were seated, the remainder hidden in an ever-darkened gray to black curtain which cloaked the inner walls. Doc seemed satisfied after a determination of the thermos contents. Tihomir, emboldened by the beer, asked the Doc, "Do you believe in curses?" Doc looked Tihomir in the eyes for a bit.

"Son, a curse isn't a matter of belief. It is a matter of science. There are elements necessary to complete the concoction." Tihomir gulped the last swig of the Schlitz. Doc went to the fridge to get another Schlitz for Tihomir, and a Pabst for himself. No lack of speed impeded the Doc from returning to the table, as he seemed to relish the pop sound of another pulled tab.

They popped the tops, saluted each other, and gulped some more of the expired beer. At this point, Tihomir felt comfortable asking one more question. "Would you believe it if I told you I am cursed?" Doc sighed, "We are all cursed." Tihomir became frustrated. "No, listen, I am really cursed, my family, for many years." Doc holds up his left hand, then speaks, "This mutation was self-inflicted, due to my own curse of curiosity, as a scientist, to explore where science has not yet been explored. My tests did the same to my house guests, the white rats, rabbits, yet I was convinced a proper dose administered to a human would work. I injected only my left hand, used a small volume of the experimental liquid, the same liquid in the tiny containers housed in this thermos, and voila."

Tihomir lost the patience for talking in circles. "Doc, I will be back, just need to make a trip down the road." Doc squinted at him over his eyeglass rims. "Okay, see you soon." Tihomir didn't know how to respond. He was not expecting to be back soon. He decided a trip to Angelina's was in order, at least for some newer, tastier beer, plus he needed a smoke, or two, or three. He stood, walked to the door, looked back at the Doc, who continued to sit, hunched over, at the square table. Tihomir pulled open the basement door, stepped into the cold night, noticed the snow had stopped falling, closed the door, and began the slog.

2

Angelina's was now closed. He would have to seek out the broken and malevolent elsewhere. The weather had taken a toll on businesses along his way. Every location was closed. Tihomir heard music further down the road, so he ventured in that direction. Perhaps Lucky Spirits, a strip joint, was open. He arrived to find the lights still turned on, and he heard the sensual music of the lonely hearted tempt his soul to enter, which he did. His yearning for solace was once again stimulated by the interior dim lights. He noticed the two delivery men were hanging out here also. They seemed to enjoy the focal point of the establishment, the circular stage centered in the low-lit, mirrored room, where female strippers in high heels swished and chirped like crickets along the stage floor. Beer mugs, frosty, frothy clanked at varied intervals of bravado and cheer for the on-stage entertainers. The delivery men sipped from glass mugs, leaning back on the ledge of the main bar while seated on high stools. They were entranced by a scantily clad, medium bosomed, long haired brunette of thin calves, thick thighs, G-string panties, spectacled pasties. She clung to a silver pole which reached from ceiling to stage floor, immobile, as she wound her body like a snake about it. Her motion was accompanied by her chosen song of sensual emotion. Tihomir, after his second Guinness dark, became mesmerized by the dancer. His trance was only broken by a curse word shouted by the delivery driver. "We were supposed to drop off two packages. We have to go back to the medical lab down the road." Off the two men jumped from the bar stools. Tihomir started to stare back at the stage floor but the music had stopped. The dancer's high heels clacked along the stage floor to the side steps to change her music. It was only then Tihomir's trance completely evaporated, only to punch him in the face with a cold realization the two delivery men were delivering another package to Doc Ziggy. Tihomir heard a door slam. He looked at the entrance and realized the delivery men had started their trip. He threw some money onto the bar top, then jogged to the entrance door, opened it, and found only the tire tracks of the delivery van in the now unoccupied parking space of the van. He started to jog back into the direction of Doc's lab, but his groin told him to pee first, so he went back into the bar to take care of nature's need.

He walked to the bathroom and up to the wall urinal inside the Lucky Spirits, unzipped and pissed. A newspaper front page from the "News Journal" taped to the wall at eye level blazed a headline, "Chinese Premier Visits Capital." He finished his necessary task at the urinal, walked over to the sink and looked in the mirror. He lamented his average look: scar under his right eye from hitting a concrete step while running as a kid; scar on his chin from falling on a concrete alleyway while running in flip flops playing step ball; and scar to the right of his eyebrow from a football tackle on a cheap, rocky, dirt practice field in high school. The newspaper headline stared back at him in the mirror, over one of his shoulders.

When he started the trek back to Doc Ziggy's lab, he just followed the tire tracks of the delivery van, to reaffirm his notion the van destination was in fact the lab. He had hoped it wasn't. He retraced his footsteps and tried to step in the footprints to make the walk easier. When he turned the corner of the lab, he found two sets of deep footprints which he followed. One set continued towards the basement stairwell, but the other set moved off towards the parking lot entrance. He noticed the van, the front end impaled into a telephone pole. He trudged over to the driver's side where the door was open. At the entrance to the driver's side a dark blue liquid oozed in great volume from the driver's seat into the snow on the ground amidst what appeared to be clothing, gloves, work boots of one of the delivery men, but no body. No living person was nearby. He wondered if a naked delivery driver was running around in the snow-battered wilderness of Townsend. He jogged over to the building stairwell and noticed the basement interior light was still turned on. He also noticed deep shoe prints of himself and the drivers and passenger from the previous entry and exit moments, but the prints showed a bluish tint to them. He started to step down along the side of the prints, along the railing side, left hand on the iron railing.

He discovered the flannel, cap, gloves and work boots of the other delivery man amidst a bubbling dark blue liquid. The liquid was squirming as if stuffed with undulating foam. A dark blue pool of liquid snaked into the bottom of the stairwell French drain. The basement door was partially open and exposed the liquid had seeped into the interior floor area. He straddled the blue liquid, tried not to step into it, and pushed open the door. He followed the snaky liquid trail into the darker recesses of the room. He spied a small box laying on one side, leaking from underneath. The heating system kicked in with a grunt. A blue haze was being sucked into the building vents and he swore he heard distant sounds of speech, a conversation perhaps, far away yet close. He tried to fathom all that he had seen. The voice sounds were an echo. It was just one voice that echoed. Since he could not see the source, he was forced to search in the less lighted parts of the room.

A long tabletop, black, supported by cabinetry below, exposed beakers, a Bunsen burner, various vials and liquid-filled bottles. Two exceptionally large boxes blocked his access to the other side of the room. A bluish green liquid he could now see laid across parts of the concrete floor, following the path of cracks in the cement floor and puddled in places. He heard a movement just on the other side of the second, larger box, like a swishing of plastic packing bubbles. The sole of a black shoe came into his focus, the heel of it partially drowned in the plastic bubbles around it, the toe pointing to the right corner of the room. He pressed onward, carefully, as

he waded through the boxes and plastic bubbles. He
reached out towards the shoe. The shoe connected to
a dark, wrinkled pants leg and showed a faded crease
like the owner never ironed it. Tihomir drew back his
hand. What if it was Doc and he touched the blue
liquid?

"Who are YOU?" an older man's voice trickled out of
the half-darkness. "Doc, it's me, Tihomir." Tihomir
leaned forward, pulled off his overcoat, and placed
it over top Doc's body to help warm him. In the
dimmest of light, almost candle power only, Doc
showed a dazed face, half open eyes, and jaw dropped
mouth. His good hand reached up and pulled down
partially Tihomir's white button-down shirt which
popped several buttons down to the belly and
revealing the odd-scripted word "Blessed" tattooed on
the upper portion of Tihomir's chest. "Doc, did the
blue liquid touch you?"

Doc started to come to his senses more. He blurted
out "Nano-chemical introduction-liquid form is too
strong, deadly..." while wincing over his sore back
and the back of his head. "Need to put it into solid
form, like a patch, to stabilize it." Tihomir looked
down at the cement floor behind him and noticed the
bluish liquid was moving towards them. "Doc, the
liquid, it is following us. Tihomir searched in a
wall cabinet to his right, found a claw hammer,
grabbed it hurriedly, crept over to Doc, cocked the
claw hammer back. Doc, still in a bit of a daze
panicked, showed fear in his face, reached out his
hands to block what he perceived as an impending blow.
Doc screamed, "No!" but the claw hammer descended and
dug into the only drywall in this part of the basement
walls just inches above the scientist's head. Tihomir
dug out some drywall pieces, some two-by-four wood
chips followed in unison and splintered against each
of the men due to the ripping motion of the hammer.
Tihomir crumpled the wall debris in his hands, then
packed it onto the cement floor surface to redirect
the blue liquid away from each of them. He continued

raking the drywall panel with the hammer, clumped it together and tossed it near the basement door to prevent more liquid from entering. He carefully dropped some of the drywall pieces into the blue liquid to sop up the flow, but the liquid seemed to have a mind of its own. It moved over, around and through the drywall, slowly, steadily, until it reached Tihomir's snow slushed shoe, then damp sock, then like a sticky molasses, spread across his shin. "Are you insane?" Doc stammered. He didn't notice what had happened to Tihomir's leg. "Doc, it's...it's on my leg. What...what do I do?" Tihomir's voice trembled. Tihomir winced, "It stings." Doc offered, "You aren't dead yet. The other two died quickly. Maybe it was diluted by their bodies." Tihomir said his leg went numb. No more pain, just numbness, now on both legs, now at his waist, up to his stomach. Then Tihomir just blurted out. "The curse, I told you... I, my family were cursed. It is a demon curse, a demon curse... my family called it Onionhead." Doc noticed the blue liquid wasn't coming towards him, it had latched only to Tihomir. "Maybe the curse, if it was real, was keeping you alive?" Doc conjectured. Tihomir nodded, "Yes, that is it. I can't die until I turn about age thirty-five...part of the curse." Tihomir's voice became shaky. Doc saw what was happening to Tihomir's body, but there was nothing he could do. He moved to his side and placed the overcoat on top of Tihomir, fully expecting him to die soon. "I will stay with you, son. If what you say is true, you should be okay. I can help you, I will help you, as best I can." Tihomir was silent. His body made no motion. It seemed to be in a cocoon state. His transformation into a different zone of existence had commenced.

Tihomir wasn't sure if he was awake or asleep. He didn't want to relate to Doc the information about his girlfriend of about 6 months' time, Marsha, distressed by his inability to focus, was moving farther away from him emotionally, fueled by his aloofness and alcoholism. Still, it wouldn't matter if he related it. He would never see the scientist again after this, so no harm, no foul. Maybe he could hear some advice he could masticate upon, discard, and drown with a few pints of Guinness dark later, if he survived. The scientist's wisdom could then filter into Tihomir's subconscious and perhaps haunt him from the boredom of daily life and the inevitable.

Doc Ziggy conjectured perhaps Tihomir's girlfriend considered Tihomir a project worthy of time and effort. Doc Ziggy decided it was time to pontificate, perhaps Tihomir could hear him, "In an Era when humans are drowning in a prism of culture-changing events and governmental controls, humanity seems doomed to collapse under the weight of their own incompetence. We all have our own demons to battle and the demons are regularly winning. Just one act by an anonymous, inconsequential soul could tip the survivability balance in favor of humanity ..."

Doc tried to stand but slipped and tripped up. Tihomir didn't realize he was dreaming now, yet he could still hear all around him, including Doc's voice and movements in the room. "Doc, Doc, I call myself Zoner. I zone in and out of reality. Sounds stupid but that is how I try to face life, my fate. I need to stay sane, don't want to hurt anyone, just get through this and go at the appointed time, but sure would like to break the curse on my family." The blank part of his dream started. The darkness descended quickly.

3

He awakened face down in a dimly lit alley between the Doc's office building and small other buildings behind it. A few green dumpsters were lined up against the back walls. Some rats gnawed at his right arm. Roaches pressed themselves in numbers on his lower back. A row of crows perched above on a nearby, wooden, electric pole wire as they peered down upon the scene. One of them braved a descent to test for edibility of the human form, attracted by the death aroma. Lightning struck nearby. The lightning strike sound scattered the creatures of the morbid opera below. Invisible gamma rays emanated from the lightning strike and rolled towards the scene. Tihomir tried to move. His body absorbed a fallen crow, some roaches and a rat much as a slice of dunked bread absorbed the broth from a soup. His body became the incubator for a new species about to spring into the world, created from the genes of each of the species attached, baked into him by the gamma rays, facilitated by the mystery blue liquid bath of hours previous. He once again lost consciousness.

He found himself seated on a stool in Owens Bar, a hole-in-the-wall place across from the strip club, in a shopping center, not aware of how he had arrived. His seat at the end of the bar nearest the long, almost wall sized front window allowed him to peer outside to recount any memory of how he had managed to travel from the origin of his transformation. The neon lights of the alphabet which spelled "Owens" transfixed him. He shook his head to avoid a hypnotic state. A face reflected towards him from the window. It was a face he didn't recognize. He noticed lone, deep footprints in the snow leading to the entrance, and the flat swash of the snow imprint of the bar door having been opened outward to accommodate a previously entered patron. He turned his head to look around the bar, and saw only a portly barmaid, and a much older gentleman seated as far away as possible, at the opposite end of the narrow room length bar.

The small, rectangular tables which lined the wall opposite the bartender's area were devoid of occupants. Three vehicles, cars, were parked outside the bar, now stuck there as the snow drift had piled up against them. Only a healthy, lengthy shoveling, or a morning to noon sun, could free them.

He turned on the bar stool to rest his elbows on the cushioned edge of the bar top. A portrait sized mirror displayed the word "Pabst" in cursive writing on the wall to his left. He kept his head down and shielded his face using the overcoat. He glanced at the "Pabst" mirror and noticed the right side of his face had not yet completely formed after his transformation. "I need a hoodie," he thought. The barmaid asked his drink choice. "Pabst", he mustered. The barmaid's buxom bottom was the only stimulation he could manage in a soul that was still dead, not yet regenerated. The old man at the other end of the bar, slurred out, eyes half open, "Hey buddy, you lost something?" Tihomir could not think of himself as Tihomir any longer. His self-appointed nickname, Zoner, seemed more appropriate, descriptive; a name for new life baptism, after his rebirth a few hours prior. The old man at the far end of the bar couldn't resist a beer induced mocking, while Zoner stared into the mirror from his left eye, "Ha-ha-half -fff yerrr fffface is mmmissssing." Zoner then noticed something. The unformed part of his face had formed, but it stuck like putty to the left of the mirror, mudded into the bar wall of knotty pine paneling; Picasso'd into the surface. The barmaid waited for the finished tap pour of the Pabst into a glass mug, but she looked over at Zoner to see if he was okay. Zoner concentrated on the left side of his face and could then see the barmaid from his left eye where it was imbedded in the wall. Time to pay up for the brew. He reached for his wallet, gone. He reached for his pocket change in the right pocket, gone. He patted the other pockets front and back, empty. He knew what he had to do. He stood up, leaned into the wall headfirst, against the left side of his face.

He emerged from a dimly lit alley behind the bar. From the inside of the wall he had travelled from the front of the building to the back. He was halfway out. In the center background of the rear wall at a steel door with a small window about head level, a face looked out towards the alley. Zoner encountered some steel and drywall nails on his way out of the wall, so as he recomposed into human form, still naked, the upper half of his body was split in two at the waist. The steel door opened, and a janitor stepped out in total shock. The janitor walked over to Zoner's severed body and started to fix things up while pushing a broom. Zoner's clothing continued to come out of the wall in a slushy mix as it slowly covered the body like warm chocolate poured onto cold ice cream. Zoner's "Blessed" tattoo regenerated onto his upper back. The deft swishing of the push broom connected the two halves of the body together again. Proud of his work, the janitor intoned, "There now."

Zoner awakened not knowing how he arrived below ground. His resting place became the sewer branches among the Pigtown neighborhood of asphalt covered narrow streets; concrete sidewalks; worn looking red brick rowhouses as stingy of emotion as an old woman's face; three-tiered narrow marble front doorsteps shiny white from moon glow; acquaintances of sewer rats. A concrete ledge served as comfort for his prone position as a pool of black water streamed to his right while his right-hand fingers dipped slightly into the streaming water, creating lines of waves. Another ledge across the water served as a track for some of the rats. They started to drop into the water and swim over to him. A crack whore wailed her disdain above his head, across the street, "Pigtown suuuuucks!" like a siren sound. Zoner laughed, "Her marketing technique needs some work."

His mind drifted among the events of the past twelve

or so hours. "No one comes to Pigtown," he thought, "Not even the cops, unless coaxed into it." The rats moved closer to him from the water and along the ledge where he rested. He raised his head to see a stream of them, in lined rows along each concrete ledge, above and below him. He imagined the rats were ready to crown him king of their domain. He remembered the displacement of his face and whether it had reconstructed. He leaned on his side at the concrete edge and looked down into the dark water. "Ah!" His face looked like a rat's face. He opened his mouth only to expose many rows of sharp teeth. "I really need a hoodie." He raised his hand from the water pool and saw what used to be a human hand was now a hairy rat's claw. He started patting his body for more confirmation and noticed his arms were not as long as they had been, yet they were more flexible. Something wiry extended out from each side of his nose: whiskers. He waggled his feet only to expose two more claws. The rats were now all around him. He tried to verbalize but only squeaks came out. He connected his thoughts to the squeaks and that seemed to work. The rat's started to move away but stayed close.

Chaos and mayhem could be heard in the distance from police sirens and women and children screams. He looked up into what was now an early morning light to spy at the street above. Through a sewer grate he viewed large tearing eyes of a small child. The child began to pout. Zoner sat up as the rats scattered from around him. His eyes adjusted to the lesser light of his environment. His vision was blurry. He waited for it to adjust. He wanted human eyes to see. His vision adjusted for human sight, but he remained in rat form. He dreaded the learning cycle necessary to call forth the parts of him needed for varied instances of survival. A pain in his abdomen told him to eat, search for food, eat. "What now? What now?" he wondered. His sewer mates' red eyes, lifeless, betrayed to him their desire to pounce like rabid demons; or perhaps he overreacted, and they were loyal servants and anxiously awaited orders. He hoped they were new-found friends of a now alone, peculiar soul. His unique body still tried to confirm the transformation activity inside it. The energy use of the process put him back to sleep.

4

His eyes opened. He still laid on his back, stretched along the concrete ledge. The black pool of sewer water sometimes revealed solid contents of food wrappings, wood splinters, dung, plastic drink bottles. Dead things like squirrels, rats, bobbled on and amid the flotsam. A revelation poisoned his mind, "Don't ... need ... anything ... now." A loud stomach growl hammer smashed the thought. "Not money, anyway." He sat up and rested back against the gray brick interior wall; left leg straight; right leg bent at knee and foot firmly on ledge; right arm relaxed across the knee. He was somewhat glad to have returned to a human form. "I don't need to buy anything. Not food. Not shelter." The rats began to move onto the ledge from side holes in the walls and creeped closer to him. They cuddled nearer to him from both sides of the ledge, almost like cats in demeanor. He was able to sense a sound frequency coming from them in unison. They were hungry. He must have been asleep a while. Street pole light filtered into the sewer from the grate above. Then an image of his girlfriend's face came into focus from his imagination. He stared at the concrete and brick wall in front of him, located on the other side of the sewer river ledge. He looked at her imagined face, the one he would never forget, of permed long blonde hair. Lioness-like eyes peered at him sideways, as a knowing smile emanated from her thin lips. He wondered if she missed him. A quite fat female rat, a dam, nudged against his chin. She clung to him as he crept along the ledge. The other rats scattered. "Guess we need to shop for curtains, Milady."

The curtains could wait. His Rattus companions needed nourishment, as did he. The word had gone out among the nest to start the march for nourishment. The mischief proceeded forward to the far end of the sewer tunnel. The group climbed up a wall and exited a grate a few blocks down the road. He was not able to fit through the grate. He concentrated his thoughts on bending around the grate impediments. He was able to go through the grate in divided form, then reattached once he was outside the grate. He was now completely in rat form. His size was a mountain among the group in comparison. The group side-tracked down a nearby alley, then raced to a series of dumpsters, too many to count, and the feast ensued as the rats covered the dumpsters like theater curtains; squeezed under the plastic hinged lids on top or penetrated through half open side doors. Once inside he and the troupe quickly devoured the supposed detritus of the Pigtown human population. The venture nearly completed; the mischief began a retreat to their underground comfort. He noticed some of the rats were still chewing on something in the back corner of the dumpster. He communicated to them it was time to leave. He wondered what they were chewing on. He moved closer and the rat group separated from the meal. He sniffed what looked like a human fetus partially wrapped in brown butcher's paper. Maybe it was a dog fetus, he wasn't sure. The fetus was already half-eaten. A sick feeling rumbled in his abdomen. He scattered through the trash, and found more fetus remains in partial decay, some already picked at by the rat swarm. His head began to pound and pound. He tried to mentally file the sight of the dumpster remains. He confided to Milady his urgent need to reconnect with a human friend. He promised to return. She looked at him, squinted her nose, then turned and moved along with the rest of the mischief.

Outside the dumpster he regenerated himself into human form. His last worn clothing of black work shoes, modest underwear, long pants, white shirt, remnants of a red tie, and the overcoat remained on him. He desperately sought out some clothing to cover his face or at least mask it in some darkness. He walked along a Pigtown street until he came across a shopping area, about two blocks long, where he found a second-hand clothing store. It was closed at this hour. He looked and sniffed around. There were no onlookers apparent. All the shops appeared to be dark inside, closed. He spotted a mannequin dressed in a black hoodie, close to the front show window. He reached his hand through the window glass, absorbed the hoodie into his hand and arm, then retracted it after making a fist. Once his hand was out of the glass, he opened it and the hoodie oozed out, then solidified into the original cloth material. He pulled down the top portion of the overcoat, still buttoned from the waist down; pulled the hoodie over his head and arms; crowded the top around his face to favor the front; pulled the overcoat back over his upper body. He used the storefront window as a mirror. He noticed his eyes were a ruby red color in the iris area. The walk to Doc Ziggy's lab, a few miles away, began in earnest. After walking a few blocks down, he noticed some crows staring at him from some of the two-story rowhouse roofs. One of them came down to him and stood on the sidewalk ahead. It cawed at him. The caw sound generated inside Zoner an energy. His body started to change. Soon his nose had extended into a beak. His ears disappeared, covered in black feathers. The hoodie and clothes absorbed into his flesh which was replaced by long feathers. His hands and arms expanded and spread into wings; his feet into springy claws of the three toes front and one in back. His legs retracted backwards at the knees. Finally, a tail fanned out in a square shape behind him. The crow then jumped up and flew back to the roof edge above. Zoner had hoped for a flying lesson.

He jumped like the crow, but he lifted so high, he went beyond the roof's edge. He descended and parked next to them. The crows rattled a sound he interpreted as mocking derision. "A little help," he rattled back at them. There were three. They alit from their perch, rattled at him some more. Then one of them came back and perched next to him, face darting back and forth, up and down, side to side. Zoner cawed at him for instructions on flight. The crow took off, flapped wings three times to gain some height to find a stronger wind, then glided around in a large circle. Zoner tried to follow along. He was surprised he could do it. He then realized the meaning of the three crows: the symbol that big changes are going to occur in his life soon. He was in the middle stage of those changes. He and his new crow mate knocked and clicked out some sounds back and forth to each other. The other crows, in unison, bowed their heads and dove towards the ground. Zoner descended onto the sidewalk. The teacher crow remained perched on the roof edge. After a few clicks of "Thanks" and "You're welcome" to each other, Zoner became airborne again and began the trip to Doc Ziggy's lab.

Zoner dropped down from his flight, behind Doc's med lab, after circling a bit to make sure no humans could notice him. He transformed back into human form. He realized the transformations were taking less time to complete. He checked to make sure his clothing was intact using hand pats all over. This time his wallet had reformed into his back pocket. The snow had melted some, started to change into slush. He noted the Chevette, parked across the street in front of his work building, was still locked in by the snow. No other cars had arrived yet likely because the side streets had not been plowed by the County. As he walked over to the staircase side of the med lab, he looked through the window near the staircase. The light was on, but Doc wasn't visible. Zoner knocked. No answer. The door was unlocked. "I need better shoes," he muttered. He pushed open the door, shouted "Doc", and started looking around.

Doc responded from another part the other room, "I want you to see something." Zoner followed Doc to a back room. The room walls were stacked about six feet high with glass cages. "What, did you start a pet store?" Zoner joked. Doc waved him closer to the shelves. Zoner didn't detect any movement in the glass cages. "They are all dead, but not before transformation." Doc pointed out. "See, this rat, I took it from the alley in back when you left. It was still alive, but I noticed a roach was connected to it. The rat absorbed the roach..." Zoner finished the sentence, "...and now it has become part of the rat, I can see the antennae and additional legs." Doc nodded yes. "And look, overhear, is another rat that mixed with a roach, but it looks more like a roach than a rat." Zoner remarked, "Crazy." Doc explained the chemical delivered to him wasn't supposed to come to him, it was meant for a Department of Defense office two blocks away. Doc continued and said he inspected the blue fluid. The fluid was a masking agent to control the microscopic enzymes housed in the fluid. "Looks like our government was experimenting on a type of military protocol to enhance the stamina of soldiers through a biochemical reaction...is the best I can tell without knowing more." Zoner was confused. Doc could see such by the expression on Zoner's face. "I am not sure why, but when the masking agent touched your body, the enzymes broke free. They should not have done so. All I can figure is something, previously unknown to me, attracted out the enzymes from the fluid and into your body." Zoner grunted, "I told you, Doc. I am cursed by a demon, as was my family, for over 500 years. The demon is inside me." Doc shook his head side to side and looked up, "Perhaps that is why you survived the en masse enzymes attack."

"Doc, there's more." Doc looked concerned. Zoner continued, "I can now become a rat, a roach, or a crow, almost at will." Doc was silent. Zoner waited to allow Doc to synthesize the meaning of the words, the implications of the reality. Doc motioned Zoner over to the last cage, in the far corner of the room. It was covered by a white cloth. Doc pulled down the cloth and it floated to the cement floor. Doc turned on a flashlight. "Look," he said. Zoner peered into the cage. There he saw a creature. The creature was part crow, part rat, part roach. It didn't move. Doc explained, "Before this creature died, it stopped moving in mid-transformation." Zoner looked long at the sight. He looked down at himself, raised up his hands into the light, felt his face. "Doc ... I can do that, too." Doc took the news as a clinician at a hospital would undertake to understand the findings of a medical exam.

"I have a plan." Doc explained an African country admired aardvarks. The scientists of that country used aardvark heart, claw nails, skin, beat the mixture with a special tree limb and wrapped it in skin and wore it around the neck, to lay against the chest. It allowed the wearer to walk through walls and rooftops. "Of course, this story is an historical myth passed down from generation to generation by the tribe who created the potion." Doc explained he could try creating the same, a potion using microscopic enzymes and when worn like a patch created the ability to mix or blend into objects like walls. "Perhaps it will help you hide for a while." Zoner squinted hard, "Doc, I can already do that."

Doc looked at Zoner, from head to toe and said, "A suggestion?" He asked Zoner, "Are you the least bit artistic?" Zoner wondered why. "I won an Art award in high school. I sculpted dinosaurs out of clay for a science project in grade school once." Doc continued, "Because when you are re-forming into human form, you are losing some of your natural appearance each time. Look at your hands, your chest...and your face!" Taken aback, Zoner questioned "What's wrong with my face?" Doc walked out of the room and came back with a hand-sized mirror. Zoner held it in front of himself and moved his head in a circular motion, "I think it looks pretty good...oh, wait a sec, I see what you mean." Doc gave the opinion, "It isn't all just you any longer."

"Maybe that isn't a bad thing. I don't want to be found." They each germinated the thoughts of Zoner's biological changes. "Can you get me some photographs of you, maybe I can hire someone to make a cast or mold to help you?" Doc asked. Zoner expressed, almost daze-like, "Means I have to go back home. I guess so?" Doc cautioned, "I don't think so. Your wife won't necessarily recognize you." Zoner corrected, "She isn't my wife." Doc reasoned, "Your pheromone scent has likely changed, given all of the elements and animals you have come into contact with." Zoner noted Doc's point. Doc scratched his head and said, "Guess I better clean this place up more. The Government people will be here to find out what happened to their men, and the thermos contents." Zoner advised, "Be back soon, Doc." Then, he absorbed into and walked through the cinder block wall and exited and reformed into the back alley. Doc blinked hard a few times, "Incredible."

Before Zoner left the area, he walked over to his Chevette across the street at his work building. No cars in sight yet, likely due to the snow. No plows visible yet either. He transformed into a roach and crawled around and over top the car, so it would become cleared of snow. He then changed into a rat and cleared a path to the back of the lot. The asphalt lot was flat, so he changed back to human form and drove the Chevette to the back of the lot. He transformed into a crow and flew towards his girlfriend's apartment complex trying to use cloud cover along the way to avoid detection.

As he approached for a landing, he noted his girlfriend's car on the parking lot. The lot was still rife with snowfall and high drifts along parts of the parking area. Her apartment was on the top floor. He melded into and through the roof; traveled in the walls. He could see ants crawl along the wooden ceiling beams, a dead squirrel in one wall, roaches descending on the vent pipe. He realized he couldn't enter the apartment as he would risk being seen by his girlfriend. He roamed around in the walls and ceilings of the rooms, sometimes bulged them discreetly. He found the closet where some old shoe boxes might hold recent photographs, extended one arm from the drywall, and picked out some recent photographs. As he held them, they melted into his hand. He then pressed his face through the drywall and attempted a glance of his girlfriend as she lay in bed. He desperately wanted to enter, hug her, kiss her silken cheek, but he couldn't do it. He didn't want to ensnare her into his new world or his new life. His heart sunk under the realization he could no longer continue a relationship with her. He retracted his physical being behind the wall and slithered his chemically modified body through the inner workings of the apartment construction materials. He began the flight back to Doc Ziggy's.

5

Doc Ziggy spent a good bit of time researching the enzyme from the blue fluid. His past research notes revealed the enzyme may have been intended for military use, administered, at first to wounded soldiers for quick repair of wounds; to facilitate their return to action. It worked like a surgery, or prosthetic all-in-one medical cure-all, unencumbered by the crafted stainless steel of surgical instruments; but the cure-all engendered unexpected effects discovered during testing. Some flaws initially confounded the researchers. Soldiers couldn't hold objects properly; their hands would meld to weapons; and their brains and central nervous system had not yet adjusted to the transformation stage to allow proper use and skill. Boots would stick to feet and legs. Couldn't remove them from feet, so trench foot environment would develop. The soldiers just needed more training and skill development, much like Zoner, who appeared and disappeared outside of his memory frame. Doc speculated the disappearance episodes were like a cocoon stage of caterpillars prior to transformation into moths or butterflies. He tried to create a patch that could be worn while the time-released enzyme seeped into the blood system. The test chemical would be applied to the patch and pasted to the skin of the subject at a significant artery area such as on the chest near the heart, or banded around a wrist, or taped to the back of the neck. There was more work and testing needed, Doc admitted.

Zoner had returned to Doc's lab. A curiosity about Doc's withered hand exposed itself, again. "What happened, Doc?" Doc explained there was not enough funding for his projects. He was pushed into the background. He worked on many half-developed projects the government pushed aside due to military industrial complex lobbyists either stealing his ideas literally or covertly; or pushing lesser effective ones to get a project through networking and spreading around incentive cash judiciously. The enzyme-patch project was one such project, but it was now about to be tabled. Doc said he didn't complete reconstruction of his own hand, not that he didn't try through experimentation, because he considered it a trophy, to remind him of his trials and tribulations, and how he had overcome them. He considered a low status state now was a triumph because he continued to work, exist, despite the trappings of the corrosive government complex system. "Doc, I need to learn more about my new life. I left the photographs on the counter." Zoner vowed to return to see Doc in a few weeks, to check on the development of a patch. "I am on vacation any way. The snow day was my last time in the office for two weeks."

Zoner spent the next few days in the Balmoral Library to research and to understand the symbiosis of roaches, rats and crows in the urban environment; how they co-exist; blend into society. He was now a part of that environment. He tried to help it in unseen ways; adapted himself to a stream of consciousness exercised by these creatures. He roamed with the vermin. He crept with the roaches. He soared with the crows. He learned how to become part of each clan. He became much warier of cats when he was in the creature form as he had learned, raising, or rather being raised by his own cat, how the feline species could exercise their skills upon his new friends.

After the library research completed, given his curiosity about his own dilemma, perhaps as a means of tapping a form of knowledge his Busia had learned from, he sought out a gypsy seer for a meeting, perhaps a reading. He arrived back at his old neighborhood. The trip was not constrained by time, vehicle traffic or weather anomalies. His current state allowed him to adapt to each of these existence obstacles. In a way, he felt his current biological state had helped him conquer the drawbacks of each. His cocoon state took less and less time, as did his transformation process. As he became more familiar of the construction materials and methods of the buildings around him, he was able to negotiate covert movements among these obstacles. He encountered unexplained difficulty in some of the building walls, but he moved around the inaccessible areas. He truly no longer needed as much the human born buildings of offices, homes, eateries, taverns. Yet it took him time to learn to utilize them for the purposes of a rat, roach or crow. It was during this time of his adjustment when he was most vulnerable to discovery or death at the hands of a frightened human or group of humans, or perhaps at the hands of the authorities. He correctly presumed the Onionhead curse would regenerate him if mortal wounds were inflicted, given his age, as he was not yet in his mid-thirties.

He consulted the same seer his Busia had consulted. It was late in the evening. The seer's front window neon light "Readings" was still turned on; murmured a soothing hum. He walked up to the front door, perched upon the third marble step and investigated the window adorned from the inside by dreamcatchers and necklaces and glistening jewelry. He saw no movement inside. He knocked. He looked around behind him and pulled his hoodie further across his face until it was masked in shadow. The door started the rattle of a greeting. "I've been waiting for you a long time," the gypsy seer said as the door opened inward. Her appearance was much younger than he expected. Her blonde and long hair was partially braided on each side of a delicate yet plump face, but her layered dress, shawl, and crystal necklace appeared familiar to him. He sensed he had been inside the environs of this establishment previously. The seer responded "Yes, you were, when a little one, clutching your Busia's warm hand." He crinkled his eyelids at the thought she knew his thoughts or purpose.

He wondered if she responded in such a manner, one almost predictable, given the long age of the neighborhood and the habits of the inhabitants. "Sit," she directed him, as if time was of the essence. He sat in the wooden, cushioned at the seat chair nearest the door. He was uncomfortable as his back was facing the door. "Don't worry," she said, "I will lock it," as she made herself comfortable in a larger, cushioned chair opposite him on the other side of the round table. She raised her left hand, turned it at the wrist, and he heard a click at the front door. He looked back but saw no one there. The seer also directed some words, Slavic in origin to his ears. There was a long mirror on the wall behind her. It reflected the door behind him. He blinked a few times while looking into the mirror until he could no longer see the door or the streetlights outside. Only candlelight kept the room absent of lonely darkness.

The gypsy seer wasted no time. She didn't ask for money or recompense in advance. He thought perhaps Busia had given her money years ago in anticipation of his return. The seer knew why he was there. "Your name is Tihomir Goralski." He was still wondering what her name was, but he listened. "You are demon cursed." He knew this. "But you don't know why, or how to stop it," she reminded him. He turned in his chair and looked back at the door which wasn't visible any longer. "Pay attention," she demanded.

The seer started to recount for Zoner the ancestral stories (previously related by me in Part First-Onionhead) which the poor fortunes of his family did not allow the time for a telling. "I will find out more from my mom and Busia, if you don't mind," he advised her. In a somber tone she stated, "You will have to wait a long time to do so." Zoner's head turned like the head of a confused dog. "Each has passed during your absence." Zoner looked down, stared hard into the brown tablecloth. He saw the faces of Busia and his mom. He started to cry into his hands. His body shuddered. He could feel a transformation at the cusp. His nose grew longer into a beak. His fingers extended from the palms of his hands into claws. His face took the dimension of an upside-down triangle. The seer, her eyes closed, didn't notice his partial transformation. "Relax," she murmured as she started to enter a trance. His transformation began to retreat. His human appearance returned.

The gypsy seer came to the point, "Something else inhabits you ... nesting, waiting to break out ... many of something else rests also there ... in the background darkness." Her body shuddered as it accumulated the visions. She continued, "Your soul, your soul ... has become dormant, hibernates ... a demon ... I ask its name ... Likho ... has become trapped." She fainted. Her head banged into the tabletop. Zoner heard a click at the front door. The wall mirror reflected the door visible again. The gypsy seer slowly lifted her head. She reached her hands out to him. He looked at his hands. They were human in appearance. He grasped her hands but some of his flesh and muscle started to mesh with her hands. She gasped, tried to pull away. Her eyes briefly reflected the Onionhead demon. Zoner let go. The front door swung open. A wind flushed in. "We are done," the gypsy abruptly said, almost breathless. Zoner admitted, "I don't know what to do." The gypsy put up her right hand and shushed him as if she heard something. She repeated it to him. "It is time to see Doc." She added she didn't know what that meant. He nodded his head to her and thanked her for the time. "You are rich in time," she concluded. He exited and began the trip to the cemetery of his relatives' final resting place.

The clouds overhead, during his walk, began to grow dark. A humid air laid thick upon his path. The cemetery was just outside of town. There was not much cover of buildings. He turned off onto a path into the wooded area, a shortcut to his destination. A rainfall came down but shifted sideways into his left side as a viral wind swept into the tree line. Thin limbs sheared off and searched like daggers for a target. He found a large oak and sat to rest behind it, and to escape nature's fury. He started to fade out as his attention pulled somewhere else. He tried to stay focused, but the wind would not let him. He started to transform but he could not stop it. In the distance, the snorting engine sound of a tractor-trailer beckoned. In a half-conscious state, he felt the transformation intensify. This time it was different. There was not much around for him to fold into, except the wind. His body became a liquid state colored black, blue, stretched like a beach resort taffy. He could not stop it. The wind carried him like ocean waves until the liquid he had become rolled into the trailer part of the tractor. Inside, his body hardened, then the cocoon state formed around him. There he remained for a long while amidst palates of transport goods.

6

He awakened in an alley, at evening. As he reformed
from the cocoon state, he realized there was a good
bit of blood, bone, and some severed limbs combined
into his outer extremity areas. He tried to shake the
human detritus away, thinking he had emerged in the
graveyard outside Balmoral. The detritus abandoned
his body as he became something, he still wasn't sure
what. The enzyme infection had begun the attack on
him at Doc's office. He did the math: human, demon,
crow, rat, roach. Apparently, his body could not hold
any more contents. He looked around and saw other
humans huddled, silent, in patches of box and trash
bags housed in the waste near dumpsters. He realized
he was in an alley inhabited by homeless people, and
further, he had just regenerated on the spot where
one of them had been sleeping, except the person he
regenerated through wore a fine suit, somewhat
business-like in appearance. Each of the severed
limbs was covered in the suit material, except the
part of the limbs that had separated from the body
to expose bone and blood. Brown cowboy boots covered
what was left of the legs. He felt sick as he had
never seen the severed remains of a corpse; he had
never taken the life of another human being. He told
himself he wasn't sure if he had killed the person
or if they were already dead before he started to
regenerate on the same spot of ground as the body.
He reached out to his sides to make himself upright
and struck a hard object, roundish, which rolled
along a few feet away from him. The rays of light
from the streetlamp at the end of the alley showed
the object to be a human head at rest on the right
side of the face, clean shaven, black hair on top
slicked back, small gold earring in the left earlobe.
Zoner reached his hands to his face and felt it all
over, lowered his hands to his neck and felt it.

A long, black limousine sprayed a shadow from the
streetlight as it passed the end of the ally where
it abutted the street. There were high, brick

buildings planted at each side of the alley. He stood
and walked towards a light of the street corner. He
heard voices as he approached. As he neared the
sidewalk a visible newspaper box identified "The
Capital Gazette" as the contents. He was in the
Capital. The tractor-trailer must have passed through
at some time while his cocoon unsealed. There was no
pedestrian foot traffic. The buildings across the
street belied any hint of habitation, reflected by
broken windows, lack of light; except the mixed
aromas of excrement and urine hinted otherwise. Many
brick pieces and chips littered the far sidewalk as
if a storm had blown through. Some voices came closer
to where he was standing. He tried to retract into
the wall to his right, back first, but his effort was
impeded by something in the wall or on the other side
of it. He flattened and spread himself as thin as he
could, but the upper part of his face could not make
it completely into the wall. He squinted his eyes,
so they would not reflect the streetlight. Three
suited men came around the corner, dashed past him,
and aimed flashlights into the alley. One of them,
the one in the front, waved the others to move back.
"Something not right here. Looks like Hawk's dealer
bit the dust." Zoner widened his eyes to identify the
purpose of the suited men. As they turned, one of the
flashlights shone across his eyes and he was spotted.
He unfolded from the wall and started to run. He
noticed the stunned look on their faces before his
retreat.

The wheels squealed on the limo, but it wasn't moving
away, it was moving backwards. Gunfire erupted. His
back began to sting. He ejected the bullets from his
back. They spit out one, two, three and clicked onto
the sidewalk. Some of the bullets ricocheted off the
storefront wall and crashed into some of the windows
to his left. As he kept running, he wondered why they
were chasing him. The limo continued racing backwards
until it stopped ahead of him, then drove over the
sidewalk and pinned him into and through the brick
of the last building. His back began to sting again

as it pressed against the drywall interior. A dark,
tinted window on the back-passenger side of the limo
rolled down. A male voice inside said, "Hey there.
We won't hurt you. Just come with us to talk for a
bit." Zoner couldn't see inside. The limo backed up
and Zoner slid from the wall in two pieces, severed
at the waist. Smoke drifted upward from his back. The
suited men then took a large tarp from the back of
the limo, rolled each piece of him onto it, and
continued rolling until he was completely covered. It
felt like the tarp was crushing him. He tried to
reconstruct but was unable. He tried to seep through
the limo trunk walls but could not free himself from
the tarp. He passed out, unable to breath any longer.

When he regained consciousness, he found himself in
an exceedingly small windowless room. He wasn't
restrained and he could see why: the lower part of
his body from the waist down was missing. Most of his
body hung in a mesh cloth, like a large shirt pocket,
as he suspended from the wall on a thick pipe. He
tried to seep out of the pocket. He tried to seep
through the pocket. Nothing worked. His left arm
hurt. Then he heard a voice, from above. He looked
up at it. The ceiling wasn't solid. It undulated ever
so slightly when the voice started. A male voice
announced, "Welcome." Zoner wasn't thinking about
responding. He was still working on a solution to his
predicament. The voice continued, "Why were you in
the alley?" Zoner continued to concentrate on any
possible mechanism of escape, but he started to hear
other voices from above. His sense of hearing seemed
enhanced. The rat in him was starting to work. Another
male voice said, "Don't ask him that. He is never
getting out of here. Cut to the chase." There was a
humming noise. It was something outside the room. The
roach in him could detect the air currents in the
room. They were all coming from above. He sensed the
location of his internment was at ground level. There
was a second story above him where the male voices

emanated from. The voice and tone of the second male speaker agitated in him the Onionhead demon. It became active in him again. Perhaps, he thought, it was better to let it out, to help him escape, then draw him back in using the power of the enzymes.

The voices continued speaking above him, yet he remained silent.

"Sir, we checked for a DNA match to the perp at the drug dealer's crime scene in the Capital. There wasn't a match."

"Weird. Someone that violent and not a match. Did you check in at the FBI for access to their database?"

"Yes sir, per protocol. No matches there either."

"Ask the FBI if they can request a worldwide search through NSA."

"Right, sir."

No voices now. The air system was still flowing. He relaxed, mentally invited the Onionhead demon to seek out those who had imprisoned each of them. He could see the demon start to ooze out of him and move towards the ceiling. He heard another voice. It was the male voice in the black limo near the alley. It was a voice a bit more muffled, yet easily understandable to him. The voice was dithering on about a plot, cooked up by the First Lady, to garner campaign cash from the Chinese. She was going to make a deal with the Chinese to allow them to obtain space technology in exchange for campaign contributions, a potentially deadly security breach, to help the President win reelection. Zoner decided to speak.

"Tell Mr. President I didn't vote for him."

All the voices stopped. His distraction worked. Onionhead had started to seep beyond the ceiling above. Zoner heard choking, coughing. Then he spoke again.

"Where is my other half?"

Zoner could hear the voices above exert an audible panic and pain. The President's voice shouted, "Open it...open it." Across the narrow room of Zoner's imprisonment, he could see the far wall start to retract and reveal a sack like his own, suspended from the ceiling, which held his lower body half. Male voiced screams above him meant Onionhead's work had commenced in earnest. Zoner exited his sack by cutting it with an extended rat claw. He then transformed his upper body into the upper body of a roach. He could hear a male voice up above blurt out, "Are you seeing this?" Zoner crawled over to the lower body sack, pulled it down using the forelegs of the roach, then retracted back into human form, squished the lower part of his body against his upper part at the waist, then waited for his complete body to reconnect. He heard a lot of chatter in the ceiling area. He mentally pulled back the energy of Onionhead, but the demon resisted. He would have to go up into the ceiling to see what was wrong, as the view in his mind was of a red glow as he looked through the eyes of Onionhead. He transformed back into a roach and crawled up the wall and along the ceiling, melted into the ceiling material, then reformed on the floor of the upper room back into human form. Onionhead was there, in the middle of the room. The demon's energy stream was still connected to Zoner, handcuffed in a way. Each was the proverbial ball and chain to the other, a crippling encumbrance to each, but together a life force of incredible strength. The walls of the room were lined by one large computer system. A table in the middle housed a view screen. The screen was blank. Small camera's and speakers dotted each ceiling corner. No living human remained in the room, but Zoner could still hear moans, near cries, as whispers in the air. Onionhead still consumed the spirits of the humans whose bodies lay slumped over the center table or on the floor. Only four in the room. None were the President. He must have been communicating through the computer system.

Zoner itched his left forearm. It sometimes had a sting to it. It had been stinging off and on since he regained consciousness in the room below. He looked at his arm but couldn't see or feel anything on the skin surface, except where his fingernails scratched it. Onionhead completed the spirits consumption. Now it was the turn of Zoner's biological mix to feed. He didn't recall when he last ate. The dead bodies in the room were fresh, still palatable to the crow, rat, roach. He allowed priority to the crow. He lay down next to one of the dead bodies, undressed it from the waist up by cutting the cloth with rat's claws he allowed to extend from his hands. Then the crow emerged from inside him to overtake his human side. The crow went about business, pecking, clipping, pulling at the face of the first corpse, then the neck, then the chest. After several minutes, the crow's efforts slowed to an almost disinterested manner. Then the rat craved to escape him and overtook the crow transformation. The rat's assault on the body was messy, full of tearing, clawing, boring into the body cavity at the area's initiated by the crow's work. The rat became fat in the body and the assault receded. Then the roach emerged from the rat form to begin tedious, nondiscriminatory mastication of all that it deemed worthy. There were three other bodies on the menu, but there was no more hunger to forgo. The satisfaction of the appetites of his co-conspirators was more than enough to satisfy him. He wanted to sleep right there, weighed down by the feast, amongst the dead, but the creature instincts of his body inhabitants recommended, without cogent thought, otherwise. A sense of danger persisted in them.

It was time to find a means of transport back to
Balmoral. His captors were likely plotting a second
assault upon him. He wondered why he could not humanly
sense any hostile activity at the exterior of the
room environs. He stood, assumed the rat form, but
now it was combined among the roach anatomy as two
long, black antenna protruded from his head to push
back the hood. He was able to penetrate the seam at
the ceiling and enter the place between the walls,
unimpeded. The rat and roach senses in him exerted
much energy until he burst from the side of the
building, spraying drywall, wood, brick pieces like
a sinister rain, as primarily the crow, nearly full-
bodied, except the roach antennae persisted. Some of
his clothes, pants, hoodie, remained upon his figure,
curled among feathers. His hands remained as rat
claws, but his feet portrayed crow talons. His flight
was aided by the crow wings as they extended from his
arms and along his spine. Another biological
adjustment, he thought. The cemetery beckoned.

While flying, a rain started. He located a truck stop.
He landed behind it. He shook the rainwater from the
crow wings and transformed back into human form, yet
still could not coax the roach antennae back into his
head. He noticed signs on poles which named his
geographical location as a town he knew to be just
west of the Capital. He had handled some insurance
investigations in this area the previous year. His
walk and senses led him to an empty tractor with a
trailer still attached. The ground was muddy as the
rainstorm had not yet abated. As he walked among the
trailers, he heard a radio weather report coming from
one of the tractors. Rain was predicted for the next
few days. He looked up to the sky, noted the low cloud
cover, calculated a need to expend energy from the
recent corpse feast, then determined he could fly
above the clouds and make it to Balmoral in under an
hour or so. The cemetery visit would have to be

delayed until he could learn more from Doc Ziggy about the potential for a healing or controlling patch.

Above the clouds the trip was easier, yet he started to doze a bit. He glided much along the wind currents but kept one eye open as a caution. His mind became burdened by random flashbacks to moments of crow, rat, roach encounters in his younger days. After flunking out of law school, he kicked a dead rat like a soccer ball. While living in a dingy apartment, he came home from a long bar hop evening only to start smacking roaches on the walls in the kitchen in a drunken rage; but he always felt he could communicate with the crows ever since his grandfather, during a long walk together when he was a child, showed him a trick involving a distant flock of white birds. His grandfather whistled, and the birds changed course, then back again on the next whistle. His grandfather winked, but never explained and left it a mystery. Now he realized his grandfather had been watching the birds for so long, he knew when they would start their turns moments before he whistled. It was a cute trick.

His daydreams were interrupted by voice whispers. He darted his head around. The roach antennae were picking up the radio signals or telephone signals from a nearby tower. He tried to filter out the whispers to find any news of his ordeal at the government building of his internment. He heard:

"Sir, we checked for a DNA match to the perp at the drug dealer's crime scene in the Capital. There wasn't a match."

"Weird. Someone that violent and not a match. Did you check in at the FBI for access to their database?"

"Yes sir, per protocol. No matches there either."

"Ask the FBI if they can request a worldwide search through NSA."

"Right, sir."

Those sounds were the same whispers he heard in the building where he was interred. He started to wonder if he was dreaming or if the transmission was delayed in some way during his ordeal. The remaining whispers concerned broadcasts from truckers, radio stations, much of it not intelligible to him. He searched for a classical music station to soothe his soul and the energy of Onionhead. Too much static interrupted his effort until he recognized Vivaldi's "Summer Presto". He concentrated on the sound. It energized him for the remainder of the flight.

7

He started thinking about sex however misplaced the passion for it may have been. The thoughts were more intense than when he was only a human entity. His human thoughts, crowded out by his creature inclinations, put the cemetery visit on hold. He visited Lucky Spirits for some gratification. The center stage was occupied, in the early evening, by a crack whore he recognized from a previous visit. He ran a tab on a credit card he pinched from a passerby along the trip and binged on several cans of Schlitz. He consumed time to discern every inch of the crack whore's bodily appearance to unlock an understanding of her soul. It didn't look like she ever took a break from her fix. Her hair was a bit knotted. Her panties were a bit too loose. The crack had consumed her physically as countenanced by her too much bone and not enough padded flesh. He found where some of the off-stage dancers relaxed, in the darker room parts at booths, lined up along the knotty pine, paneled walls. As he walked by the promenade of booths, he noticed most were unoccupied by customers, yet each one presented the assets of a woman seated behind thin linoleum tabletops that abutted the vinyl covered wall-length chairs. The typical seated posture of a dancer exhibited either legs spread or crossed, bare except for the hint of a bacon slim thong waistband below the abdomen, and an enticing connect-the-dots view down to the feet which were adorned by long-stemmed high-heels glistening at the open toed areas, pocked of black, red or white painted toenails. He was dismayed to find his favorite dancer, Lovey, was not among the dancers visible. Maybe she was off tonight.

For a second, he felt like he was in the meat section of the grocery store, checking the packages for expiration dates, tenderness of product, and price.

Each table was adorned by the preferred drink of the host; some thin but tall champagne bottles; some exotic foreign beers, and at one table a Schlitz. Some of them smoked a thin cigarette. Some coolly snarled a grunt. Some sipped at a bottle of their joy juice (alcohol). Some, like the dancer whose booth he selected, ruffled her hand in a tiny, glitzy clutch purse as if looking for a lost treasure. He seated himself first by accessing the narrow space between the adjacent booth and the seat of his chosen one where the red and green and white lights of the stage deflected off her Schlitz can. A more so, but barely, clothed woman waitress of wrinkled visage, clicked her heels over to the booth; offered a drink request which seemed to require an obligatory, affirmative answer. "Pabst", he intoned. The waitress clicked back to the bar area, not lacking in the least a bit of sensuousness even in her experienced age. There was some small talk exchanged between him and his interim booth friend.

He tried to convince her, Amy, to sleep with him, which of course, was not required. She only wanted to see the cash. He orally expressed he had no money. She took that as an insult, so she insulted his manhood. He then belched out, "Want to see the goods?" Since he was a bit looped, he unzipped while still seated and showed her two tools: one he, the other rat. A smaller one just above the larger one. Her astounded lips opened wide to reveal a dental view a few teeth short of a ten-pin reset; then she protested "Screw you dick wad!" Not bearing any sense of decorum, given his intoxication state, he exaggerated an off-key response as, "Usually a guy has to be married and wait until age fifty to get that kind of respect from a woman." The Pabst was delivered at a cost five times convenience store price. Zoner uttered a derogatory word. The waitress snapped fingers at the front door to trigger a burly bouncer response to the commotion. The bouncer commenced an assault upon the table; picked Zoner up by the shoulders, pushed him forward toward the front door.

He staggered and bumped into the bar stools sentried around the raised dance floor; caused a few of them to roll over. Once out the door, the bouncer dragged him by the hoody along the side alley towards the dumpsters. The hoody caught under his neck. The dragging piqued the demon inside him. The crow, rat and roach of his new biology stirred. By the time the two reached the dumpster, Zoner had reformed as parts of each. The bouncer didn't notice, just picked him up and dropped him into one of the open dumpsters.

His body was thus expunged from the cheesy strip joint heaven. As had begun a sleep coaxed by inebriation, seasoned by the despair of his Capital ordeal, he realized there was a cyclical comity to each of his bodily inhabitants. Over and over the impulses occurred to him, but more strongly when he was transformed into the form of crow, rat, roach: food, shelter, breed; food, shelter, breed; food shelter, breed. It was involuntarily shelter time.

He heard a noise outside the dumpster. Someone had opened the side door and tossed in a soda can. He was overwhelmed by a pleasant scent, one he recognized as Lovey. The door remained open, so he peeked out of it, strained beyond restraint about the scent origin. It was her, Lovey. She was a young woman, perhaps early twenties age, just under average height for a female. She casually walked away from the dumpster. Her hair was cropped short. On stage she usually displayed long, black hair. Her tight jeans movements just below the waistline pulled upon him as if she held a fishing rod, casted it into the dumpster, and hooked him through the lower lip. Her scent further pulled him from the dumpster, even as she moved to at least 100 yards away. Her personality around him always seemed pleasant, but he hadn't wanted to become involved in her personal life, until now. The creatures within coaxed him onward. His heart pounded in pain. His groin ached. He adjusted his pants.

He climbed out of the dumpster. He could no longer

see her, but he followed her scent path. He knew there was a place around the corner, named Scoops, that served mini-hamburgers and French fries. Her scent led him there. He stood across the street from the burger joint and looked through the large front window. She was seated, alone, in a booth at the far back end of the narrow, rectangular shaped eatery. Most of the booths were empty, given the time of the early morning, before sunrise. He needed a shower, bad. There was a downspout still leaking out water from the rains at the edge of the alley near him. He transformed and slid snake-like through the spout, then slid back out. He reformed and sniffed again. Not bad. A bit better. He felt his face. He tried to make it handsome. He scooped back his hair. He needed a blow dry. He found an exhaust fan on the roof of the burger joint and stood in front of it until he was dry. He also smelled a bit like burgers and fries now.

He climbed down the back wall and tried to contain his lust. He walked down the side street next to the burger place, passed a few parked yellow Taxi Cabs, then turned the corner and entered through the glass front doors. He walked to the back and sat down in the empty booth just in front of the booth where Lovey was seated. He pretended not to notice her. Her scent was so strong in his enhanced hybrid being, he wanted to crawl over the table and press himself upon her. She crunched some bacon in her teeth. A piece of the bacon remained stuck to her fork. She was lefthanded. A waitress idled over to his table as if not interested and asked his order. "Coffee, black." She left the table. The squish sound of her shoes faded forgivably.

"Hey there, stranger," a friendly voice uttered. He looked up and saw Lovey staring at him. "Come on over here." He scooted along the plastic seat but tried not to show eagerness. After an ahem, he responded, "Good to see you." Lovey answered, "Same." They talked for a while. His coffee arrived at their table during the conversation. He ignored it. She softly blew on her tea. It rippled like an almost calm sea. He swore, in his mind, he could feel her breath upon his face. The creatures inside him enjoyed it more. She offered to him a piece of bacon, which he voraciously wanted, but declined. He kept telling himself not to act too eager. He tried to help evolve the conversation around to the idea of intercourse. He knew nothing about her, except her aroma, her incredibly soft-hearted eyes, sweet voice, and the beautiful skin in which her slim yet curvaceous body was encased. "Taking a break?" he inquired of her. She finished munching the crisp bacon, then sipped down some tea. The cup clicked onto the saucer. "No ... I'm off."

As he tried to connect the conversation dots in his mind into a bed scene that would entice her, she asked him for a ride. "I missed my bus." His hand shook a bit as he pressed the warm coffee cup to his lips and sucked down half of it. "Sure, I can help." His car was on the north side of town, if it wasn't towed yet. His apartment, if the locks were not yet changed by the landlord, was halfway in between Scoops and his car. He briefly enticed himself on the idea he could carry her on his back and transform into the crow. He realized, right before he let it out as an idea, it would serve as a non-starter and likely a deal breaker, if she was at all interested in a sexual liaison. "Oh, I forgot, I took the bus down here." Some moments of silence quashed the plan, then she said, "A cab. One of the drivers knows me."

She paid for her meal and his coffee, then left a modest tip on the tabletop. They walked towards the glass doors. The back view of her walk, particularly

the view of her well-rounded buttocks area, enhanced
the sexual thirst in him. He took a deep breath. The
second Taxicab from the corner was occupied by the
driver who knew her. "Where to?" Zoner hesitated. He
gave his apartment address.

During ride he checked for his apartment key. It was
in his right pants pocket. He also wondered why Lovey
never asked his name. He looked over at her as the
streetlights intermittently invaded the back-side
door windows along the trip. She stared out the
windows. Almost there, she reached her right hand
over to his left hand. She placed her hand upon his
hand. Her hand was warm, almost moist. The skin was
smooth. The trip took about twenty or so minutes.
Lovey paid the driver. Another view of her from the
back fueled in him the adrenaline and the creatures'
needs.

The entrance to Zoner's second-floor apartment was at
the back of the building. They walked side by side,
still connected at the hands. There was an ease of
the soul for each of them in the compression of the
grasp. They became physically familiar with each
other rather quickly. An energy seemed to flow
between them. Their hands squeezed and receded yet
didn't break in grasp, at a similar regularity as
their beating hearts. At the second-floor landing, no
larger than a vestibule, the ceiling lightbulb
flickered a bit. He tried the doorknob key. It still
worked. Inside the darkness they went. He found the
table lamp and pushed the switch. The light
illuminated a small portion of the room yet allowed
the few roach invaders on the walls to remain somewhat
docile. He led her to the bathroom where there was a
light switch and flicked it up and looked back at
Lovey, "You first, if you need it." He then went into
the bedroom and turned on a table light. More roach
friends moved over to hide behind the window

curtains.

He let the hoodie jacket slide from his arms onto the floor, then kicked it up onto a corner chair. Somehow, he got along only wearing a tight tee shirt. His pants remained on, but he untied the shoes and flicked them with each foot under the same corner chair. He lay back on the bed. It was covered by a single sheet. He almost never used anything else. He couldn't stand to be bound by covers for any length of time. He heard the trickle of urinary excretion in the bathroom toilet; then the sound of streamed water from the shower head.

After a few minutes, Lovey entered the bedroom, only wearing a black thong. She lay next to him on the bed, each on their back. They tested their sense of touch against each other's body, starting from the face, head, hair area; and then slowly descending upon the neck, shoulders, arms, breasts, abdomen, loins, hips, thighs. Each in turn moved and skimmed the skin surface of the other. She had already allowed her sensuous energy to emerge. He remained restrained, afraid his inner creatures would attempt to emerge during the stimulations. She turned from her side to lay face down. His vision, his hands explored the regions of her body again, from the head down. He was now completely erect and still in human form. His skin no longer desired the body's conformity. His fingers told him she was moist and ready for penetration. The ballet began. He joined into her body. His stimulation, intensely nurtured by the moist warmth of his penetration into her, increased tenfold. Her audible sounds indicated a pleasurable experience. Louder and louder his breath grunts became, so he slowed a bit to extend her opportunity for pleasure, then sped up again to gain advantage over her sensations, to corral them, then set them free.

He realized his fingers became longer, narrower, sharper at the tips. He was careful not to scratch

her back or arms. His elbows dug into the bed mattress
to support his upper frame. The heat between their
bodies beamed like the rays of a new morning sunrise.
A large cardboard box, a few feet to the left of the
bed, started to stir the noise of feathery scratches.
The roaches had become stimulated. The roach inside
him likewise responded. A quick tapping sound moved
across the ceiling, likely a rat in the rafters. A
crow alit on the window ledge to his right, feathers
ruffled, then settled. Each of these moments stirred
the creatures inside him. They wanted to emerge, but
he did his best to hold them back. His back grew fine
rat hairs as did his hands. His hair distended into
crow feathers and tried to surround his head and face.
The antennae of the roach extended from the top of
his head. His thrusts became more powerful as his
knees gouged into the mattress and pushed her body
slowly towards the wall at the top of the bed. She
pushed her hands against the wall to steady her body
and prevent the top of her head from banging into the
wall. Finally, he exploded his bodily fluid into her
loins. The symphony of pleasure had reached a
crescendo in mutual moans; then slowly receded into
the long fall of endings; as a sea of sweat, heat,
ecstasy calmed. The darkness of the early morning
began to recede, then filled their minds and allowed
the respite of slumber.

He awoke, unsure of how long he had slept next to
her. The gnawing hunger of his unwelcome bodily
guests nagged him. His human side ignored them as he
needed to recontact Doc Ziggy for an update on the
curative patch. In fear he may be transforming too
frequently, he resolved to walk in human form for as
long as his energy level would allow. Lovey was still
asleep. He kissed her on the cheek. He took a shower,
dressed, then left.

His arrival seemed not unexpected to Doc Ziggy. Doc
told him some completed preliminary tests determined
the enzyme absorbed into anything except lead. There

was a caveat: the lead concentration in air, soil and water was not toxic to him due to the small concentration; the hazard was primarily in building and home construction where the concentration was much denser. Doc thought at some point, like normal humans, Zoner's body might become adjusted to the higher concentrations in artificial products. "Oh, I forgot, here are your paint chip test results." Doc tried to hand Zoner a packet with the test results of the paint chips. Zoner's hand instinctively retracted as he felt a burn to his hand. "Shoot, the chips contain concentrations of lead in the paint." Zoner responded, "Maybe I don't need the results anyway. Looks like I may be out of a job by the time my vacation ends. I can't adjust to the needs of the critters inside me." Doc said he would hold onto the paint chips. "Anyway, here's the patch I've been working on. Pull up your shirt and I will tape it to your chest." Zoner complied. "That reminds me," Doc noted as he taped the patch. He explained he came up with a new species name for Zoner. "I am honored," Zoner mocked. "Cratch," Doc stated, matter-of-factly. "What?" Doc spelled out, "C-R-A-T-C-H. You are part CRow, part rAT, and part roaCH." Zoner wondered about the name. "But I'm still human ... right ... right?" Doc wondered, "We shall see ..."

Doc's patch spawned some surprises for Zoner: tiny parts of him like skin and body hair were left at certain places as more and more of his human physical being deteriorated during transformations. The crow, the rat, the roach each engendered and consumed a part of him. He felt like them sometimes; he saw what they saw in his daydreams. He felt like he was going crazy, plagued by the sting of multiple thoughts and scenes in his head, to the point where he sometimes was temporarily blinded to the happenings of relevant and current real scenes and moments. Perhaps the infliction of the Onionhead curse, modified by the enzyme cells regeneration, changed him more than he could fathom. He went over and over these thoughts in his mind: "I was Tihomir, now I am a Cratch, a hybrid form of human and insect and rodent and bird. I started as a human, cursed by the Slavic Onionhead demon who inhabited part of my human spirit; then infected by military grade enzymes. These mutations allow me to walk through walls and inside other large structures. I can transform, become rat-like, of long teeth, long nose, pointy ears, hairy, yet standing in human form, somewhat hunched, a tail attached behind me; or mutate into a roach as the rat jaws, partially open, twist as they change into the sideways jaws of a roach; the ribs, hip bones, knees distend into roach legs, and the tail disappears and antennae appear from the forehead edges; then the roach transforms into a crow-like creature, the legs retracting, the shoulder blades expanding into wings, the roach jaws twisting back to a beak proportion, and they chop up and down like hedge clippers. Body hairs become feather-like hairs. Then the final transformation: the full hybrid, incorporates roach-like two legs, a tail, shortened antennae, feathered wings."

His thoughts attacked him vigorously. Each moment of incorporation happened previously, when he was first combined; when he was near death and attacked by roaches. He then tried to overcome the roach influence, because he was so disgusted by it and torched by a need to find food; and he was attacked, or let himself be bitten by many rats, who were competing for the food he was consuming. Then he chose the crow influence, to experience the vision and joy of flight. When he was a rat, his hair collected moisture from the air, so when it was hot, steam emanated from it. He could claw and bite through concrete and steel. When he was a roach, a foamy ooze dripped from his mouth. He could crawl along any obstacle and cling from any angle. He could fall from great heights and not suffer injury. When he was a crow, he pooped at opportune moments. His body movements emulated these creatures: a crow's side look; a rat's to and fro; roach rapid movements and ability to sense danger. He communicated with each of these creatures. He was each and all of them.

In the Roach Domo, the mantra was "ignorance is bliss." At least that was his human interpretation. They communicated to him "We don't know what that means." When Zoner moved, the roaches near him moved in unison. There was nothing more unnerving to the human psyche than the discovery, in the home, of that random pepper-stream of roach eggs. They were a sign of an invisible invader, but now, as one of the invaders himself, his temperament towards them had changed. Still, the din of the Roach Domo was deafening to him. There was a constant, near-silent, low-level buzz in his ears. They hid in the big, junk box next to his bed when he lived in the old apartment; under his bed; in the kitchen cupboards; in a cereal box; under the sink in the kitchen.

He almost wished he had not mixed with the Roaches. Their music was helpful in communications, but a nuisance, like a Chinese water torture after a while. He glared at the roaches on the walls. He tried to understand their noise, closed his eyes, blocked out all other sounds, but their calling and constant work-search for food, sex, search for food, sex, search for food, sex, search ... for ... food, ... sex, ... became a circuit he could not break. He raised his hand, felt like squashing all of them under the fat pad of the palm.

In the Rat Domo, the mantra was "sex, food, and rock and roll." The Rats he knew well, from his old City neighborhood. They were larger than life, almost as big as cats, but they slunk around, hid in the shadows of corners, readied to move when the humans were not watching. He became accustomed to looking at the corners, and he could see the black ball of their noses and thick, sewing needle-like whiskers peeked out from the edge of shadow plane. They moved in the corners of his eyes. Sometimes he wondered if only he noticed them. He almost never saw them eye to eye;

it was either nose and whiskers, the eyes still
covered by shadow, or their rumps and long tails
dragged behind them as they skittered into the next
shadow, as if the light would burn them. He liked to
sit on the run-off banks and watch them drop into the
water for a bath, especially on a well-lit moon night.

In the Crow Domo, the mantra was "liberty is freedom;
our belief in it sets us free." The Crows were daytime
creatures, looking for the remnants of the nighttime's cruel actions. How the carrion got there, in
the space the Crow spied from above, was irrelevant.
He heard the "Caw-caw" communications up above. He
wished he could think that way. What I need, I need;
how it got there was irrelevant; but for his mind,
there was relevance to everything, so much so that
every movement, every sound, every action and object
around him, dripped heavy from a healthy dose of
relevance. He must understand all around him to feel
comfortable; to reach a calm, emotionless, non-
threatened daze state. The Crow, having found his
breakfast space, went about to his business, once it
determined that all around it was calm, emotionless,
in a guarded state.

Zoner had a place to live, but his more frequent
transformations into a Cratch required a less
conspicuous spot. An abandoned fertilizer factory, at
the end of the night world, was located on the edge
of a Highlandville neighborhood where a shipping pier
poked out into the river. Pigeons lived in the roof
where most of the below ground had been dotted by
pigeon droppings. Nutria lived under the wharf where
they plunked like bowling balls into the water when
disturbed during a food search. He settled into this
quaint, forgotten place.

8

Zoner transformed into the Cratch just before dusk as creature sustenance had commanded a journey. He knew of a Roman Catholic Church nearby, likely rife with varied food sources given the charitable donation collected among neighborhood parishioners. He had spied out this location for some time. Rodrigo's "Concierto De Aranjuez/Adagio" played softly in his mind as he went about daily feeding business. Once inside the Church, he stuck to the ceiling transept, well above the nave, only his dark and yellowish back visible, in a shadowed corner to the left side of the central Altar. He looked down, flicking roach antennae like whips. A young Hispanic woman, seated in one of the front pews, hands clasped in prayer, noticed a stir of the shadows as the dimming sunlight filtered through the high and narrow stained-glass windows. Zoner's rat instinct told him to search for satchels and boxes; or closets and upper level walkways; and hallways that served access to the choir and modest organ. He scouted out a bountiful harvest in the upper corners of the hallways, especially near the bell tower.

Some other parishioners entered. Among them was a middle-aged man and a young boy. They slowly walked hand in hand, against the wishes of the little boy, along the nave and up to the front area of pews. After a long week of work, Pop had some venial sins to confess, most generally some orated curses due to bursts of pain to his limbs, particularly at the joints, while working as a roofer. The young woman seated near the front pews was his cousin. She had agreed to watch the little boy while his father took care of his own soiled soul restoration. Pop directed the little boy to sit on the pew, then Pop knelt beside him. After a few minutes of solemnly contemplated introspection, Pop stood and walked to the Confessional Box, slid the black curtain open, entered, then slid the curtain closed. All present in the pews, few at this time, usually the much older women displaying a disconsolate visage, who knelt or sat with clasped hands wrapped by Holy Rosary beads, knew what the opening words uttered were, once a soul entered the Box. "Bless me Father for I have sinned. It has been (fill in the blank) days, months, years since my last confession." Then the oration of the sins sprung forth from the sinner; then the Priest's direction for Penance requirements ensued, usually a series of prayers of Our Father, Hail Mary, Glory Be, and if an egregious amount of time or villainy had been proffered by the sinner, a Holy Rosary. It must be noted the Holy Rosary could be said by anyone on behalf of others, or to pray for living or deceased souls' good fortune or fortitude in overcoming transgressions self-imposed or otherwise. The elderly women had perfected the art of Holy Rosary prayer and oration. Their speedy whispers of the words in Church were almost unintelligible, except to one who knew which words were to be uttered in each prayer related to each bead. Many of the elderly could say the prayers in Latin or Polish, Italian or German. The elderly in this Church whispered in Spanish. Cratch was aware of the whispers of the Rosary as he had said it many times as a child, after learning it from his Busia. He would listen to its recitation on the early Sunday morning radio broadcast at breakfast.

Not long after sitting in the pew, the little boy started gazing around the Church, particularly the ceiling. Cratch noticed the boy's sounds such as laughter, and motions such as a mimic of crawling. The little boy had noticed Cratch walking upside down along the ceiling beam. Cratch crawled into the side rooms which were no bigger than closets as they were used for storage. The bounty had been found. He began foraging. He called to his fellow rats in the neighborhood, but the frequency of the sound was unable to be heard by the humans below. They responded in kind and were on the way. Additional parishioners also entered during this time, seated themselves in the pews on either side of the main, center nave and pulled down the kneelers which echoed a clunk, to begin prayers for themselves and family, and to ruminate about transgressions better left unsaid, except to the Priest in the Confessional Box. The sun had reached a near full descent in the west allowing more shadow than light.

Yet, Cratch sensed other movement outside the wide and high solid oak doors at the Church entrance. The creak sound of the iron door hinges served as an overture for the acts to come. The once again opened oak doors unmasked a group of three young adult males, all dressed in black from hoodies covering most of each face to slacks almost skintight. Arm sleeves rolled up to the elbows revealed the inked symbols of a local gang. The noiseless athletic shoes, except to Cratch, were a red color, fit for an All-Star, and splayed down in brash steps. The hands of each entrant were wedged into the hoody pockets on each side, but the pockets were not vacant of mischief.

The first act began as the males stood in the middle of the nave, church pews on each side of them. Then, Pop exited the Confessional Box in the adjacent aisle. Cratch sensed a tense air among the humans below, so much so that he stopped his sloppy mastication in mid chomp. Something was wrong. He peeked his rat head out from the closet darkness. No human words could he hear. The candles at the Votive Stand, lit for deceased souls, burned at the wick a soft and hoarse tune that arose from the glass holders. Words gruff, demanding words flowed from the mouth of the three-pack leader. Then, Cratch could hear a soft click, then a loud bang. Pop fell where he stood, in the nave just feet away from the center Altar, onto his knees, his head slumped down. A loud gasp emanated from the parishioners in attendance. The two other gang members pulled out guns from their pockets and demanded money from the Offerings boxes.

One of them was halfway across a left side pew eyeing the Votive Stand box. There was the sound of a door opened near the Confessional Box. The other gang member fired his gun at it. The exterior wood splintered upward.

An urge, an angry urge, as if heated like a blow torch, arose deep inside Cratch. Although he was all rat at this point, his body started to change into crow. The roach antennae grew long and thick. A human adrenaline rush overtook him, and before thinking what to do, he was halfway down into the air of the Church center, boring straight as an arrow for the first attacker. The other gang members then fired off shots rapidly. Blood spattered from Cratch as he continued his descent upon the demon gang member in the center, until Cratch landed on top of him. All the way down bullets entered him, splattered off parts of him. The blood loss fell as a red rain. Drops bounced onto pews and the nave floor. He still had not completed transformation. His face was now mostly crow, but also part rat. It was the rat teeth that found their mark on the neck of the lead gang member, who was now pinned to the floor. A loud crunch and rip evidenced the fate of the gang member. His head was near bitten off at the neck. His body writhed. The gang member at the Votive Offering box had already shot the box open and proceeded to sweep up in both hands the currency and coin that flew out, but the opera was not yet completed.

A choir of rats entered the center nave of the Church, saw the commotion, and descended upon the gang member at the Offering table. He was quickly consumed of flesh, blood and muscle. His remains looked like a bulgy bloody rag of splintered bone, sinew, flesh, torn organs. Cratch could hear a loud mumbling all this time. As his adrenaline slowed, he realized the mumbling was screaming and shouting. The little boy had also been shot. His last gasps of breath were evident. Cratch had heard them once before, when his Aunt died. It was the death rattle. In his loudest voice, tears running from his now partial human face, he roared a sound that sent the parishioners in the rear of the Church out to the street as they scrambled into and through the rats who were still streaming inside. The roar echoed like thunder from the Church ceiling. The side windows shook. Then the crows came in, through the front door. They could sense the adrenalin rush of Cratch.

The last gang member, who had disappeared in the commotion, came from behind the confessional, gun pointed at the head of the Assistant Pastor. In the other hand, the gang member held a heavy sack of money. A second rage of adrenalin struck Cratch even harder. Just before he could make a move towards the last gunman, a hand reached out to him from below. Pop grabbed him at the rat fur in the waist area and begged, "Please, sir . . . please . . . save my son." Then Pop slumped to the cold floor on his right side in a blood pool. Cratch looked over at the gunman. The gunman started to run down the right-side aisle along the windows, but the rats ran like cattle over him until he fell as they ripped his flesh from head to toe until only the rats could be seen. Cratch's crow wings had fully formed and were extended somewhat. He retracted them towards his body and walked into the pew where Pop's son and cousin had been seated. The cousin was kneeling against the pew seat, stroking the little boy's head, holding his hand. The cousin's face was strained at the muscles, reddened, soaked from the tears she wept. Cratch could still hear some breathing, but the cousin whimpered, "He is dead."

Cratch then bent down, opened his wings to cover the cousin and child. He extended a roach leg forward and into the chest wound of the little boy. He allowed his own tears to enter the boy's chest wound. The roach leg steadily pulled out the bullet. Cratch then shared some of his blood with the boy, letting it drip into the wound. It was just a drop or two of blood, but the boy started to slowly breath louder and more steadily, until he sucked in a large amount of air. Cratch retracted his wings and exposed his hand, pulled a handkerchief from inside his rat skin cover, and placed it on the wound point. The cousin held it there. Sirens started to blare in the distance. The Priest must have called the police. Cratch realized he had to leave and with him, the rat hoard. The crows did their best to clean up the mess and remains of the three dead gang members, but the remains were stubborn and persisted in staying. As Cratch stood, the cousin asked, "What do they call you?" His reluctance to respond suffered defeat to her voice. "Cratch", he said. That was all he could think of for a name at the time. Not his birth name Tihomir; not his self-imposed name Zoner; but Cratch, because now, that is what he only was, what he had evolved into. He turned to leave and saw Pop was still breathing and conscious. Pop had managed to crawl over to him; patted his lower leg and whispered, "Thank you." Cratch smiled a bit from his combined rat and human lips, but it was a crooked smile.

The sirens became louder. The authorities were approaching the Church. Cratch led the rats and crows from the front entrance and disappeared into the night, but he could still hear and sense what was happening in the Church, despite his efforts to erase the thoughts from his mind. He left the rat pack and flew up to the bell tower to check if everyone was okay. He looked down, then crawled down taking roach form, to listen, yet his human eyes remained in the sockets to see and his rat ears remained on each side of the triangular roach head, so he could hear. One of the old women walked over to the statue of the Virgin Mary on the left side of the Altar to ask her for help. Then the old woman noticed a drop of blood that had leaked down, about three inches or so, along the breast area of the statue. The old woman kneeled in front of the statue and began to sing and sob Schubert's "Ave Maria". Other parishioners then gathered around her and each was stunned to see the blood on the Virgin's breast. Their weeping sounds echoed throughout. One of them whispered, "It's a miracle."

The police and ambulance crew arrived and scoured the church for clues and victims. The old women were still huddled in front of the Virgin Mary statue. Some of the police took photographs of the scene. One of them asked the women to leave. They explained to an Officer who had come over to them they could not leave yet. They were in communion with the Virgin Mary. One of them pointed to the blood on the statue. The Officer looked at it closely. He then looked around, down, behind and up. There were bullet holes everywhere, pieces of chipped wood from one of the columns directly behind where the statue stood, broken window glass on the floor, but no other sign of blood near the statue. The Officer then asked if the women could at least step back, and they did. The Officer walked around carefully. He could not see any sign of blood near the statue. As he moved closer to the first pews on either side, he could not see any blood. The parishioners outside had told him about the raining blood, so it didn't quite make sense. It was only at the third pew from the front there was blood, from Pop's wound, and on the pew where the little boy, Pop's son, had been seated. The remainder of the blood was pooled and spattered at the remains of the gang members. The Officer interviewed the Priest who was presiding over the confessions. He said he didn't know how the blood came to be seen on the statue. He had gone to the side office to call the police and ambulance. When he came back to the Altar area, it was quiet except for the singing of the old women, and cries from the young woman who was holding the little boy. A Forensics Team then interrupted them and returned to their business of evidence gathering. One of the Team members told the Priest there was a media crew outside the Church, looking for story details. The Officer stared at the Priest hard but didn't utter a word. The Priest walked towards the front doors. The Officer moved back to the old women and again asked them to leave. They relented but not without a significant chatter amongst them. "Get a swab of that blood on the statue," the Officer directed in a shout to the Forensics Team.

Cratch's enhanced ability to hear sounds in the air detected, through the roach antennae, a conversation among police officers outside the church. They talked about how their take on the drug trade in this neighborhood could be reduced now. Cratch's heart burned inside. The chaos launched upon the church had just revealed to him about the corrupt nature of some in the police community. He wondered if his father's death resulted from such corruption. The thought pounded into his brain. Then he heard what he had feared. "At least we know Goralski wasn't here to ruin us again." Another officer's voice chimed in, "That's for darned sure. It took us a long time to get rid of him." Then sounded a choir of laughter.

The media pharisees outside the Church began a predictable engorgement of the spectacle unfolding. Cratch looked down, from his distant perspective, at the Virgin Mary statue. He could see the blood. He hoped it was not his, as he didn't want to be discovered. He now needed time to plan his revenge.

9

About three months later, as evening descended upon the rooftops of a line of Balmoral rowhouses, ringed by chain link fences, another neighborhood adventure started for him. The houses were connected by a web of electric wires emanating from tall, wooden utility poles spaced every eighteen or twenty houses in length. A cement alley split the backyards of the houses like a dry riverbed. The chain link fences seemed to spring up on the alley boarder like metallic foliage under the dim streetlights. A barking dog stood stout at the end of a chain-link fenced yard behind one of the Balmoral rowhouses. Another dog trumpeted a series of barks, ruffs, snarls. A shadow of a dark clothed creature raced down the center of the back alley, not quite on two legs, more like on four, amidst the dim, yellowish light. A dog in another yard jumped the chain link fence. The chasing dog betrayed ahead of it a moving four-legged shadow of short tail, whip-like in appearance, as a long black overcoat waved like a flag above the tail of the shadow.

A middle-aged man displayed a roundish gut which burst from the bottom of a white wife-beater T-shirt; pock marked by irregular holes; rimmed at the arm pits by yellowish stains; and stained on the chest area by chili goo as it dripped off a wooden ladle the man used to eat his late-night feast directly from the cooking pot. The man peered out of the back-porch screen door of the rowhouse to check out what was the ruckus causing the barking of the dogs. "What the hey?" The man's spoon tipped down as his face spread a shocked look while the chili dripped a familiar line of blotches onto his shirt. The chasing dog caught hold of the black shadow's overcoat end in a frenetic leap. The dog and shadow tumbled down the alley.

The Cratch further transformed in the shadows; became rat-like of long teeth, long nose, pointy ears, hairy, but stood in human form, somewhat hunched, extruding a tail as long as the body. A humid evening allowed the rat to collect moisture from the air onto his own body hair and made it more difficult for the dog to hang on. The transformation continued into the next faze as a roach. The rat jaws, partially opened, twisted sideways as they mutated into the jaws of a roach; ribs, hip bones, knees distended into spindly roach legs; rat tail retracted into the body as antennae extended from the forehead edges; a foamy ooze dripped from his mouth. Then the roach transformed into a crow type of creature. The legs retracted then extended into crow claws; shoulder blades expanded into wings; roach jaws projected into a horny beak proportion, then chopped up and down like crow hedge clippers; body hairs widened into feathers. Then the final transformation: the full hybrid of connected parts of each creature. Crow wings lifted it up, then poop dripped down and down again upon the dog's head, blinding it. The dog stumbled, then slunk down and frantically retreated towards the opposite end of the alley. The Cratch started a flight towards downtown of the City.

A Robinson helicopter whir disturbed the piecemeal city sounds on this evening in downtown Balmoral. The copter hovered above the Circuit Courthouse on Culvert Street. In the center of the wide street, stood a granite monument built to honor one of the City leaders a century ago. Crows sat on top of it. Rats lined and crowded the monument base. Roaches perched on the sides. Pockets of nearby neighborhoods were unlit. A blackish gray blotch bubbled up on the three stories high Courthouse roof edge. The rooftop scene reflected from the somewhat tinted front window of the helicopter as it tilted downward to get a closer look. A male TV News reporter sat in the passenger side of the helicopter and reported over the air, "We are trying to determine the cause of the power outage ... no storms on the radar reported, so something unusual has happened ... apparently."

A flock of crows, red-eyed, whizzed by the front window of the helicopter, nearly hitting it. "Caw! Caw! Caw!" The pilot gasped, "What the hell?!" The pilot pushed the cyclic control. A panicked look emerged on the TV News Reporter's face as the helicopter veered to the left side. "Look! Down there! On the Courthouse roof!" The Pilot shined his spotlight onto a mutilated figure of a man rising through the top of the roof near the rooftop ledge closest to the street below. First the head emerged in a dark hoody; then red lifeless eyes peered out of where the face would be, but the hoody and the darkness allowed no vision of specific facial form. Distance and darkness denied any view other than a blurred mask of a face. The figure continued to press out of the roof top goo puddle, as up came the waist. A black overcoat formed around the body. The arms in the long sleeves asserted an appearance on each side of the trunk. The Pilot reported to base, "Not sure what we have there."

The hooded man, birth name Tihomir Goralski, self-appointed name Zoner, and biological designation Cratch, became fully visible. The dark wool overcoat revealed cut slits on each side along the shoulder blades and down the length to the bottom which reached about knee length; no shoes, as they were still absorbed into the shins. His feet were rat and crow-like but indistinct as if they didn't know what form to take. The hands revealed black and gray hair, long fingers and longer nails pointed at the tip like tiny spears. A distended nose and jaw poked out from the black hoody. The TV News copter pilot squinted to see better.

Gunfire erupted from a building roof across the street. Cratch dodged and swatted at the bullets but they viciously met their mark. His form was streaked and dotted by red tracer lines as the burning projectiles started to reach the target. Blood oozed

out of the ripped portions of his coat taking some
flesh with it. His face transformed to part human in
the lower half to expose lips. Cratch heard a voice
from another ascended helicopter identify as FBI,
then the voice told the News helicopter to leave. The
News helicopter veered away again.

Cratch could see police cars start to line up below
on the street. A Balmoral City Police Commander
looked up at the roof line; had a perplexed look on
his face. The Commander held a bullhorn near his face.
Spotlights from the ground were focused on Cratch
from left and right. "I know what he did!" Cratch
bellowed down at them. A grizzled-looking, lean FBI
Agent snatched the bullhorn from the Police Commander
and shouted, "Give it up Goralski! There's no hope!"

Millions of roaches began to climb from the buildings
and scaled the outer walls. Thousands of rats emerged
from the sewers and surrounded the humans on the
ground. Hundreds of crows flew in, to perch on the
edge of rooftops. Cratch looked down at the bullhorn
origin. If they knew his real name, he thought, they
knew too much. His tension heightened as dark slime
dripped from his body at the point of bullet
penetrations.

"I know what he did!" Cratch shouted again.

Cratch spied the Police Commander and FBI Agent next
to each other, three stories below at ground level.
His roach antennae picked up their voice signals.

"Who is he?" asked the Police Commander.

"It isn't true! There is still a chance!" was the FBI
Agent's response to Cratch.

The two men glanced at each other. The FBI Agent clued
in the Police Commander, "Goralski thinks POTUS put
a hit on him."

The Police Commander responded, "Weirdo."

Bullets whizzed by Cratch's face, scraping his left cheek, tearing a line through it on the surface. Blood oozed, and the bullet continued and ripped off the upper part of his left ear where it poked through the crow feathers at the arc. His enhanced reflexes and hearing allowed him to dodge the barrage of bullets from any angle, almost. Cratch winced. A bullet scraped across his upper back, opened another red line of oozing blood. A dazed but glaring look formed on his face as some of the crow feathers receded back.

"He must pay!" Cratch bellowed in a vengeful tone.

The FBI Agent looked up at Cratch. "Not today!"

Cratch's roach antennae detected a phone ringing down below. The FBI Agent's car phone hummed only a few feet in front of him. He reached into the car and pulled out the phone. The roach antennae on Cratch's head tapped into the phone conversation. Cratch could hear POTUS' voice on the other end of the line asking if the deed had been done. The deed of course, was to assure the capture, or even the terminal incapacitation of Cratch, retrieve the body and bring it in for analysis.

The FBI Agent performed a bad impression of pretending to talk to his wife, to not alert the Police Commander of the FBI's true intentions.

"Right, Right, almost done," the FBI Agent blurted in an exaggerated tone.

"Who was that?" the Police Commander inquired.

"Wife, I am late for a PTA meeting."

The Police Commander felt a pain in his lower leg. Cratch could see from up above, a rat had skulked over to the group of Police Officers. "Ouch!" Cratch had set the rats upon the Police to chase them away. He didn't want them to die on his account, although he knew some of them were complicit in the City corruptions.

Cratch transformed some more. He sprouted crow wings, leapt upward and disabled the engine of the FBI helicopter above, caused it to spin wildly and crash into half of the Police vehicles below. The explosion on the street created a seeming volcanic eruption as heated metal bored into the pavement and asphalt and ruptured a gas line. Another explosion in the line erupted halfway down the street, creating more chaos. Cratch fell back down onto the courthouse roof, because part of one of his wings were partially crushed during his assault on the helicopter. His wing also caught fire. He dropped and rolled and retracted the wing at the same time to allow the fire to extinguish. Shock waves from the street level explosions knocked unconscious most of the people below. There was silence, except for one sound that only Cratch could hear. His friend, Lovey. She was pregnant with his child. She never told him, but the creature inside him could sense it. It had only been about three months since their only sexual liaison. His roach sensibility detected her voice pitch that sounded like cries of significant pain. He followed the sound in haste.

Cratch half flew, half jumped, from building to building, because the wing was still crushed from the copter incident and not yet repaired itself. He traveled through two neighborhoods and disabled electrical transformers located near the top of the utility poles. Each neighborhood progressively went dark. He reached the hospital building. He disabled the transformer for that building, but a generator kicked the power on again after about thirty seconds. One lone light remained turned on, at the fourth-floor level. He transformed into part roach and scaled the outside of the building, to the fifth floor, entered the fourth-floor ceiling through the fifth-floor room and worked his way through the duct work, finally stopping in the fourth-floor ceiling. He oozed through a seal in the sheet metal, headfirst, so he could use his human eyes to see the room below, where he sensed Lovey was in danger. The light was dim in the room, but he could see everything as it happened.

He saw a doctor about to stab a long needle into the brain of a newborn, as the newborn lay just outside of and between the legs of the woman on the table. Cratch strongly sensed the newborn was his offspring daughter. A nurse stood near the doctor. The nurse noted curiously, "Doctor, this fetus is fully formed, yet the time of conception was just 3 months ago." The doctor shrugged. The anesthetized woman on the patient table, his friend from the strip joint, Lovey, whispered "Help me." Cratch crashed through the ceiling, behind the doctor. The doctor, surprised, instinctively covered his head as ceiling debris fell upon him and the nurse. The doctor was knocked down semi-conscious and fell to the floor. Cratch reached through the doctor's scrubs at the back area and penetrated the chest cavity, grabbed the heart and held it until it stopped beating. Cratch's hand, somewhat gooey and bloody, slid out of the doctor's back. After disabling the doctor, the nurse fainted.

Cratch cradled his daughter in both of his deformed and morphed hands. Lovey was still on her back on top of the table. She was partially unconscious, having been anesthetized. He checked her hospital bracelet. It read "Patricia Magnon." He checked his daughter for wounds and determined she was bleeding from the head, but suddenly, the bleeding coagulated, and the skin started to become grayish black, and covered the wound. Then from the head down, the baby skin turned to gray. Cratch looked into his daughter's eyes. "Hello, little one …you're alive … knock on wood. I

should call you Sylvia. You are a strong one." Sylvia
looked back up at him, almost smiling, a reddish tint
in her eyes."

Cratch heard a commotion of police cars, flashing
lights, men shouting. His rat sense sniffed the air.
He looked around, found a closet door, opened it, and
inside found a big hospital trash bin, the kind on
wheels, which read "Waste" on the outside. He looked
into the bin, saw a mass of tiny, bloody, mangled
baby body parts, some still intact, all recently
dead. His rat sense sniffed the air again. He was
stunned. A single tear trickled down his cheek. He
reached down into the bin. He pulled a female
stillborn out about the size of his daughter and put
it on the metal stand next to the table where Lovey
was starting to regain consciousness. "Lovey, Lovey,
can you make it?" She shook her head side to side and
held her abdomen with both hands. "I think so." Still
cradling their daughter, Cratch bent over and kissed
Lovey on the right cheek. He thought Lovey must be
her stage name. Her real name was Patricia. Then he
helped her off the table. They slowly departed after
he reformed into only human form, at least in his
hands and face. They walked down the hallway which
was still dim from use of only emergency lights. The
elevators didn't work. He found a janitorial closet.
They waited in there for a while, until he could
regenerate his damaged wing.

The authorities had entered the hospital. Their noisy
search seemed to interest Sylvia. Cratch cradled her
against his chest, under his coat, and called out
Lovey's birth name. "Patricia?" Lovey looked up at
him from her seat on an overturned cleaning bucket.
"And yours?" She joked. "Tihomir, but that was a long
time ago." His eyes looked into a near vacant past.
The FBI hospital halls and rooms hunt died down.
Cratch could hear their footsteps and government
trained jargon from many places and floors. They were
far enough away from the closet to make an exit
possible. He hunched down. Patricia grabbed around

his neck and hugged against his back, cradled her legs around his waist, winced in pain at the movements. "Trust me," he told her. He slowly opened the closet door. They departed along the hallway and entered another hallway on the left. A large window beckoned escape potential. Cratch extended a rat claw and cut the glass, then punched it out cleanly. He stood on the window ledge, cradled Sylvia tighter, transformed into primarily roach form, then crawled down the outer wall. Once upon ground, he transformed primarily to human, except for the rat feet.

The roach antennae poked out of his head to allow him a check on the situation inside the hospital. The Doctor, still dazed, had regained consciousness and stood up. He realized he didn't remember exactly what happened, but he saw the dead baby on the metal table tray and the nurse still on her side at the floor, covered in drywall pieces and dust. He walked over to a wall phone, dialed a phone number. Reluctant to admit any form of failure, he stated, "We had an accident here, lost power, but yes, yes. It is done. The child is euthanized, the procedure completed, but the mother is gone."

10

Patricia's sudden, tragic death changed everything
for the future of Cratch as it set off in him a rage
that he could control less than his ability to reign
in the creatures and demon that inhabited his body,
mind and spirit. If there was ever a slight hope of
restoration, reconciliation between Cratch and the
outside world, that hope vanished on this night.

Cratch visited Patricia's neighborhood to check on
how she was doing and to see Sylvia. They were staying
with Patricia's grandmother along a sweet looking
block of Balmoral house's in an otherwise rundown
part of the City. Some of the house blocks matured
into rose bushes, but some were vacant, wildly
sprawled weeds, devoid of human occupants unless
temporarily occupied by barely sentient drug addicts
or unfortunate homeless who sought the solace of
shelter, however squalid a condition it may offer.
Cratch lived not far from this location, in an
abandoned government building marked by the graffiti
of a local drug gang.

He communicated to a group of crows sitting on the
telephone pole and attached wires. One of them
swooped over to the second-floor window of a house
in the middle of the block. The crow began a
systematic beak tap against the glass surface until
the curtain was pulled back to reveal Patricia. The
curtain moved back to a stationary position. Cratch
waited in the back alley. Patricia came out onto the
rear, wooden porch. A cool evening enveloped their
touchy emotions. "Doing okay?" Cratch asked her as
she opened the metal gate and swung it back with a
bang. "Where have you been?" in a low growl tone she
fired at him. He explained he was waiting for things
to settle down, he didn't want to risk discovery,
leave any evidence of himself anywhere, anytime,
anyplace. She seemed to understand but wasn't happy
about the explanation. "How are you and Sylvia doing,
okay?" She tried to hide a frown. "No." He thought

perhaps she missed him, but her response continued as, "I can't work right now, no money coming in. My grandmother is driving me crazy about acting responsible ... stuff like that." He wished he could do more. She didn't seem to understand the gravity of their situation. The Feds were still looking for him. She could end up a target. She moved closer to him. He put his arm around her shoulders, and they walked. The feeling of human touch and companionship, no matter how slight, no matter how long the separation lasted, was a huge reward to his current state of existence. He relished it. He was selfish about it. He felt the energy regenerate inside him. The hidden creatures of his existence felt it too. He started to hear their chatter in his mind.

Then he heard the rev of a car engine to his left, on the street out front of the end of the rowhouses where they stood. The headlights beamed a hurt into his eyes. Patricia looked to the side and put her arm up at her forehead to shield the light from her view. Two men, close to each other, stood on the basketball court to their right. The car headlights beamed into the court area, on the two men. Cratch and Patricia were in the middle of a drug deal gone bad. The rear door of the car opened. A man stood up and fired an automatic weapon at the two men on the court. Cratch pulled Patricia to the ground as one of the bullets grazed his right shoulder. The creatures inside him were ignited by the impact pain. He tried to resist transformation. The gunfire went silent. Cratch didn't sense any life remained in the two men on the basketball court. He thought it was over, but it was just beginning. The energy jolt from the gunfire sounds and his fear of harm to Patricia, and the viral fear of the creatures inside him could not hold him back. His left arm transformed into a crow's wing and popped through the cut slit of his overcoat. The roach antennae had popped out of the sides of his forehead. His shoes disappeared as his feet became rat paws. The stage left headlight illumination stopped. A tall man in a leather overcoat and Woolrich hat upon his head, exited the car. The man's shoes were shined to a Sunday social perfection. His hands were buried deep in the coat pockets. Cratch could tell there was a gun in the right pocket as he heard the safety switch click. The man continued to walk towards him and Patricia. Then Cratch noticed that Patricia wasn't breathing. He shook her a bit; he turned her head and saw a blank stare in her eyes. He sniffed at her. A blood pool had already formed outside the left side of her chest. He listened. No heartbeat sound at all could he sense.

"Hey, sorry Bud. Just business." The well-dressed man turned and walked back towards the car as his heels clicked the cement alley. The man then flipped over his shoulder a rolled-up wad of money. "That's for her funeral."

When the wad of money bounced and scraped along the cement, the man's heel clicks went off loudly in Cratch's head. The clicks became louder, and louder, and still louder. Cratch's human sensations were overtaken by the creatures inside him, by tenfold. He lifted off the ground in full view of those in the car and transformed in mid-air to a part of each creature. His enzyme altered biology instinctively determined which part would be most useful, most deadly. He thrusted forward in a horrific rage; rat jaws opened beyond wide. The jaws snapped shut on the walking man's neck, severing it half off. The head dropped down onto one side, held up only by shreds of muscle tissue and skin. Bone chips split threw the air. The engine roared on the car, the wheels squealed, the headlights beamed, as the front end zipped towards Cratch who was still airborne, parallel to the ground, unstoppable in flight at this point, crow wings half extended. The roach antennae folded back smooth along his head. The top of the hoodie flew back from the velocity of the forward movement. Then he landed on the windshield, pulled it back until it hit cement ground after scraping along the hood. Gunfire erupted from the vehicle interior but the impact to his body only enflamed his emotions more. He dove into and through the driver's chest, the driver's seat, and into the chest of the shooter in the rear driver's side passenger seat. Cratch's wings folded away to reveal a left arm sharp as a dagger's tip. The arm jolted into the face of the rear passenger's side occupant. The front passenger side occupant opened his door and tried to flee. Two roach legs extended from Cratch's mid-section and wrapped around each of the occupant's legs at the ankles, then spread the legs wide until there was a rip sound at the groin and waist level. The car interior could only be described as carnage. During the melee, the car had continued traveling forward and crashed into a telephone pole, cracking it but not toppling. Some of the electric wires stretched too far. The neighborhood lights flashed; the connections failed. The only light came down from a clear night three-quarters moon.

Cratch transformed back into mostly human, exited the car, walked back to the well-dressed man who laid like a fallen tree limb on the alley surface. "Hey, sorry Bud. Just business."

I, Brother Henry, was informed by the Archbishop to visit Patricia's grandmother, Nana, for the purpose of offering support during the grieving period. I also first encountered Sylvia at this time. She was advanced in size and intelligence for her age of just under three months. Grandmother informed me the little one had not yet been baptized, so that matter was taken care of not long after Patricia's funeral. I stopped in from time to time the check on Sylvia. Eventually, Nana and I discussed the issues she and Sylvia would have to face in the future, regarding the family curse as well as her father's biologically altered state of affliction. The likelihood of Tihomir's aberrated genes passed on to Sylvia was yet to be determined. Only time, testing, and observation

would tell. I offered my services in that regard, to
help raise, to help teach, to help discover who she
was, her potential, starting some time near in the
future.

Tihomir had disappeared, but he was not yet finished
his work. The City media had deemed him a menace, yet
some in the Church community considered him a
protector, like a Saint Michael. There was as little
balance in the public perception as there was in
Tihomir's personal efforts to accept his altered
state of existence. My hope was for him to allow me
to encourage in him a purpose that would allow a
coming to terms with the afflictions of his life:
those he could not change; those he could resolve;
and those that would hopefully, one day evolve into
a peacefulness for his soul.

11

Balmoral disintegrated into a mob scene at the downtown area. The authorities' search for Cratch would not relent. The local Police and the President's FBI handyman determined Cratch to be a pariah unsuited to the community; an indiscriminate killer, who must be found and stopped at all costs. Murderers, drug dealers, gangs, bag men, contract killers were fine to tolerate, it seemed, based on how the local prosecutors handled those types of cases, but Cratch was deemed intolerable.

Cratch raised an army of roaches, rats, and crows to descend upon City Hall to rain down a plague upon the tormentors of his and his family's existence. The City leaders defense argument just used the occasion as another excuse to claim Federal Government funds. Soon, the Mayors of other urban areas in other parts of the country began the marketing approach needed to squeeze more Federal Government funds from taxation of the largely unwary populace. If there was this Cratch in Balmoral, they reasoned, there could be more Cratch species in other urban areas. The country's President abused the crisis as an opportunity to rally political support and further his own financial benefit. He promised additional government funds to combat the fabricated crisis and to boost his popularity.

Cratch and his army of roaches, rats and crows headed for Balmoral's City Hall not for profit or popularity, but for vengeance. He intended to take over the City. His desire was to make it pay for the treatment of his new family. The creatures inside him desired a treasure trove of edibles. His child, Sylvia, needed protection from the nefarious Feds and protection from duplicitous State actions to control a potential gold mine of power in the recruitment of Sylvia to their way of thinking. The roaches and rats surrounded and protected Cratch. The actions of the roaches, rats and crows surprised police. The hoards appeared to follow silent instructions from the creature Cratch.

Cratch was surrounded on the roof at the City Hall, but the crows rose up from their circling of the building. A SWAT team encircled and swarmed on the roof. Cratch's message to his creature friends, roach and rat, "Food for all." Cratch moved to the center of the rooftop. A SWAT team encircled him from a distance along the edges of the roof. The roaches and rats crawled up the building walls, then flooded upon the SWAT team members, covering them like living blankets. The guns fired randomly, the trigger pulls induced by first the shock of the mass of creatures, then further induced by the stinging pain of bites and tears to clothing and concealed flesh. The creatures entered them from all places of access to the body, then entered each body during the mauling, then each body crumpled, then perished in a heap of fevered insect and rodent mastication. It was the time of the roaches and rats.

Overhead helicopters of the Police, Swat and FBI were swarmed by crows as the band crashed headfirst into the most vulnerable portions of the human-made instruments of power and subjugation. It was the time of the crows, and the crashing down of the government iron fist. Three helicopters went airborne and three helicopters came smashing down on the outskirts of the building in blazing crashes that sprouted bands and bits of metal like fireworks.

Police personnel below, on the ground, stationed behind their cars which lined and barricaded all streets leading to City Hall were not spared. The roaches and rats virulently swarmed them. Any gunshots fired at Cratch were deflected by walls of roaches and rats that formed around him. There were many deaths on both sides of the conflict. Finally, when all was done, and a carpet of human and creature carcasses rested on the grounds below and the roof above, rows of survived rats and roaches created a path from top to bottom of the City Hall, where Cratch followed triumphantly down and over to the regal front steps and declared in a confidant, "This city is mine now."

The FBI had been monitoring all the proceedings and reported info to the White House. The US President was now worried. A government experiment had gone horribly wrong, and now an average US citizen had single-handedly taken over a City in one evening; a citizen who knew the treasons committed by the President of the Country. This citizen must be stopped at all costs. Cratch's roach senses picked up the radio chatter to this effect. He further detected a phone call received by one of the FBI Agent survivors in a car who had been monitoring the battle events from half a block away.

FBI Agent: What is it?

Caller: You're not going to believe this.

FBI Agent: Try me.

Caller: We ran the DNA found in the blood of an unknown perp at the Catholic Church were three gang members were murdered.

FBI Agent: Spit it out, will you?

Caller: Sure. It seems the DNA sample is somehow different now.

FBI Agent: What do you mean, different?

Caller: Well, as in, evolving different.

FBI Agent: Have you ever seen this happen before?

Long silence.

Caller: No.

FBI Agent: What does it mean, man?

Caller: We are dealing with an unknown species, of
something.

FBI Agent: What the!

12

Many more months passed. The City had begun recovery from the Cratch destruction. Many blocks of buildings burned during the City Hall confrontation. Many funerals were held for the losing participants. Much mourning and introspection resulted. The local media had convinced the public that Cratch was a pariah, a disease, and must be identified, captured and punished. The scene for Cratch's destruction became the old, long unused railroad tunnel in a deep, dark part of Balmoral City.

An explosion echoed into the night from the tunnel. Cratch, in human form, staggered out, dazed. He had been found and was about to be eliminated by the government's local Police and FBI forces. Their guns were cocked and pointed at him, but it was dark and difficult to see. It had recently rained which left mud and puddles of water on the grounds outside the tunnel. A puddle of seeming dark water bubbled. Shots were fired at it to no avail. Cratch had disappeared. His intended executioners looked all around along the grounds as each of their footsteps weighed them down in sloshy mud. Each step played a removed suction cup sound. They backtracked to their original spot, around the dark water, then a wind from above made them sway. They looked up and found a larger than life crow descending upon them, from out of nowhere. The Officers and Agents fell, unconscious, but not before unleashing a barrage of bullets upon the flying target. The crow, shot up badly, fell to the soft, wet ground. Tihomir could hear the crow's thoughts. Tihomir transformed from crow into human form as he tried to eject the bullets from the crow's body.

I, Brother Henry, found myself upon the scene while out for an errand to help a member of the Church. The sight of a human like creature laying on the ground, the smoke pouring out of the railroad tunnel, frightened me, yet I felt drawn to help. I pulled the old Buick onto the dirt lot near the tunnel. I ran to what I assumed was a man's body. His body from head to knees was covered by a dark cloak. It was the man who would become known to me as Tihomir Goralski, father of Sylvia Magnon. There were burn holes the size of oranges in parts of the back of the coat. What I could see through the holes wasn't flesh or blood. It was a yellowish ooze surrounded by a reddish-brown sheen of skin. I moved part of the cloak and noticed parts of him were missing in the midsection, but that area was crisscrossed by black feathers. The cloak still covered his face, until he rolled over towards me. What I saw was incredible. I will never forget it. His nose was protruded forward, covered by long gray hair which ran up to his cheek and along the jaw line. His arm was only visible at the wrist and hand area, also covered by long hair but there were sharp claws extended out where a human hand should be. His lower left leg was shredded but where a foot should be there also protruded long, sharp claw nails. He rested on his left side. "Please, get me away from here," he moaned in a raspy voice. His thin upper lip betrayed curved fangs on either side of the narrow chin.

"To where?" I stammered. "Doc Ziggy," was his desperate response, and further, "He can help me, and perhaps you?" I was not sure of his complete meaning by these requests. A large flock of crows came to the ground and formed a circle around us. Even more rats charged forward and enlarged the circle. More roaches than I had ever before seen extended the circumference of the circle. Some suited men and women, official-looking in nature, some were police officers from the community, came running over to this odd enclave of human, insect, avian and rodent crew. Tihomir then blurted loudly, "Defend!" I didn't know what to think of his command, but the roaches, rats and crows understood. They increased the circumference of the circle. One of the police officers blurted out, "Are you seeing this?" The other officers and suited humans were still trying to comprehend the vision before them, but it was too late for them to retreat.

A bolt of lightning struck a nearby power transformer on one of the wooden utility poles behind the officers. The wires ripped from the pole and as the pole went down towards the ground, sparks of electricity rained upon them. Since it had rained, puddles of water lay all about them, only to be energized by the electrical current. One of the suited men stepped sideways to avoid the sparks and his step culminated into a puddle. His body started shaking and his gun started firing randomly. Some of the other officers and suits were struck and started to go down like dominoes. The roaches and rats charged at the armed humans, pouncing upon them as balls of vermin. I had never seen such a coordinated action by rats and roaches. They, too, were electrocuted as the humans, panicked, began to dart and run everywhere, some to be electrocuted, some to be feasted upon by the vermin, and some came straight towards Tihomir and myself. The crows had alighted on the right, en masse, and the crows behind us flew over our heads, en masse, and pelted into the gun-wielding humans. Then, it was over. What was once life lay all before us like a blanket of death. As an educated man in the oddities of the world, I yet was stunned, but I didn't stop calculating the significant events of this sliver of a moment in my life.

I placed my hand over Tihomir's forehead. His forehead was cold and sweaty. I placed my hand on his neck area. He had difficulty breathing. He tried to speak. "Help . . . help my daughter . . . she is a child . . . she doesn't know . . . she doesn't know the curse." I tried to console him. I told him I knew who he was and what had happened to him. His expression was too desolate to indicate any sensible understanding. He used every ounce of strength left in him to continue his plea.

"Help her . . . Sylvia . . . my daughter . . . Magnon . . . help her . . ."

The sirens of the government screeched an alarm. The sounds came closer; descended upon the morbid scene. All the power went out in the neighborhood.

End Zoner

PART THIRD - AVE MEGIDDO

1

I received a communique from the Vatican, written in the ink of the Holy See Himself, after submission of my report about the cursed Goralski family. The communique required me to recruit Murker, a military mercenary expert in siege warfare; Sylvia Magnon, an archaeologist and anthropologist; Vivaldi, a long ago deceased classical music composer; and Triglav, a pagan Slavic demi-god rumored to still reside in the mountain area of a Slavic country.

I was expecting such a communication after I learned a group of Russian archaeologists discovered a footprint in the Holy Cross Mountains of Poland. The media was told this find was a footprint of the oldest dinosaur. What had been covered up was the footprint wasn't made by a dinosaur. It was from a demon, an ancient Polish demi-god, Triglav, whose presence lost favor among the Poles once their tribes began conversion from paganistic practices towards Roman Catholicism many centuries past. Triglav then went into hiding, of his own volition.

After the authorities carted away the remains of Sylvia's father many years ago, I searched for his daughter. I was uncertain of Tihomir's fate, but I managed to later identify his connection to Dr. Zygmunt Zeis and then become appraised by the good doctor of the biological affliction Tihomir had also suffered. I reported my findings to the Holy See and was subsequently instructed to find Sylvia and help care for and educate her on the trappings of the curse she inherited at birth.

My investigation into Tihomir's genealogical heritage helped me uncover knowledge of the Onionhead curse, and something else, a scientific anomaly inadvertently discovered and accidentally inflicted upon Tihomir, which eventually resulted in his transformation into a new species, a Cratch. Sylvia inherited those abnormal genes and so was born the second Cratch.

At age 25 now, Sylvia had earned a reputation, in the
employ of the Holy See, as a brilliant investigator,
commencing and concluding many cases around the world
primarily involved in the search for demon signs of
intrusion. The following narrative and communications
are related to the circumstances and consequences of
her assignment to an area of the Holy Cross Mountains
in Poland. Her experiences and subsequent escapades
follow.

2

Schubert's "Ave Maria" played on a clock radio
stationed next to Sylvia Magnon's twenty-five years
old head. The radio sat on a nightstand next to the
mantel of her bed. She crumpled up in her bed covers.
Her brownish hair tinged by blond strands fell to
about shoulder length. Her skin was a light gray. She
was fond of wearing a low cut, red T-top, and white
Capri's. She did everything in them, including sleep.
Her feet were usually adorned by root-beer colored
Brahma boots, her one fashion obsession. A green
utility belt, designed by her, wrapped around her
waist when used. A left thigh strap tied just above
her knee added three pouches for her arsenal of tools.
A long pouch held a flat trowel and thin paint brush.
The waist part held dual pouches just inside each hip
bone at the front. A smaller pouch held a cigarette
pack, and a narrower pouch held her lighter. The boots
sometimes were not removed as she fell into deep rest
slumbers at irregular intervals depending on the work
schedule. She now encountered one of her many
unexplained dreams about distant lands and demons.
This dream scene, one of many she had related to me,
showed an open, wide field, bordered by thick Oak
forests on each side. The view was from an overlooking
slight hill. The terrain ahead gradually dropped into
a flat point of ground, and off in the distance,
brownish gray mountains peeked through thinly layered
fog. In the middle of the field, strangely, a large,
ashen-colored, leafless Willow tree reached out
branches in four directions. The thick trunk almost
glowed as if haloed by a descending fog stimulated
by the rays of morning sun climbing over the distant
mountains.

Sylvia Magnon, a certified anthropologist and
archaeologist, awakened from one of many unusual
dreams that had plagued her sleep for as long as she
could remember.

"Aaaaaa-veeeee Mariiiii-iii-aaaaa…", beamed from the

radio speaker.

The sweet sound of "Ave Maria" emanated from a local Balmoral from radio station as the DJ's frothy, silky baritone voice announced a start to the just-dawned morning.

"Good morning Balmoral . . . as we hail the beauty of the coming day from WCKD."

Sylvia's upper torso thrashed from beneath her covers to suck some morning air from her cramped studio apartment. Thoth, her tabby cat, remained asleep on his side, curled against the back of her blanketed legs, averse to the morning ritual in any conceivable fashion. Sylvia's left boot jutted out from the blankets and sheets mix overhanging the lower ledge of the bed. Her simple face pleased Thoth, her cat friend and protector. As the back of Sylvia's head pressed deep into the pillow, her hair sprouted in clumps, like the Willow tree in her dreams. She reached out and patted the top of the radio. She sat up, a picture of disarray. Her hair assumed the same color as the early morning low light attacking the window above her bed. The light glistened partially on the back of a cockroach, which scurried into the shadows of the window frame projected on the side wall. Up and out of bed she went to service her needs and those of Thoth.

After a packet rip, spoon swirls and microwave subjugation, she seated herself at the apartment breakfast table, spooned into her stale, dry mouth some moist, warm oatmeal to satisfy her stomach, and started to read the local newspaper to stimulate her brain. The radio played Barber's "Adagio for Strings". The sound soothed her soul for now. Thoth entered the arena of the kitchen table and seated himself on the far edge, which wasn't far away given the tight quarters. Sylvia gorged on the newspaper's headline and read it to Thoth, "Oldest Dino Print Found in Poland." Thoth stood up on all fours arching his back. A cell phone rested on the table near Sylvia's right hand.

(Reader's Note: Much of the conversational text for the remainder of this history will be written in comic book script I learned from reading Sylvia's comic books. It has become much easier in the present time to write exactly what transpired in communications given the ease of audio and video recording and given the capability of mobile phone text message documentation. During much of Sylvia's work she was able to record her interactions using her mobile phone, or text significant results to me that allowed timely reports I then forwarded to the Holy See administrators.)

THOTH: Yeoooww!

SYLVIA: Whoa!

Sylvia's cell phone buzzed. She reached for it with her right hand, still intently reading the newspaper. The radio sound of Vivaldi's "Summer Presto" energized her a bit more into the morning routine. Before the phone buzzed off the table edge, Sylvia snatched it and pressed it to her right ear.

SYLVIA: Yep. Saw it. Guess I'll be getting another call of duty soon from His Eminence.

Thoth seated himself on Sylvia's lap as a means of reminder his attention superseded that of the electronic device. Sylvia gently stroked the back of his head with her left hand.

SYLVIA: Looks like the Holy Cross Mountains in Poland. Never been there before, either.

Thoth frowned, sensing that he will not see his friend for some time. Sylvia smiled at him.

SYLVIA: Glad you worked the advance team. I'll look

you up when I get there.

Sylvia clapped the phone flaps together. A now depressed Thoth looked away, then reached up his left paw and extended two claw nails gently into the back of Sylvia's left hand.

SYLVIA: Looks like we need to make a visit to Nana.

3

At the Vatican in Rome, a wall-sized dusty tapestry displayed eight Apocalyptic Beasts in a dark room. A doorway to the left corner of the room shined in gold-colored light from the hallway. A golden plaque mounted just underneath the lower edge of the tapestry entitled the artwork as "Apocalyptic Beasts". The tapestry frame design displayed Dwarfish nature spirits called Ohdows (impish body, roundish eyes popping from the skull, lizard-like yet smooth skin, frog-like legs and arms, pin-like digits) which managed the underworld's Beast realm. The central (centered on the Tapestry) demon was known to humankind as Romanus, the Scarlet Beast. His Eminence, The Pope of Roman Catholicism, sat in a regal chair, stared at the tapestry-covered wall. Reading glasses, over which he peered, adorned his nose. The Pope concentrated on each Beast.

The Pope's vision was first concentrated on the central Beast, Romanus. He was depicted as seated on a wood-hewn and gold-laden throne as a red-orange fire emanated from his body. The beast was large, man-like muscular, scarlet-reddish skin color, bull-faced and dual-horned, the horns curling upward from each side of the large head, and each horn had a series of dark rings around it, symbolizing the thousands of years that had passed since the time when demons tried to take back Earth. Piles of gold and silver, jewels, man-made offerings were strewn around him. Romanus, the Scarlet Beast, embodied the sin of greed.

On either side of Romanus were Taetin and Eirantka. Taetin, on the left, rose from the sea, the body of a leopard, feet of a bear and seven heads like the hydra, each with lion's jaws, each head had ten horns, bearing ten crowns. Taetin embodied the Sea Beast.

Eirantka, on the right, had a similar appearance to the Sea Beast but sprouted only a single head, its horns were shorter, and it exhibited the neck of a dragon. Eirantka embodied the Earth Beast.

In the foreground, forming a semi-circle, were other Beasts. Bahamut appeared like a muscle-bound elephant having a hippopotamus type head out of which jutted a ruby. His bull type back hair bristled. His eyes showed a powerful lust. Bahamut, aka Behemoth, emanated the sin of lust. He coveted above all the love of Leviathan.

A Sea Serpent represented Leviathan, eel-like, having multiple dolphin-like dorsal fins running along the spine, and wing-like flippers close to the head. Her eyes betrayed envy. She was the guardian of Hell. Envy ruled her demeanor. She especially coveted Bahamut.

Hayoth exhibited a human torso with oxen feet and ox tail, four wings covered the front and two in the back; four faces—a human in front, bull's face to the left, eagle's head behind and lion's face to the right. Hayoth lurked in the background as a demon warrior leader.

On the left and right of Hayoth were Asura and Triglav. Asura appeared as a titan-like size, of human, androgynous appearance, four arms on each side of the torso, holding various war and pleasure implements like knife, wine chalice, sword, club, bread, salt, as the sin of pride dominated in four human faces on one head showing expressions of wrath, pride, boasting and bellicosity.

Triglav was the three-faced goat man, exhibited by a goat in the central face, human on one side and crow the other, topped by circular ram-like horns. The horns curled down the side of each cheek of his face, ending in a sharp tip just under the jaw line which sprouted goat-like hairs to form a thick goatee. The other faces curved around from each side of the central face, completing a roundish triangle. The faces were human, a mixture of human-goat, and a mixture of human-crow. The goat and crow faces were reflected in a pool of water or ornate glass on each side of his face. A roll of golden hair rested on the top third of his head making a half-halo appearance almost from temple to temple which triangulated around his foreheads. He was massive in size, muscular, olive-skinned, his feet three-toed, like a large bird, but the heels were human. Triglav, an ancient Slavic god, the sin of idolatry exuded from his being.

The Pope leaned forward in his chair, squinted at Triglav's face and spoke.

THE POPE: My old friend. We are going to need you now more than ever.

The Pope's stare remained for as long as he remained seated. The time length of his gaze would have created an uncomfortable unease for any guest in the room, yet he still stared up at the tapestry, alone in thought. On the Pope's lap a newspaper headline displayed in large words, "Stunning Find in Poland Mountains".

THE POPE: And so, it begins.

A larger perspective of the room revealed a doorway in the distance, to the left of the tapestry, where hallway light filtered in. A short, thin man in a black robe stood in the doorway motionless, head bowed, as the bright light of the hallway attempted to model him as a shadow or apparition. The Pope, still seated in the chair, also appeared, from the back, to exist as merely a dark apparition.

THE POPE: Come in my friend.

Gregorio, the black-robed assistant to the Pope, entered the room and stood across from the still seated Pope. A white cord of rope acted as a loose belt around the Pope's waist, tied at one side. Only the dusty bottom portion of the tapestry could be clearly seen as the entire configuration exerted a domination of the room's atmosphere. Gregorio stared up at the tapestry.

THE POPE: Contact Ms. Magnon. Let her know we have a new assignment for her.

GREGORIO: Your Eminence . . . it is written by John in Revelations that a woman will ride the Scarlet Beast to power and to the ultimate destruction of humanity.

The Pope looked over top of his reading glasses at Gregorio.

THE POPE: My friend . . . let us hope John was mistaken.

Close-up of Gregorio's face.

GREGORIO: Shall I alert the Monk at the Holy Cross Monastery?

Close-up of The Pope's face.

THE POPE: You know he doesn't have a mobile phone.

Gregorio looked like a revelation had hit him.

GREGORIO: Ah, yes . . . better call Tratsch.

RRRIIINNNGGG!

A Gargoyle, gray green color, wings partially visible, held a mobile phone up to his head.

TRATSCH: Holy Cross Monastery. Tratsch here. How can I help you?

Tratsch, smiled, looked over at Hugo, the Monk, who

was seated on a wooden stool at a large laboratory-like rectangular table, books piled high all around, papers fallen like leaves on the floor, and multiple lap tops and plugs distended from them into various nearby wall sockets. Behind the Monk were two, high, glazed windows, an arch at the top and a stone ledge a foot width and three feet length at the bottom, about chest height from the floor. Hugo was a smallish man, somewhat nerdy in appearance, wore a brown overly long-sleeved shirt, and a brown skirt-like lower piece of clothing falling to the ankles, tied at the waist by a white cord. Blue and white Nike's running shoes he pressed hard against the bottom rungs of the stool. He intently investigated the depths of a very thick, old and large book. The entire far wall in the background and to his right was covered in bookshelves, books stuffed into them along the shelf, on top of the shelved books, and poked out irregular intervals.

TRATSCH: Brother Hugo. It's for you.

HUGO GROTIUS: Oh crap. I almost have it!

Hugo reached out for the phone with his left hand, still staring intently at the pages of the thick book.

HUGO: Thanks, Tratsch.

Hugo held the phone up to his left ear.

HUGO: Are you sure? Yes. Yes. I will begin preparations immediately.

4

Sylvia and Thoth arrived at Nana's, lifted the front door knocker and let it drop a few times.

THOTH: Meow.

SYLVIA: Nana?

NANA: Come in dear, it's open.

Sylvia entered, carried a small, black plastic pet carrier in one hand. The kitchen radiated older accouterments as visible in the black stove, the wall pattern of beige tiles on the countertop backsplash, gas burners on top of the stove, dark brown and grease stained cabinet doors. Potted plants crowded the counter along the backsplash. Sylvia's maternal grandmother, "Nana", perched on a metal, cushioned chair at the rectangular kitchen table next to the wall on the left. Her visibly worn face remained serene in the elder stages of womanhood. A mug of hot coffee rested before her. A page-worn, white-covered Bible rested three-quarters open on the table just below her visage. Reading glasses assisted her view. The window above the kitchen sink was open, and the curtains allowed through a light breeze.

Sylvia immediately moved to the middle of the room and opened the carrier to allow Thoth's escape onto the scene. Sylvia walked over next to Nana, bent over top of her, and kissed her on her left cheek as Nana cocked her head to the side to make it easier to receive the kiss.

NANA: Where to now child?

SYLVIA: How did you know?

Thoth had jumped onto the table and was sniffing at Nana's right hand.

NANA: Seems you only come to see me when you are about to leave out for somewhere.

SYLVIA: Fortunately for me that is many visits. Thoth doesn't seem to mind.

Nana remembered she wanted to give something to Sylvia. It was an Aardvark necklace. It looked like a beige piece of dung, a special charm which protected the wearer.

NANA: That reminds me. I have something for you.

Nana opened her clenched right hand to reveal the necklace, attached to a leather string.

NANA: Some say it allows the wearer to walk through walls when necessary.

SYLVIA: Not quite the freshest smelling thing, is it?

NANA: Just wrap it in a tissue.

Thoth creeped over to take a sniff, but his hind leg knocked over Nana's mug of coffee which had about two sips left in it. The coffee stream flowed under Thoth's legs, touching the left front paw. Thoth took a careful step forward with the left front paw and leaned towards the Aardvark necklace after Sylvia placed it around her neck. It dangled just above the small cavern separating her breasts. Thoth's face gave a wincing opinion. Nana turned her head in a manner to demonstrate a look of knowing wonder at Thoth's actions.

NANA: Thoth gives his blessing, I see.

Sylvia looked somewhat down at the tabletop below her chin, where Thoth had left an imprint of his coffee stained paw. Sylvia formed a sad face, looked towards Nana.

SYLVIA: Nana . . . Nana . . .

NANA: I know what you want to ask me child. He is not important to you now.

Sylvia's face revealed a look of frustration and almost anger.

SYLVIA: Why has no one told me about my father?

NANA: He was a bad man . . . just remember that.

Sylvia responded, even more frustrated.

SYLVA: How so? I'd like to make that judgment myself.

Her frustrated look was enough to express her feelings, but she slammed her left hand flat onto the table for emphasis. Thoth's back raised up and his hairs stood on end.

Nana winced, knowing what questions would follow.

NANA: He almost destroyed this City.

SYLVIA: But how? Was he a politician? A drug dealer? A bad cop?

Nana wanted to hold back what she was tempted to say. She had been holding back a truth she feared Sylvia wouldn't understand. Nana blurted it out anyway.

NANA: He was a MONSTER!

Sylvia was shocked. She had never heard Nana become so upset. Nana dropped her head into her hands.

NANA: He met your mother while she was working...on the Block ... as an erotic dancer.

SYLVIA: My mom was a dancer?

Nana looked at the ceiling.

NANA: Yes . . . she was young. We were living in the old housing project, Douglas Homes. She tried to get out and help us.

Nana's lips curled in a look of disdain.

NANA: They had a brief relationship. And you were their blessing.

SYLVIA: What happened to my mom?

Nana choked up. She didn't want to reveal the evening in the alley behind her house, when Sylvia's mom died. Nana remembered the evening alley scene but didn't go into all the details.

NANA: Child, you were only two months old. Your father came to visit her. They were in the back alley when a neighborhood drug deal went bad. Your mom . . . was struck by a stray bullet fired by a drug dealer's gang.

Sylvia started to tear up.

NANA: What your father then did to the drug gang, the gang leader . . . there was not much left for the police to identify them.

SYLVIA: What happened to my mom?

Nana tried not to break down.

NANA: She . . . She . . . died ... instantly.

Sylvia sank deep in pain. Nana struggled to keep herself together.

NANA: I fainted, and I didn't remember much.

Sylvia cried. Thoth buried his head into her chest,

tried to comfort her.

NANA: I didn't see your father for a long time after
that. He came to visit one day when you were a little
girl, while you were in school.

NANA: He wanted to take care of you. But his condition
would not allow it. He was extremely sick.

Sylvia settled down a bit.

NANA: He wanted to see a picture of you. I showed him
some pictures. He noticed something in one of the
photographs that made him curious.

SYLVIA: What?

NANA: The birthmark. The strange thing about that
birthmark was . . . your father didn't have one like
it. But he had a tattoo identical to it.

SYLVIA: That doesn't make sense. A tattoo on one
person can't be transferred as a birthmark to
another.

NANA: I told you. He was very strange, and sick.

Sylvia's lower back, as a child showed a small
birthmark that looked like an ambigram of the
Blessed-Cursed tattoo of her father.

Nana apologetically.

NANA: I know he was your father, but girl, there was
something odd about him. He was like a walking science
experiment. Rats and crows seemed to follow him
around, not to mention the roaches.

A long silence ensued. Nana remembered and related to
Sylvia a conversation with Sylvia's father, during
one of his visits. He handed her a golden broach. The
broach was about two inches high and one inch wide,

almost flat, no more than a quarter inch thick, shaped
like a shield. Embedded on one side was an upside-
down horseshoe upon which stood a crow or raven. The
broach opened along a hinge. The inside of the broach
connected to a very pointy pin. The sharp point was
protected by a clasp shaped like a human skull adorned
by curling horns on each side. Nana examined the
broach. She looked up to Sylvia's father, but he was
leaving. He walked through the front door . . . while
the door was still closed.

NANA: He was like a ghost, disappearing on you in the
middle of a sentence, when you thought you could still
see him out of the corner of your eye.

SYLVIA (thought): I can do that too. I guess not
everyone can do it.

Sylvia, almost afraid to ask, mustered the courage.
Nana's face showed apprehension, but she relented and
answered as her memories faded away.

SYLVIA: What . . . what . . . was his name?

NANA: I suppose it is time you should know. Tihomir.
Tihomir Goralski.

Sylvia was anxious now.

SYLVIA (thought): I must google his name. But Nana
would object if I did it now.

SYLVIA: Well . . . I guess it is time.

Nana, worried, reached out her hand to clasp Sylvia's
hand.

NANA: He left this for you. Nana released the broach
into Sylvia's hand.

SYLVIA: What does it mean?

NANA: He said it was his family's Crest. The horned skull clasp is kind of creepy.

Sylvia, thinking like an anthropologist, tried to figure out the meaning of each aspect of the broach. Thoth sniffed it and knocked it out of her hand. It landed next to his coffee stain footprint on the table, on the one quarter inch side. A long pin popped out the back. Sylvia and Nana looked at each other, a bit amazed. The odds of the metal broach landing to a stop on the thin side was remote.

NANA: He said you would need it one day. All I know is the underside and inside is so shiny it works like a mirror.

SYLVA: I wish you had told me these things before.

NANA: I was waiting for you to be ready to handle it all.

Sylvia, fumed, frustrated, didn't say anything. She reached for the broach. The pin receded quickly into the casing. Nana didn't notice.

NANA: Child, you take care. Remember the gifts God has given you. Use them well. Use them well.

SYLVIA (thought): I will do more than that.

5

A dig site in Holy Cross Mountains, Poland was underway. The site had become known for discovery of pre-historic footprints recently exposed by harsh rains which flooded the low-lying fertile plains of the land, home of The Polan tribe of Slavs for over a thousand years.

Sylvia Magnon specialized in ancient and prehistoric god myths. Most of her associates thought of this specialty the way Astronomers and Metaphysics prevaricators pondered the existence of outer-space Aliens--an interesting hobby--nothing more. She arrived at the dig sight, started to unpack and make camp.

"What do you have there?" an elderly looking, white bearded tall gentleman barked to some young, addled, trainee earth brushers.

"I . . . I don't know . . ." said a baby faced thirty-something aged digger.

The old man limped up to the crest of the site carved at the base of an outcropping of rock extending from the nearest mountain, known as the Holy Cross Mountain.

"Unbelievable" he murmured. Suddenly, everyone stopped. The experienced diggers knew him to be a cynical skeptic, practiced in the art of understatement. The unexpected word choice of the old man stung their ears. Some were confused.

The old man took over the brushing, squinted, requested a magnifier by reaching out, words unspoken. A magnifier was slapped into his hand as he pointed, gazed, then grinned.

"So, it is true." Everyone wanted to hear his explanation of what new truth could finally have fallen upon their body of science. "Dinosaurs roamed here long ago," he stated in an exaggerated tone, "identified by the fossils we previously found. The only oddity is the print is not as deep as would be thought, due to weathering in this god-forsaken, remote environment, perhaps. Enough time spent. We are out of here tomorrow." The diggers looked at each other, then cheered. Two weeks in this place was too much for them.

Sylvia awakened. It was mid-day, but she had been up all night, having gone about many preparation tasks while the others slept. She had taken a morning cat nap to rejuvenate. She knew the team working the dig sight was close to something, despite the team member's sullen attitude. The findings up to this point were typical of the area, but deep in her bones she felt that something else, something magnificent, unheard of was about to be unearthed. Her advance research determined this area was full of legends, stories of pre-historical tribal tome's, passed down by word of mouth, because those passing them down feared, at the time of print, that these truths to them, would result in disaster rushed upon their culture from the powerful in the world. She stumbled out of her near earthen tent, which she constructed more like a lean-to, so she could see the impending light of evening stars, planets, moon, her only truly enjoyed entertainment for many years, given she was on the go traveling so much, mainly housed away from the trappings of technology like microwave ovens, laptops, television. She looked around.

The only thing that mattered in her world was her work. it was a near mission for her to find the things she learned about during her own research into the ancient, pre-historical god legends and myths. She poured a cold, mud like cup of coffee from her thermos into a weak tin, slurped and gummed it like cold fudge, tossed the half empty tin into the Slavic earth, and trekked in her work boots up to the dig site. It was too quiet. Something was afoot, she mused.

As she approached the dig site, a commotion was suddenly upon her. "You won't believe it. We can finally go home for a while," one of the interns gleefully spouted at her.

Sylvia trudged to the base of the dig, having heard these words hundreds of times on sites, were findings turned out to be duplications of prior finds, or of marginal significance after research and debate had cleared.

The old man announced that perhaps they had discovered the oldest known dinosaur footprint, unusual yes, since there were no other identical findings within hundreds of miles of this location.

Sylvia looked at the finding in the ground. "That print looks humanoid to me," she murmured.

The old archeologist scoffed. "There you go again, finding ancient myth in physical science. It only has three toes for Christ's sake. And it is too close to the surface."

A roll of thunder could be heard in the distance. Sylvia would not be convinced as she offered her reasoning.

"The depth of the print is more conducive to a lesser weighted creature. No other similar found prints nearby as I noticed on the walk over. I am not even sure this print belongs here. This area has been excavated and searched for over a hundred years."

"So how did it get here?" the old archaeologist inquired skeptically.

Without hesitation, Sylvia surmised "Someone or something put it here".

In Rome, on a dank, cool day that looked like dusk before night, black clouds finally unleashed a rain shower of significant torrents. In a large room at the Vatican, bedecked in reds and purples, The Pope squinted at his reading material, entranced by the words long ago scribbled on the brownish, tattered pages of a manuscript, leather bound.

His assistant interrupted. "Your Eminence. It has been found."

"Unbelievable." The Pope responded. "What now? An unusual, mythical finding, at the dig site? Who is there?"

"Some American and Russian archaeologists, some student interns from France, and of course Sylvia. She arrived there today. Sylvia reports there are dinosaur prints and bone fossils at the site, but nothing unusual found yet. The American government group is leaving tomorrow." The Pope pondered. "Ah, so the Americans are involved, too."

The underling was silent as The Pope's countenance moved to and froe, from squinch to stretch, his eyes disappearing in the elderly folds of his brow, then popping out as if newborn orbs had formed in the sky. The underling squirmed, but remained motionless, awaiting the slightest sign of speech from His Eminence. There was no verbal sound.

"Good, good. Sylvia will have the site to herself. She has proven quite adept at discovering overlooked nuances."

"Your Eminence, anthropologist Magnon is somewhat looked down upon by her peers because she takes on the most difficult, controversial and impossible investigations, willingly. It appears her peers scoff at her efforts as useless and unnecessary."

Words slowly formed at The Pope's lips, and his voice resumed, almost from a quaint distance, "Well, her government and their military must have had a good reason for having their own archaeologists at the dig site. Perhaps Sylvia's presence scared them away."

Sylvia's official assignment, hers alone, began in earnest at the spot where her government's archaeological team had packed up and gone home. She determined to investigate further the footprint imbedded in the moonscape-like terrain, bordered by far off mountains, spots of brownish-green grass, caves, patches of trees. She stooped down and began brushing away the ancient dirt at a mid-level mountain plateau. Dust and invisible microbes settled below her feet. A footprint frozen in the rock-hard stone terrain tempted her curiosity. The print was three-toed, like a large bird's footprint except for it had a human heel, but the print was somewhat larger than even a large-sized man. A nearby trowel and thin paintbrush beckoned her use. The beautiful view of this lonely land stimulated the sounds of "Night on Bald Mountain" by Mussorgsky, to play in her head.

SYLVIA: Well, what have we here?

As she photographed the footprint with her cell phone, a male voice from behind her, calmly and almost quietly, unassumingly spoke. He was Triglav, an olive-skinned, seemingly mountain-sized and goat-faced man, wearing a black cape sprouting an oversized hoodie covering most of his head and eyes. He had two other faces--one man-like and the other crow-like, which formed a triangular head. He used the hood to hide the other faces from her for now. Because curved horns protruded from the sides of his head and down to near under his chin on each side, the upper half of the hoodie had a curved appearance. Sky-blue shorts covered his lower trunk and legs to the knee, jagged edged at the bottom, and a red, thick cord knotted in the middle hugged at his waist.

TRIGLAV (thought): Hmmm.

From a perspective looking from the front of the stooping Sylvia, but behind her stood Triglav, somewhat hunched over her. His head was a bit raised; now revealed a face serene yet inquisitive. His shoulders massively bulged, almost unnaturally, from under the black garment. Since the Sun was behind him, in the west, a large shadow covered the stooped Sylvia and part of the rock print.

TRIGLAV: What did you find there?

SYLVIA (thought): Looks like rain coming. I didn't notice it was so cloudy.

From Triglav's perspective, he looked over top of her.

SYLVIA: A print, probably dinosaur, could be bird.

She stood up and bumped her head into his chest which arched over her head. She was startled.

SYLVIA: I thought all the government hires headed out of here already. What, did you miss the bus?

She turned around to find a visage, almost twice as large as hers, moonlike in the afternoon hot Sun. The Sun was bright over Triglav's shoulders, his face regal, chiseled and covered partially by a black hood. Connected in one piece was a shawl-like open robe draped over his massive shoulders and along his arms, ended just below the waist. His mouth was surrounded by an overgrown, shaggy gray white goatee, extended to below his chin, but his skin was an olive-green hue. Sylvia's jaw dropped down to reveal the hollow of her mouth. Triglav looked down at Sylvia. The footprint could be seen beyond her shoulders.

SYLVIA: What? I mean, WHO, are you?!

He stood fully erect and completely blotted out the
Sun, low in the sky behind him.

TRIGLAV: I am Triglav. I have lived in these parts a
long, long time.

Sylvia's face showed a perplexed reflection.

SYLVIA (thought): Triglav? No one names their kid
after Triglav. He was the disgraced pre-Christian god
of the Polan tribe. And ninety-seven percent of
Poland is now Roman Catholic in religious belief.

Triglav sidestepped her and bent over to further
peruse the footprint.

TRIGLAV: I know whose print that is.

He put his massive arm out to brush her back a bit
from the spot as she stepped forward, then he intently
sized up the print.

TRIGLAV: I think.

SYLVIA (thought): Whose? Doesn't he mean what's?

TRIGLAV (thought): Is it? Could it be?

Triglav inhaled, expanded his chest wide, the black,
shawl-like garment started to slide off his
shoulders, but the hoodie stayed fixed on his head.
Sylvia was behind looking down at his heels. His
facial cheeks expanded into two bubble-gum blown
puffs. Sylvia couldn't believe what she saw.

SYLVIA (thought): Three toes?!?!

Triglav exhaled and pretty much sandblasted away
while putting his face close to the print. His focused

breath stream cleared the ancient dust and soil. As it blew wildly into the air, the entire massive footprint was revealed. Sylvia peered from around him, eye level at his waist, holding onto the back of Triglav's garment as if she held the sides of a ladder, but his body width was more than twice hers. He lifted his left foot, the underside revealing crusty, scaled flatness. Sylvia intently focused on his foot. He put his foot down into the print. It matched perfectly. Sylvia, stunned, began to sag forward, eyes half closed, as her body turned sideways. Her one word trailed off weakly.

SYLVIA: Impossible . . .

She fainted into Triglav's arms as he turned around.

TRIGLAV: Oh no . . .

6

Around a campfire they sat. A small distended part of the fire showed flames wafting upward toward a metal tripod cradled in the middle a pot of steaming hot water. A small tent tempted solitude and rest in the background. Wooden crates, archaeology and paleontology tools and implements were scattered about. Triglav sat on the ground, legs crossed Indian style, arms rested along the thighs. His massive hands sprouted pointy fingernails draped over each knee respectively. A near full moon evening, long thin strings of clouds trailed across the clean sky but didn't block a view of the Big Dipper star constellation. Sylvia sat on a log opposite Triglav, at the other side of the fire.

Triglav started the conversation, staring into the heart of the campfire flames. He still wore his cape-like gown to cover his head.

TRIGLAV: I love this world. Are you feeling better?

She quickly shook her head up and down.

SYLVIA: Yes, thank you. Too much sun, too soon, I think.

TRIGLAV: Need to hydrate a bit more, perhaps.

SYLVIA (thought): I can't believe this. I'm sitting in front of a fire across from a strange guy, or something, that thinks he's an ancient Slavic god.

Triglav's voice toned a bit of wonderment. Sylvia supported her head, her left hand acted as a crutch, her left elbow propped on the edge of her left knee. She desperately clasped a tin cup from which the steam of a hot beverage massaged her face.

TRIGLAV: Why are you the only one way out here?

SYLVIA: Long story. You sure you want to hear it?

He stared directly into her eyes. Triglav's visage demonstrated extreme thinking. Sylvia was taken aback by his elegant gentleman-like nature.

TRIGLAV: Nothing else to do now, really. We each have long stories . . . but you first . . . if you could so graciously indulge my curiosity.

SYLVIA: Well, then, where shall I begin . . .?

Triglav's face and demeanor demonstrated empathy. In the distance, the black form of a Neuri (human-like wolf), stood on a mountain cliff, against the large, yellowish moon background, looked down upon their scene. After some minutes of conversation later, Triglav summarized.

TRIGLAV: It so appears we have something in common. Neither of us ever really knew our father.

SYLVIA: What? How would you know that?

TRIGLAV: Lucky guess, I suppose.

Sylvia stood up to stretch. A small, near wafer-thin, gold-colored broach case fell from her person and came to rest halfway between each of them on the ground. Triglav tried to pick it up. She quickly snatched it up with the speed of an adrenalin shot.

SYLVIA: NO! . . . I . . . I . . . I've got it.

Triglav's jaw dropped open as he defensively backed away, hands spread out before him.

TRIGLAV: That must be especially important to you.

SYLVIA: Yes, yes, it is. My father gave that to me.

TRIGLAV: I thought you didn't know your father?

SYLVIA: I didn't, at least I never met him or spoke
with him. He left this for me when I was a child, so
it is special to me.

Triglav showed an expression of understanding, sort
of.

TRIGLAV: Yes, yes, I understand. It is your only
connection to him I suppose.

Sylvia yawned, put her left hand up to her mouth.

TRIGLAV: Well, it has been a long day. Off to slumber.

Triglav trudged off into the darkness. Before Sylvia
could say goodnight, as she was looking at the broach
case, when she looked up, she found herself alone.

SYLVIA (thought): Goodnight.

Triglav looked back from the darkness to make sure
Sylvia was okay. Sylvia squeezed into a pup tent. Her
waist and her upper body were inside the tight tent
opening as the bluish yellow tip of fire light danced
off the round curves of her somewhat plump, buxom
buttocks. From a distant hill, the dark silhouette of
a lone, overly large man-wolf, a Neuri, stood up on
two legs, barrel chest pointed upward to the moon,
arched back, howled loud and long. Triglav heard the
sound and realized Sylvia would be safe. This man-
wolf had befriended Triglav long ago.

Inside the tent, Sylvia curled up in her sleeping
bag, looked at the broach Nana had given to her. She
fingered and opened it at the clasp. A light glow
emanated from it. What was inside could be seen from
a small mirror hanging on the back part of the tent
just above her head. Inside the case were two
compartments, one half held a whitish rouge type of
dry paste. The other held a black and white photograph
of a male and female. Under the male name a pen mark

indicated "T"; under the female name the mark indicated "P". She looked at the photograph a long time.

The Pope stood in a high-ceilinged room of the Vatican, looked out of the window, onto the city below. He fingered the Solomon's ring worn on the middle finger of his right hand. He rubbed with his left-hand fingers a "V" shaped, thin, sliver groove cut out of it many, many generations ago. "The Ritual Fire Dance", by de Falla, played from the four speakers mounted on the top corner of each part of the room. He spoke to himself out loud.

THE POPE: I hope she is doing well on her most important of missions.

The broach lay opened on Sylvia's stomach. She was asleep in her pup tent. Morning light shined on the broach.

Gregorio entered the room and approached The Pope from behind, stopped, and spoke. The Pope didn't turn around.

GREGORIO: Your itinerary is completed, Your Eminence.

THE POPE: Good. I shall be gone for a while.

Musical notes continued to emanate from the ceiling corner speakers.

GREGORIO: Music has existed for virtually all human time. Early humans created music to mimic the sounds of the nature environment which surrounded, enveloped the environment of habitation.

THE POPE: Gregorio, our only hope is this ring, Sylvia and her broach, and the music of the monastery.

GREGORIO: To think that the fate of our humanity hinges upon the use of these simple objects and sounds, and the chorus of chaos you have recruited, as weapons, is incredible.

Gregorio wished him well on his journey. The Pope turned around to address Gregorio directly.

THE POPE: Yes, the world as we know it has always danced seemingly on the head of a pin, like the Angels.

The post-dawn light had not yet aroused Sylvia's sleeping beauty. Her hand still clutched the broach. The pin side was upturned and glistened. Disturbing dreams had plagued Sylvia since she reached puberty, perhaps because she was a recipient, from her father's genes, of the Onionhead curse. In this dream, she remembered her friend, Thoth, her tabby cat, and their first encounter, relevant to her life in more than one way.

Sylvia at age twelve exuded the early appearance of a woman in a child's body. She frequently wore her favorite clothes of stirrup pants, skin-tight, white in color, and a red tank top which hinted at the first signs of her puberty in the breast and hips areas. Her blonde hair, streaked by a natural light red tint, was fixed in a ponytail which she rubbed in her right hand as it flowed down her right shoulder to just above her right breast. It was June, warm, and the howls of overly excited boys were heard stinging the air as they played American football on the playground asphalt. The girls stood on the side, watched the boys' ritual of attempted impression-making replete of scratches, cuts, scrapes; except

Sylvia lingered at the edge of the whole affair, looking off in the distance. She heard a soft yet desperate sound.

THOTH: Meeeooowww... Meeeooowww...

Sylvia escaped from the sour boy shouts; her attention drawn to the meow sounds. She stood under a middle-aged oak tree, looked up into the branches. Midway up the length of the oak trunk, she spied a tabby kitten clutched tight to a limb.

SYLVIA: Aww! How did you get up there?

THOTH: Meeeooowww!

A brownish, pug-nosed pit bull, not leashed, hair on its back raised in a dark stream, stood next to her, growling.

PIT BULL: Grrrrrrrrrrr!

Sylvia looked at the pit bull, directly in the squinted glaring eyes, a big mistake if Sylvia had not been empowered by the demon inside her.

SYLVIA: Scoot!

The pit bull did not accept the challenge, slowly backed away with a squeal, because it sensed the eerie demon presence in Sylvia. Sylvia's body in the eyes of the pit bull revealed a skeletal appearance, particularly her face. Some of the other girls became distracted by the pit bull growls and took notice of what was happening.

PIT BULL: EEEEhhhhhh!

Sylvia began climbing up the tree as the boys and girls on the playground came running over.

A BOY IN THE CROWD: Did you see that? She scared off

a pit bull!

A GIRL IN THE CROWD: I am not surprised. Look at her.

ANOTHER GIRL IN CROWD: Freak!

The boys in the crowd intently admired Sylvia's courage and round buttocks framing her skin-tight stirrup pants.

A BOY IN THE CROWD: Yes . . . look at her.

Girls in the crowd stood mixed among the boys, taking temporary advantage of the opportunity. The girls' looks displayed envy. The boys' faces exposed puppy-love wonder. Sylvia reached out towards the tabby kitten with her right arm, the rest of her body pressed tight against the tree trunk as she straddled it with her thighs and held onto a branch with her left hand.

SYLVIA: Come on now . . . just trying to help you.

Sylvia's hand clutched the tabby as it let go of the tree limb. The boys cheered. The girl's frowned.

BOYS IN THE CROWD: Yeaaahhhh!

Thoth, a tiny ball of fur, looked up at Sylvia, then buried his chin into her chest as she clutched him close, as if to say, this humanoid is right for me.

The morning light broke her from the dream. Sylvia's eyes opened as she lay on her back in her sleeping bag.

SYLVIA (thought): Thoth . . . thanks for visiting me in my dreams.

Sylvia closed the broach and stood up, then slid it into her side pocket where it left a slight impression through her pants. She pushed back the tent flap and stepped into the new day. Holding her crotch, a squint of slight pain and anxiety wrinkled up on her face. She looked for a place to go to the bathroom. Half-awake and somewhat disoriented, hair pushed to one side on top, in the distance she spotted a tree which appeared to bear the mark of upside-down crosses on it. As she scurried closer to the tree, she noticed the veins in the large, thin, reddish leaves made an upside-down cross shape.

SYVIA: Darn! I really gotta go.

She somewhat waddled over to the tree, squatted against it, rolled down from the waist her skin-tight white pants, and let go of the pressure in her groin to release the relief of a morning pee. The steam of the warm excretion wafted from the tree trunk. Some of her menses also escaped as it was her time of the month to release the microscopic human female unfertilized egg. The tree groaned, started moving, because Triglav was clung to the other side of it. He spouted in a horrific, tinny voice.

TRIGLAV: Ewww!

Sylvia sprung forward, tripped up by her lowered pants bounded at her legs as she fell face first into the ground, scattering the dirt all around her. Triglav apologetically spurted out a greeting.

TRIGLAV: Uh . . . good morning.

Sylvia started spewing expletives, and wetted dirt chunks as she hurriedly pulled up her pants to cover her curt, roundish buttocks and private parts.

SYLVIA: What the frack . . . Jesus, Mary and Joseph . . . gosh darn it.

She jumped up and looked around. Triglav, blushing, shook his head as the tree reduced to his humanoid form. A red stain adorned the lower calves' area at each of his legs.

SYLVIA: Geesh! You could give a girl a warning!

TRIGLAV: Sorry, guess I didn't get a chance to tell
you too much about myself last night.

Sylvia was embarrassed and verbally overcompensated
to mask such.

SYLVIA: Like the part where you're Anamorphic?! That
could have been helpful.

They headed back to camp where Sylvia began packing
a knapsack.

SYLVIA: I must go now. Rome called.

Triglav looked skyward. Sylvia expressed a confused
look.

TRIGLAV: Rome doesn't necessarily like me.

SYLVIA: Rome knows about you?

Triglav looked at her again.

TRIGLAV: More than you know. They would not greet me
with open arms there. They are the reason I am here.

SYLVIA: Why don't you come with me? Perhaps I can
help them to better understand you. Who, or what you
are.

Triglav displayed some discomfort. He realized it was
"who he was" and not "what he could be" that prevented
consideration of such a thought. Still, he remembered
a long-ago The Pope of Rome had indicated one day
there may be a future need for his service. He was
ready, if needed. Holed up in a mountain cave for
generations on end was losing its charm.

TRIGLAV: I can take you on a shortcut if you would like?

Sylvia pointed to her Jeep.

SYLVIA: I have a shortcut. It's called a Jeep.

Triglav still appeared uncomfortable.

TRIGLAV: You need to know some things before we go.

Triglav could hear Chopin's, "Etude No. 12 in C Minor Op. 10", in the air. A meteorite streaked across the sky, and the sky responded with a resounding "boom" as the atmosphere was invaded by multiple orange-red streaked fire balls.

Boom!

TRIGLAV: Hurry, this way!

Triglav shouted and he reached out, grabbed Sylvia just as she finished putting on her knapsack, and practically strapped her to his back using his massive arms. The meteorites whooshed all around them. He ran, while carrying her on his back, as meteorites bombed all around. At a distance, the shock waves almost knocked him sideways, and the heat of them seared all in their path, including the campsite and nearby trees. Large craters and burn trails scarred the landscape as the meteorites "whooshed" into the ground. The Jeep was struck and turned into burnt toast.

Boom! . . . Boom! . . . Whoosh! . . . Boom!

Finally, after dodging and darting, and Triglav swatting away ashes and nearly molten debris, a cave was seen in the distance.

Whoosh! . . . Boom!

Triglav and Sylvia disappeared into the cave. Sylvia, in near shock, pressed against his back, facing the remnants and destructive aftermath of the meteorite shower which sprayed into the cave. Triglav bent on one knee and loosened his grip so Sylvia could slide to the ground. They seated on opposing rock outcrops. The cave ceiling was high and dark. The walls were ribbed by unusual rocky outgrowths. Sylvia wondered.

SYLVIA (thought): What was that all about?

As if he could read her mind, Triglav answered. Sylvia wears a surprised look.

TRIGLAV: Could be they were after me, or after you.

Another meteorite strike near the cave entrance sent orange-hot stone chips streaking into the cave which bounced off the walls in every direction. Sylvia gasped as the flame from the embers sucked air out of the cave.

Boom! Hiss!

SYLVIA: Ack!

Triglav grabbed her and cloaked her to prevent rock chips, dust, heat waves from consuming her. His skin visibly vibrated and bubbled in parts due to the heat waves. He breathed into the top of the cloak to give her air, since it had been sucked out of the cave by the heat of the meteorite blast.

TRIGLAV: Huff, huff!

When things calmed down, Sylvia verbalized the experience, eyes-half opened as if in a drunken daze. Triglav nearly laughed.

SYLVIA: That was some kiss.

TRIGLAV: A kiss of life. I hope you don't think me too forward.

Sylvia winced. Triglav smirked.

SYLVIA: A bit stinky though.

TRIGLAV: You like my stink?

Sylvia blushed.

SYLVIA: Yes. I like your stink.

Sylvia became more curious by the moment. Triglav stared at the cave floor.

SYLVIA: How did you know about this place?

TRIGLAV: Look down there.

He pointed to the cave floor. It showed his footprints embedded all over the floor, looked like a dance studio floor. Sylvia looked down and noticed the footprints, amazed.

SYLVIA: Looks like you were practicing The Watusi.

TRIGLAV: I have been coming here for a long time. Is the Watusi good meat?

Sylvia laughed, but she wasn't sure if Triglav was kidding or not. He resumed his serious, almost monotone voice pattern.

TRIGLAV: Since you are a scientist, uh, anthropologist, uh, archaeologist, sorry, hope I got that right, I anticipate you will find interesting what I am about to tell you.

SYLVIA: I suspect I will have to suspend the temptation towards disbelief.

Triglav began the history.

TRIGLAV: Our ship haphazardly landed, millions of earth years ago near what modern humans call the Yucatan Peninsula.

SYLVIA (thinking): This guy is a crazy old Slavic hermit, tortured by dementia.

Sylvia tried to change the subject.

SYLVIA: You really think these meteorites were sent by some higher intelligence?

TRIGLAV: Unfortunately, the planet did not take well to our landing. Most of the terrestrial life was extinguished.

A rustling stirred outside the cave entrance. Triglav hunched over and whispered, then raised a long, pointy-nailed finger placed perpendicular to his wide, puffy lips. Unusual sounds filtered into the cave entrance.

Swiiishh, Proooshh.

TRIGLAV: Shh. Spies, trying to find out if they hit their target . . . me.

Sylvia looked at the cave entrance where a dim light shined through but didn't reach the rocks they were seated upon.

SYLVIA (thought): Geesh. He seems to think it is always about him.

TRIGLAV: They already know about you, it seems. They are probably wondering why a human has ventured to this place and has associated with me.

Triglav stroked his chin again and wondered if he should tell her this part of history. Sylvia, still looking for signs of entry by the spies, noticed a shadow of them streak a side of the cave wall. The shadows showed a thick girth and long, multiple tentacles.

TRIGLAV: I am not as I seem. In my ancient world, far beyond this solar system, this galaxy, many galaxies farther, we are all balls or blobs of energy, which would appear to you as blindingly bright light.

SYLVIA: But I can see you and no light, now. How is that possible?

TRIGLAV: Don't be afraid . . . I will show you.

Triglav morphed into a ball of energy by sucking in the parts of a humanoid (limbs and trunk) and goat-man-crow (faces, horns). The forms were enveloped into a ball of light, then the single light form transformed back into Triglav.

Sylvia considered his claim of blinding light a bit exaggerated as it didn't blind her. Triglav wondered why his natural form light didn't seem to affect Sylvia's vision. He thought she must be a demon, or at least possessed by one?

TRIGLAV: Eventually we had to mutate into an extant species appearance. Otherwise we could not interact with the objects and things in this world.

Triglav sounded like a historian. Sylvia, now interested, analyzed.

TRIGLAV: I suppose that was part of our punishment. Banishment, and cursed to inhabit a mortal body or bodies, mammals primarily served our purpose to survive.

SYLVIA: Our gift is a mortal body. Although some believe that we can still exist for some time as spirits.

TRIGLAV: When new living species began to re-inhabit this planet, we had to interact with them at some point; thus, the transformation. Your Sun would have destroyed me long ago if I had remained in my true physical form. Otherwise, we were merely light to their vision, a light that over time became as a destructive energy to their gaze; hypnotic, hallucinatory. Human writers have authored stories of fantasy and horror about the condition. Psychologists, sociologists have written treatises trying to explain the destructive process at work in the human mind. Basically, the existence of my being, and those who were sent along with me to this planet inadvertently became a destructive force to humanity.

SYLVIA: What do you mean by "punishment".

TRIGLAV: My world was very structured, down to the last syllable of communication. Too much unauthorized communication, interaction resulted in banishment, for myself, my mate, and a few others. We were loaded into a "spacecraft", an energy field, then ejected out of the galaxy, landed here, during the age of earth dinosaurs. Our crash into the earth world wiped out over ninety percent of the living creatures.

SYLVIA: We? Are you alone, now?

TRIGLAV: Now, yes, but your time calculation of centuries is comparable to seconds of time for my kind. Even here, where I settled, I became banished by one of your Popes, many centuries ago.

SYLVIA: Then for you this place is what we would call Hell, in a way. Was there a time when you were not alone?

"A Whiter Shade of Pale", by Procul Harum, played in her head.

TRIGLAV (sad faced): I had a mate. Her name was (he doesn't say). She died in the last cosmic battle for humanity, almost 100,000 years ago now.

Triglav stared at the floor of the cave and recalled the images of his mate's demise.

TRIGLAV: The battle was won, by the humans and humanoids, at great cost of course. Dead and dying earth beings and what you might call demon spawn littered the plains of what would one day become Poland. The last great, warlord demon, Romanus, also one of the punished from my world, was about to be sealed with his cohorts into a prison Realm, which I helped construct, when he saw her . . . my friend, my love. He struck her dead. Before she died . . .

A tear that glistened like a nighttime star slowly rolled down his rough-edged cheek.

TRIGLAV: Standing tall amid the dead, she transformed herself into a beautiful Willow, so that the dead could be commemorated, and the dying could have one last glimpse of beauty before facing their Judgment.

Sylvia had difficulty connecting the dots on everything Triglav related to her. A war 100,000 years ago? What kind of technology existed then enabled construction of a prison able to seal a demon for so long? She was not aware of any archaeological records of any tribes, clans, or human civilizations able to physically combat a demon army. There was no such record of these events in the known earth history. The closest human literature to what Triglav described sounded like the events iterated in the Hindu sixth book of the Mahabharata known as Bhagavad Gita.

Triglav looked up at the cave ceiling. He described for Sylvia some more of his story. Romanus hurled a huge bluish-white fireball on a beeline towards the beautiful Willow. Dead and dying humanoids lay all

around on a large flat plain. In the distance was a
mountain range. Humans now call this range The Holy
Cross Mountains.

TRIGLAV: I've learned the rules of this world over
the eons. When we transform into an element or object
of the world we inhabit, we are subject to the rules
of that world unless we can change back to our natural
form before mortal death takes hold.

SYLVIA: What happened to the Willow tree?

TRIGLAV: Here is the rest of the story.

Triglav told Sylvia about the scene on the plain after
the great battle. He was buried in a near mountain
of human and humanoid bodies. He crawled towards the
Willow tree. Fireballs, like the ones that just fell
upon him and Sylvia, tried to find him, but missed
and struck near the Willow. He could hear a scream.
There were many screams coming from the many bodies
around him who lay dead or dying from the battle. He
was able to get close to the tree and cover it with
his body to douse the fire.

Triglav's face revealed tears that drew from his eyes
like a rain shower. The plain of the dead and the
Willow tree became muddy, soaked by his grief. He
told Sylvia he had the power to control thunder and
lightning if in the right mood, an angry mood, a
frightened frame of mind. He looked skyward and
commanded with his intense eyes a thunderous boom.

BOOM!

He drew back his right hand behind his dual-horned
head and grabbed a huge lightning bolt as it emanated
skyward from the ground behind him. He heaved it with
all his might at Romanus, shouting the Scarlet
Beast's name. Romanus saw the bolt coming. He dove
into the large, cave-like hole in the side of the
mountain, not before he beamed a look of panicked

glee. He fell into the prison Realm of a parallel dimension, free from the vengeful retribution of humans and humanoids.

TRIGLAV: Romanus! His name became a curse word to me.

Triglav's shout echoed in the cave where he and Sylvia were hiding. He continued the story. His consciousness seemed to revert in time as he told the story. The hurled lightning bolt had shattered against a windowpane like door, melding it shut.

PFHISSSHHHUUMMPP!

TRIGLAV: Later characterized in the literature, as the Seventh Seal of Revelations, it is not unlike any other construction form. It requires maintenance. It was forged by me and my friend, the Willow. We had previously traveled to the other places of the world where some of our prisoner companions also waged mayhem and war for their own pleasure. There are six other Seals, all constructed for the same purpose: to imprison those of my kind, "species" in your tongue, who would destroy this earth world for their own foolish desires or authoritarian machinations.

He was concerned he had said too much, but he realized this human, Sylvia the scientist, was in this part of the country for a specific reason, even if he didn't yet quite understand the certain nature of it.

TRIGLAV: The Willow is still standing to this day.

Triglav looked over at Sylvia as her stunned facial expression started to show extreme sadness, if not concern.

SYLVIA: I'm so sorry.

Triglav's massive hands covered his face and head. His elbows bored into his thighs at the knee area. His back hunched solid. A crow outside the cave called out.

Caw! Caw!

TRIGLAV: It is safe now.

Sylvia was dying to ask more questions. She waited for a sign from him that he was ready to address them.

TRIGLAV: Sorry. I have said too much.

Sylvia attempted to add some levity to the troubling moment.

SYLVIA: Not at all. I don't often have my scientific specimens engaged in conversation.

TRIGLAV: I can see you have questions. I'm not impaled on your butterfly board yet, so let me have it.

SYLVIA: You mentioned a prison Realm.

TRIGLAV: Yes. Your Earth has been our prison Realm for eons. The banishment capsule primarily encased us in a state of suspended animation, not unlike some of your earth creatures when the weather becomes unpalatable, except our status existed for a much longer earth time. Eight of us were banished here to serve our sentences. My mate snuck aboard to join me.

SYLVIA: What were your crimes?

Triglav removed his hands from his face.

TRIGLAV: My crime was challenging rule by the Elites. Their rule benefitted only them and those they chose worthy of their generosity. All others suffered at their expense.

SYLVIA: And the crimes of the others?

TRIGLAV: Refusing to suffer at the expense of the

Elites. They sought to overthrow the Elites, not out of some benevolent motive, but purely for their own self-interest.

Sylvia wondered. She asked again about his time in this world.

SYLVIA: How long have you been on Earth?

TRIGLAV: Since the time of what you call the dinosaurs. Our landing destroyed them all, which opened the door to further development of mammals, of which your species is one. Over the course of millions of years, our craft's cryogenic mechanism deteriorated, which allowed us to seep out, emerge into your world, then search for a means to survive. The vessel maintenance system stopped working, apparently not long after entry into your planet's lower atmosphere, but the records of entry were intact which allowed us to tap into the data to learn about this world in order to better navigate for shelter, food and avoid hazards to our biological anatomy.

Sylvia's mind now swirled in the wonder of gaining so much knowledge of Earth first-hand. She was almost as much convinced of his veracity as he seemed to be. Still, the thought, "musings of a madman" tempted her doubt pangs.

SYLVIA (thought): God! I'm dying to ask him so much, but better stick to the present for now.

SYLVIA: Do many of you have horns, goat faces and human torso?

Triglav scratched his head at Sylvia's question.

TRIGLAV (thought): That wasn't the question I expected. What a cunning human.

He searched his memory and verbally related to her a

perspective of the earth he first experienced. He described what she interpreted to be a prehistoric world, barren earth, seas bubbling of marine life.

TRIGLAV: When we first arrived on this rock, we needed to find a way to interact in the environment. For thousands of years, there were no suitable species.

Sylvia stroked her chin.

TRIGLAV: We possessed some of the ocean creatures, but we didn't find a need to remain in the water when land creatures started arriving. We began to possess them. Goats worked well for my ephemeral needs.

SYLVIA: And humans?

TRIGLAV: There were no humans in existence yet according to our biologic history data. My first attempt once I found one did not go so well, unless I mixed as a hybrid with another species. The human DNA is difficult to possess for any length of time in our chemical structure. The human cell structure learned to resist the intrusion.

Triglav's feet started to wiggle a bit, to Sylvia's fascination.

TRIGLAV: My appearance is the product of a goat, and a large crow-like bird that happened upon the scene, and the strongest male of a tribe of humanoids nearby.

SYLVIA: That explains the feet.

Triglav gloated.

TRIGLAV: Humans thought I was a God, or Demon, depending on the culture.

SYLVIA: You're not?

TRIGLAV: Well . . . not really.

SYLVIA: Then what are you?

TRIGLAV: Just another life form, not indigenous to this planet.

SYLVIA: I suppose one tribe's Demon could be another tribe's God.

TRIGLAV: We have been portrayed one way or the other in every culture around your globe.

SYLVIA: Some humans here, on Earth, are not so sure there is a God.

Sylvia tried to connect the dots.

TRIGLAV: You mean the scientists? They can't explain it, so they don't believe it.

SYLVIA: Well, something like that.

TRIGLAV: The scientists believe there is a Universe. Yet they cannot see all of it. Why do they limit their thinking? Thank goodness for Copernicus.

SYLVIA: A roommate of mine in college was from Africa. She told me about the African Spirit myths. I have not experienced the presence of Spirits, but I believe the theory is plausible.

TRIGLAV: So, you believe in things you cannot see or experience.

SYLVIA: I am just trying to make sense of things.

TRIGLAV: Know this. Women are strongest.

Triglav smiled.

TRIGLAV: It is a characteristic of humanity I have "discovered".

SYLVIA: Truth is stronger.

TRIGLAV: Except what is truth has been as malleable as the heated metal the blacksmith's hammer is applied to, depending on the discipline in which the hammer is wielded. Even atheists wield a mentality hammer. Too many "truths" have been held onto until the rope tied to them has broken.

Sylvia was skeptical.

TRIGLAV: It is time for you to continue your journey. Perhaps I can be your guide. You see, Sylvia, humans cannot come close to understanding their mortal world unless they take a drink from Religious theory. It is the science of the spirit world, much like quantum theory in the discipline of quantum mechanics, or physical cosmology as a branch of astrophysics.

SYLVIA: I am not so sure about that. You posit a heretical concept in the science world.

TRIGLAV: Hey, I was there. Modern humans carved and built temples from limestone. Religion is the reason the modern world exists.

SYLVIA: Hardly. Farmers, many of them women, started the first societies. The idea for Religion developed as an offshoot, to organize the increased numbers of population which resulted from the more readily available food sources.

TRIGLAV: No. It was the concept of Religion, as an organizing principle, which caused the people to come together. I was there. The need for farming started as a way of supporting the larger groups drawn to the Temple tribes. Your Science ignores this truth.

SYLVIA: Isn't it possible the need for food and the advantage of enhanced survival ability in a large group created the concept of Religion. The leaders of the groups needed a means to cement their bond to the group. Each needed the other. Religion was the glue. But as history of every Religion shows, Religion can be as lethal as the sword when used improperly. I was raised Roman Catholic. Science and Religion are not mutually exclusive. We know we can't prove the existence of God. God is beyond all that we can know about existence. Our Religions agree on that point.

TRIGLAV: At least you have given yourself a chance to understand. I've seen many "gods". I was considered one by those who needed my help. I gladly helped, but silently declined the "god" principle. Then I was cast aside by those who wielded a knowledge of a god they deemed supreme.

Sylvia, perplexed.

TRIGLAV: There are fights for the human soul happening daily, happened daily, since the beginning of the human form, whether humanity recognizes it or not, even amongst the religious leaders.

SYLVIA: Why is humanity so important to the universe?

TRIGLAV: I am hesitant to tell you.

Triglav measures his response.

TRIGLAV: In this great, wide chasm of energy, dust, and nothingness in between, the soul is the one thread that gives the rest of us the greatest hope. It is the tie that binds all of us. It is the tether to the unknowable. It is a meaning cloaked in mystery, yet deeply sought after, from the beginning of life until the end at death.

SYLVIA: That is a real revelation.

TRIGLAV: That it is . . . a Revelation . . . one that many envious and power-hungry beings would like to bury as the concept itself reduces their power and influence.

Sylvia felt as if she was sitting in an Anthropology class.

TRIGLAV: The human is the least among the sentient beings, in terms of intellect, strength, ingenuity. Yet the soul is the ticket to the highest level of Universal solitude, if the soul is properly prepared. Perhaps my friend Buddha had it right. Seek what is in oneself to achieve the highest plain of existence.

TRIGLAV: The Hindu's subjugated whole groups of people under a caste system.

TRIGLAV: The Muslims subjugated half the known earth by treating women as lesser beings.

TRIGLAV: The Roman Catholic elders considered their women as incapable of leadership.

TRIGLAV: The Jews considered themselves the only righteous people.

SYLVIA: What about Mother Theresa? She went to the Hindu world, to work among the least of those, wholly content in her spirit.

TRIGLAV: We need more Mother Theresa's in spirit.

SYLVIA (cynically): Or we need more responsible human beings.

TRIGLAV: There are many of those unheard, unseen, or this world would have fallen already, like so many others.

SYLVIA: My world of late seems to punish the most successful and charitable and deify the destroyers and takers.

Sylvia started to walk away, towards the mouth of the cave (invaded by daylight).

SYLVIA: Well, I need to get back to Rome. Report my findings.

TRIGLAV: I can help with that. The road is long, and dangerous. First, we must visit The Murk.

The two stepped outside the cave entrance now. Devastation of the ground and trees rested everywhere.

SYLVIA: We? Why? Where is that?

TRIGLAV: I would like to warn my friends there. It is on the way to Rome.

SYLVIA: I really need to get back now.

TRIGLAV: It is extremely dangerous for us to travel in these parts. Remember, we had to hide in a cave not long ago.

A reluctant look overtook her face.

SYLVIA: And The Murk?

TRIGLAV: It is also a place to find some warriors who may help us, and the only place on earth where life and death exist on the same plain.

SYLVIA (thinking, "you've got to be kidding", but verbalizes it as): I have a feeling I am once again about to make a seminal discovery.

TRIGLAV: Which must be kept a secret. I hope fame and fortune were not in your sack of life goals.

They began to walk. Triglav walked behind her. He felt good to have a purpose again.

SYLVIA (thought): Nightmare-less sleep will do.

As it was now near dusk, a gray, crystal clear, star-dotted sky looked down upon them, as if the whole universe wanted to be a spectator.

"Summer Presto", Vivaldi, played in Sylvia's pocket. The sound helped to energize her spirit. She reached into her right hip pocket, unsnapped it and slid out her phone.

SYLVIA: Yello.

MALE VOICE: You are not going to believe this. I mean, what I have discovered.

Sylvia cradled the phone to her right ear. Triglav's massive, cloaked back loomed in the background.

SYLVIA: I have something big, too. I suppose this discovery of yours is the reason you didn't make it to the dig site yesterday.

Sylvia's phone-covered ear twitched for a decent comeback response as she wished she had remembered to bring a Bluetooth.

MALE VOICE: Never mind that now. This is the most incredible discovery in the history of paleontology. I am sending my live, phone camera feed.

SYLVIA (thought of "I doubt that" as she looked back at Triglav and smiled): Okay, I'll call you back after I view it.

She focused on her phone screen, cradled it in her right hand. The screen showed a riverbank at the edge, the phone camera lens seemingly pointed down at the edge, and a reddish, gunky liquid substance slowly flowed by the camera eye. A local deer is seen standing at the edge, head bowed to take a drink of the water, but sniffing it first. Then, two long, scaly arms, smeared by the gunky and red liquid, reached out from the river towards the stooping deer. The arms, dripping of red slime, enveloped and pulled the thrashing deer in, until the deer disappeared in the liquid.

SYLVIA: What the . . . ?

Sylvia heard the ground brush rustling which came from her phone video. She squinted harder to try to see what happened.

"Lose Yourself", Eminem, played in her head.

Triglav now towered above her, looked down over her shoulder, a worried look on his face. The male voice, in a whisper, exclaimed as his phone camera angle spun around.

MALE VOICE: Oh crap!

Sylvia could see the camera frame on the male voice's end falling sideways to the ground. She could hear his footsteps (rustling and shuffling sound) rapidly getting farther away.

SHRASH, SHRash, SHrash, Shrash, shrash.

The male's phone camera now pointed sideways at an area of low brush near the edge of a forest rim, to the side of the river bend. Two thick, hairy legs which were only caught in the camera from just above the knees downward started to creep from the brush. Sylvia shouted but the male voice couldn't hear her while she viewed her phone video.

SYLVIA: A wolf! Get out of there!

Triglav still looked over Sylvia's shoulder.

TRIGLAV: Well, I guess the story is telling itself. The Rivers of red sludge mean the Seals are breaking.

The Demons imprisoned there, in what you call the spirit world, are trying to break through.

Sylvia showed an astounded look on her face, while Triglav still looked over her shoulder. Sylvia still looked down at the live video feed on her phone screen for something, anything to help her reach a conclusion about the episode transpired in the video.

SYLVIA: What? Wait, there is more.

Sylvia and Triglav observed two hairy wolf-like legs stalk towards the camera lens, then accidentally kick it, spin the lens back towards the red sludge riverbank.

TRIGLAV: A Neuri . . . part human, part wolf.

SYLVIA: That would explain why we are seeing only two legs. Wait, what am I saying, a MANWOLF!?

Triglav tried to making light of the goings on.

TRIGLAV: Congratulations on your third seminal discovery in two days. There is truly little time.

Sylvia spied a blurry view on the sideways camera frame again.

SYLVIA: There's more.

The video stopped and went dark. In the distance, above the tree line, Triglav spotted something and pointed Sylvia to look at it. They could see what appeared to be a large, winged creature, a gargoyle, holding a dangling male human in its claws, flying up into the air and away from them. Sylvia's jaw dropped, and her mouth forned an "O". Triglav's visage revealed that of resignation. Another gargoyle appeared above the tree line, dropped down upon the deep area of the bushes. They heard the loud howls and ferocious struggle of the Neuri, then dead silence.

RRAAHH! EEEGGGAAA! UUUHHH! . . .

Triglav whispered to himself in a low tone.

TRIGLAV: Revelations begins.

7

The Pope directed his assistant to contact Sylvia using a video feed. She and Triglav had set up camp after a long walk. She rode piggy-back on him for a good bit of it. When her phone rang, she went into her tent for a bit of privacy. Gregorio advised His Eminence wanted an update and passed the phone.

"Well," strummed The Pope's voice. "How are we doing?"

Sylvia looked puzzled, wondering what her real purpose was for such a call.

"You have found it?" He inquired.

"Found what?" Sylvia sheepishly retorted.

"The thing that could not be found, until the right time. The evidence that changes everything."

"The footprint?" She wanted to tell him the old archaeologist white beard at the site thought it was a significant find, a pre-historic dinosaur footprint, the oldest known finding of such a print. But that was all, even if a fib.

"Now, now," The Pope knowingly chided. "You know what I mean."

She did know but could almost not believe it herself. "My theory would be laughed at, you obviously know."

"Humor an old man," The Pope indulged.

"It, it, I can't believe I am saying this. My theory is it isn't a dinosaur footprint. It . . . it is the print of a humanoid."

"Ahhh." The Pope sounded as if he were thinking deep within his soul, reaching down for a piece of knowledge, like a book hidden in the smallest, darkest room of the biggest, most grandiose Bibliotheque known to mankind.

"I have a request," he said. "You will go to a monastery we have there, in Poland, and do some research for us. The most ancient writings of the Slavic world are housed there. The writings have only been seen by a handful of scholars in the last seven hundred years. The knowledge had long been forgotten, but my advisors think the materials you encounter will explain the footprint."

Sylvia pondered this request. She had wanted rest away from the world for a bit, perhaps this would be a good place to get away, a monastery. It should be quiet, remote, serene; but deep inside, her better instincts warned against an immediate acceptance.

"I have unfinished projects set up from now until, well, for a few years," she somewhat stammered, half-heartedly. The Pope gave her a slow, wry smile. "At my request." Sylvia did not respond, as if she didn't hear. Her mind seemed wandering onto some other issue. Her left hand gently strummed the broach in her pocket. The Pope sensed her nervous apprehension.

"Are you familiar with the Propugnaculum Christianitatis?" The Pope asked.

Sylvia seemed thrown for a loop in her thinking, the musical sound of the words pulled her back to the conversation.

"Yes, my mentor, Brother Henry, told me about it."

The Pope counseled, "Numerous members of your ethnic clans of Sobieski, Goralski and more have come before the holders of my title for centuries. Not a one has refused a request of their Pope, regardless of the sacrifice or the task."

Sylvia understood this counsel, but was not
necessarily swayed, as she was used to going against
the grain of thought or action as it conventionally
stood or was known.

The Pope removed his white, zucchetto cap with his
right hand, then overturned his hand and opened it.
The cap lay upside down, but deep inside, at the base,
was stuck a tiny silver pin, identical in shape,
design and size to Sylvia's broach pin. The Pope
slowly moved his cap filled hand, "Hold on a sec, I
will send you a picture of something I hold in my
hand". Sylvia then heard a "click" sound, then after
thirty seconds or so, she received the image
notification on her phone. She looked at it. She was
stunned. She immediately stopped strumming her
broach. Something was happening here she didn't
understand. She must find the reason. An
understanding of her very existence as a human on
earth was about to unfold for her. "I will go."

The Pope gave her a brief history about her broach
pin. The Pope sent it to Brother Henry, when Sylvia
was a child, for safe keeping until such time as she
would appreciate and understand its meaning. The Pope
indicated the pin was forged from a sliver of King
Solomon's ring, allegedly given to Solomon by Michael
the Archangel, as a weapon for combat against and
capture of demons. There were similar broaches and
pins made, but not distributed for reasons The Pope
didn't go into.

The Pope then added, "I trust you've made a new friend
on your exploration?"

Sylvia still confounded by the conversation,
indicated, "Yes . . . yes."

"Tell the Big Guy I said Hi." The Pope's phone then
went silent and the video feed went blank. As Sylvia
tried to put all the conversation together into a
fathomable mix, she received a text message from The

Pope. It was a smiley face.

"Will wonders never end?" she said to Thoth, a picture
of him now in her head. She forgot to tell The Pope
about the side trip to The Murk, but she suspected
he already was aware of it, and the purpose.

8

Sylvia stood over the grave and cautiously wondered,
"How did it come to this?" She had dozed off in her
tent and the rhapsody of another dream played in her
head, as follows. It was a time when the dead were
safer than the living. The silence of death no longer
rang like a deafening bell which drowned out her
existence. Death seemed solemn, peaceful, resigned
for so long to her. But it was not always like this.

The gravestone, gray and sheened, read "Sobieska" at
a cemetery just outside of the Balmoral City limits.
It was the final resting place of her great, great,
. . . so many greats she no longer remembered
grandmother on her father's side, a descendent of the
legendary King Jan Sobieski, who had helped rescue
17th century Europe and Rome from the Ottoman Empire
hordes.

She feared a different horde was on the brink of
overtaking all that was in the human domain, but
accessible through deceit and cunning by, depending
on the belief system, fallen angels from pre-time, or
beings from another world, or life forms from another
dimension, or perhaps an entity not yet conceived by
earth-bound human minds. Whatever caused the
intrusion upon the human world on earth, she was in
a unique position, as one descended from a demon
possessed father, and born of a human mother who
incubated her as the second Cratch, to make a
difference for the fate of this earth world.

While Sylvia was in Poland, I sent to her a manuscript
I had created to give her some background information
for her new assignment. She would read it when she
arrived at the Holy Cross Monastery, but it turned
out the monastery monk, Hugo Grotius, sent one of the
gargoyles to drop it off in the darkness of evening.
She texted me about it and I apologized for the

spectacle of an air dropped package in the middle of
nowhere. I have captured a summary of it below.

Onionhead Line

When the Huns showed up on the Eastern doorsteps to
Rome, it was almost an accident. They trekked from
somewhere beyond the Steppes of Russia, nomads,
looking for soil to call their own. This journey took
them across the rich Slavic soil of The Polan and
Czech and Uks, but they could not find a soil that
suited them. It was their blood, not pure enough for
the soil. Wherever they set down, a poison enveloped
the growing things in that area. The most dangerous
plant grew a beautiful red and yellow flower, but it
was really an onion-like bulb, which when eaten raw,
as it was many times by a near-starving Hun, put the
victim in a trancelike state, causing the victim to
lose all sense of reality, neglecting hygiene and
health, but increasing the testosterone level
immensely. These beings no longer resembled humans
but looked more like skeletal bats sans wings, ivory-
white in color, developing massive jaws and razor-
sharp teeth because of an ever-present chewing of
bark and tree branches. They ate anything that moved,
including their fellow Huns. Thus, the Huns began to
avoid the Slavic soil as if it were a plague upon
them, not bothering to loot, rape, or many times
breathe the world around them until they could
traverse the plains and forests and end their curse
of the soil. Hence, they crossed the Slavic tribe's
territory speedily, bumping against the Italian soil
of the Roman Empire, a more forgiving environment.

Slavic Line

There is much Slavic blood in the world. In the 14th
and 15th centuries, the Princes of Europe traveled to
Krakow Poland, land of the Polan, to find a bride
amongst the reputedly most beautiful women in the
world. Slavic blood then mixed with the Royal houses
of Europe.

While reading the manuscript Sylvia had dozed off for
a little while. When she awoke, she emailed to me
some details of her dream visions, as described
below. Some of her later emails tested my view whether
she was gifted of exceptional foresight.

At the edge of a forest, looking out into a plain, a
computer tablet is laying on top of a flat rock,
opened, the user is distracted, suddenly through the
tablet screen, a tableau of beings and creatures is
seen crossing the plain.

During her visions her mind allowed her to project
scenes into her head as she read the words. She heard
music, Prokofiev's "Romeo and Juliet-Suite No. 2 Op.
64", Dvorak's "Slavonic Dance No. 4", then "Waltz
Masquerade" by Khachaturian. (Perhaps her radio was
still turned on while she was reading?)

The vision continued. Spirits of Auschwitz danced
with demons in a red slime river, a dance to the
DEATH! At the end of the music, the Demon Lord who
hosted the event didn't realize a good portion of the
Demon army leaders had been vanquished in the Waltz.
That's what an offering of vodka, from guest Sylvia,
accomplished.

Sylvia's vision then transformed, through a clouded
veil, she saw another Demon Lord. He apparently could
see through the eyes of other demons who helped pursue
this Lord's needs and demands. A Gargoyle was one of
the demons affected by this Lord. Sylvia heard the
Demon Lord boast he knew exactly what was about to
happen, and "they" should give up. She didn't know
who "they" referred to. The scene changed again. On
the eve of a great battle, all seemed lost, her
stomach ached. Someone in her battle group revealed
one of the secrets in the Slavic Book of Curses that
he who controls a Gargoyle can also see through his
or her mind. The aforementioned Demon Lord had been

fed false information by the Gargoyle about her group's battle plans. Near her end to the dream visions, she encountered Vampires, Werewolves, Katyn Forest Polish officers, Winged Hussars, gypsies, Russian warriors, unidentified beautiful women spirits, and the musical sounds of Vivaldi performed by the spirits of deceased Nuns. A brief snapshot glimpse of a portrait of the Black Madonna floated into her vision.

The battle lines were drawn as such: on the Demon Lord's side are all the souls and demons condemned to hell (or a dimension comparable to the human description), now promised a chance for paradise (control of the earth world?). The remaining red slime surrounded the battlefield. On humanity's side are a varied mix of Polish and Russian Vampires, Neuri werewolves, some Gargoyles, Revenants, deceased Polish Officers and Hussars, deceased Russian Officers and Soldiers, living gypsies, townspeople from the nearby villages that ringed the area at a distance, remaining lost souls of Auschwitz, and the Vivaldi music weapons of the spirits of Nuns.

Upon receiving these email messages from Sylvia, I forwarded the information to the Holy See, thinking perhaps some sense could be made of it. I awaited a response.

9

The manuscript also contained a summary (below) of
Triglav's entry into the human world. I assumed by
now Sylvia had met him, tried to shake off her
skepticism, and proceeded forward on the needed work
ahead.

A cylindrical spacecraft shot through the Universe,
unleashed by a distant alien civilization. A prisoner
transport it was. It randomly sought a rock to dump
prisoners aboard. These prisoners were memorialized
on the tapestry (mentioned earlier) in the Vatican.
The spacecraft entered the Milky Way Galaxy, then the
solar system of the human designated Star known as
the Sun. As the craft passed the planets of this solar
system, it neared the rock called Earth. On the way,
it clipped the moon, breaking off a piece of landing
gear, which randomly altered it onto a course that
crashed it into the Yucatan Peninsula off the coast
of what is now called Mexico, but not before it
ejected some of the spacecraft contents of glass like
spheres which housed the prisoner beings. The spheres
scattered across the earth.

Bahamut's sphere crashed into what is now The Middle
East. Asura crashed into the Indus Valley area now
called India. Triglav and his mate, Helene, crashed
into the area now referred to as The Balkans. The
Scarlet Beast, known as Romanus, landed in the area
now deemed Mediterranean Sea. There were other beings
as noted on the Vatican tapestry previously.

Sylvia was asleep in the tattered remains of her tent
just off the path Triglav had forged for them. The
clearing gave way to a semi-circle of tall oak trees.
Curled up in her sleeping bag, she drifted into the
next dream.

In her dream, Sylvia had just about reached the age

of puberty. She wore a frilly, white dress in celebration of her Confirmation as a Roman Catholic. Her shoes beamed a shiny black, but bore some scuffs resulting from the walk back to Brother Henry's Study from the Church.

The Hells Point area of Balmoral, seen from an aerial view, was crisscrossed by asphalt streets. Chalk white sidewalks lined each side of the street. Abutting these sidewalks were rowhouses (townhouses) which sported flat, gravel-topped roofs, and steel chimney heated exhaust pipes, and ceramic exhaust pipes for the bathrooms. Some were still decorated by utilized TV antennas. High wooden telephone poles sprouted at every two hundred feet or so in the narrow cement alleys which separated the houses in the backyard areas. From each pole top, connected black wires carried electrical current. Cars were jammed together on both sides of the asphalt streets. The houses, red brick, were grouped six together in a row. A shoulder width wide alley also separated the houses in every group. The alley extended from the street to the cement back alleys.

An end house, slightly wider than the others, benignly rested at the corner of two intersecting streets. It was the home of Brother Henry, Sylvia's mentor. He schooled her in the ways of the Church, daily life, and helped her navigate the idea that she was a rare human being. Sylvia's profile could be seen in the side window, from the intersecting street, at ground level, looking down, because the Study of Brother Henry was in that portion of the basement.

Sylvia sat on a long, black couch in her white dress and polished shoes. She heard footsteps coming down the staircase which lead from the kitchen to the basement. She demonstrated a somewhat brooding mood, arms crossed.

Brother Henry and a younger looking Nana entered.

Brother Henry spoke as Nana smiled. Brother Henry was dressed in his typical all black suit, open collared, button down black shirt. His jet-black hair was combed the 1950's way (a wave of hair crossed the top of his head). Nana's left arm was bent at the elbow and her hand pointed to the ceiling, as her pocketbook dangled heavily at the crease of her arm. She wore a bright flowery patterned dress.

BROTHER HENRY: Congratulations Sylvia.

Nana looked intently at a long wall, lined by bookshelves. All manner of books cluttered the shelves from floor to ceiling.

NANA: My goodness! So, this is what you two have been up to these last few years; book learning upon book learning.

Brother Henry privately trained Sylvia in the ways of Archaeology, Anthropology, and the World's Religions in this Study. Nana was busy still looking over the room. Brother Henry had his hands folded together at his chest. Hope beamed from his face. Sylvia's right arm at the elbow was embedded into the large couch arm. The right side of her face she pushed almost flat into the palm of her right hand. A half scowl overtook her facial expression. Something bothered her. She looked around the room for Thoth, but he had yet to make an appearance.

SYLVIA: Brother Henry says I am going to be a fine Anthropologist someday.

BROTHER HENRY: Sylvia has already read most of these books about Archaeology, Anthropology and the World's Religions.

Sylvia pointed to a dark far corner of the room, where gray, plastic milk crates were stacked on end against the wall in a few rows. Comic books were squeezed into them.

SYLVIA: Much more interesting than those comic books.

Brother Henry wasn't sure what bothered her. He tried to make light of it.

BROTHER HENRY: That's the lighter side of the Sylvia I know.

Nana walked over to the comic books' makeshift shelf, picked up some of them, began reading some titles. Many of them were titled "The Adventures of...", and "The Incredible Feats of...", and "Amazing Stories of...".

NANA: Well, this would explain the muddy shoes and clothes I have been scrubbing all these years.

Brother Henry opened a black door at the far end of the room. He and Nana entered an Anteroom. It was a room Sylvia never realized existed. She had seen the door many times, but thought it led to a closet. Before the door closed, Sylvia noticed even more books in the Anteroom, and many metal filing cabinets. It smelled musty, old.

BROTHER HENRY: Sylvia, please wait here.

Only the black door could be seen from Sylvia's view. She was surprised to hear a lock engaging after the door closed.

Clunk. Click.

Sylvia, still seated, somewhat curious, would have gone to the door to listen, except something inside her, inside her head, her bosom, her torso, started beating rapidly. She at times had to fight back tears. Her hands clenched into fists which now grinded into her thighs. She could not stand the unknown mystery of the room interior. She then tried to relax and took a deep breath. The deep breath allowed the whispers from the room to increase in volume. She took another deep breath, and the room conversation volume increased in her ears. Somehow, she had enhanced her hearing ability. Brother Henry told Nana how he found Sylvia's father. Brother Henry was now worried about the Onionhead curse asserting itself upon Sylvia as she neared biological womanhood. He encouraged Sylvia to become interested in science, the greater world around her, so she was not so lost when she learned she had to deal with something no other child her age must confront.

Sylvia was angered by the secret conversation. She knew the many mysteries of childhood remained to be suffered, by age degrees, but still she was hungry to become an adult and get on with her life. The frustration of not yet knowing enough about her field of study, and life in general, pained her greatly. She snuck out of the study to go for a long walk as a means of placating the simmering rage inside her gut.

The seeds of the Onionhead were passed on to her at birth, unlike the condition suffered by her familial predecessors, because of the enzymes inherited from her biological father. Sylvia had been wondering if the biology of her mother could also have been an issue, as Sylvia had been secretly reading, at the Balmoral Main library, about a medical condition recently discovered at a local hospital. The condition affected small numbers of the populace. She had suspected someone on her mother's side of the family was a carrier of the condition, a sort of virus, passed along, perhaps from the place of her ancestors' homeland, Ethiopia. The virus could kill those infected, but in a small group of the afflicted, the virus attacked foreign infections and killed them off before they multiplied into a fatal condition.

During the walk, Sylvia became lost in thought, and lost in physical direction. She concentrated to escape the cloud of cogitation that had afflicted her

and found herself on a sidewalk near a wooded area.
It was at this time the Onionhead curse was born in
her, for the first time. She heard footsteps along
the sidewalk, behind her. She was distant from the
last group of rowhouses. She turned around, but
nothing was there. She walked back along the sidewalk
and started to notice red splotches, quarter-sized,
on the concrete. Then she felt herself below and
realized her loins were moist. A reddish mucous had
oozed into her underpants. Nana had told her about
this moment a few months before, the first menstrual
period.

Two arms grabbed her from behind, lifted her up, and
pulled her into the alley a few feet away near the
last rowhouse. She tried to scream, but something
stopped her, inside her body. She was pushed down
upon bags of garbage that residents had set out for
the trash pickup the next morning. She flung her arms
back to break the fall. Once stabilized amidst the
mess, a large man bent down and pressed against her
body. Sylvia could see up to the roof's edge of the
house and noticed crows perched there. A trail of
roaches appeared next to her head on the right, at
the center of the alley. Rats emerged from the pile
of garbage bags stacked further into the alley
depths. A loud animal screech, from a cat, echoed in
the alley, off the walls, filtered into the tree line.
Thoth leapt and attached himself to the face of the
male molester. Sylvia suddenly felt a flood of energy
erupt inside her, into every limb.

Her body began the first transformation from mostly
human, to the humanoid form of a Cratch, like her
father before her. The attacker lifted himself up
while trying to extract Thoth's grip from the sides
of his large head. Sylvia noticed blood start to
trickle, in fine lines, along the jowls of the large
man. She no longer considered him a man. She
considered him a predator. She realized she was the
prey. She felt her face transform to a near skeletal
state. The large man grabbed Thoth and pulled him off

along with threads of skin from the man's face. Thoth
went rolling down the alley several feet. The large
man's panic excited in Sylvia the enzymes inside her
anatomy. Her mind unconsciously summoned Onionhead at
the sight of Thoth's treatment by the man. The man
then became angry. He went down upon Sylvia even
harder this time. "I will have you red eyes."

Sylvia saw herself in the man's eyes, he was so close.
Her eyes glowed like red traffic stop lights. Her
face bubbled subtly. She could smell the alcohol on
the large man, from his mouth, on his clothes. More
energy changed her body as the enzymes crafted her
further transformation. Just as her body rumbled and
writhed as the enzymes found their rightful place
among human chemistry and amidst the Onionhead demon
presence, her teeth became pointy and greenish. Her
fingernails and toenails extended into razor sharp
points. Her hair matted, then grew distended like
messy corn rows, colors of black and blonde
intertwined. She roiled a sound from deep inside
almost as powerful as the fabled banshee of folklore.
The large man began to realize he was no longer the
predator, but it was too late for him, for his soul.
He was mutilated beyond recognition by swift, fast
attacks from the teeth and hands of Sylvia Magnon,
the second Cratch. Sylvia crawled away to let the
transformation lapse into a steady state, then
guiltily joined the feast of the man's corpse. The
crows, rats, and roaches assisted, to finish off the
meal.

No one was the wiser. Not even Brother Henry.

10

Triglav poked his head into Sylvia's tent.

TRIGLAV: That must have been some dream.

SYLVIA: So how do we find The Murk?

TRIGLAV: Funny thing, that. I don't remember.

SYLVIA: The Earth's fate hangs in the balance and you lost your memory?

TRIGLAV: But I do know who can help us.

Sylvia was skeptical.

TRIGLAV: Baba Yaga. She can give us the Key.

Baba Yaga, an old crone gifted of magic, sooth-saying sensibilities, ability to cross over, mentally, into the undead and other spirit worlds, lived in a house stilted on chicken legs. She cannibalized humans not for meat mastication, but for her work, as any knowledge she could dredge from the other worlds required payment, not usually in the common currency of the time. Once they arrived at Baba Yaga's house, they were close enough to see it, but it stood up and ran away on chicken legs. They came to realize the means to enter it was to ignore it, then curiosity would entrance the house to come over to them. Once the house was calm, it could be accessed by those of the outside world. The house settled, they entered, but Baba Yaga wasn't happy, or perhaps she displayed her happy mood and they didn't realize it as they were unable to parse her countenance and demeanor in comparison to any previous actions, since Triglav had never met this Baba Yaga, only an ancient one, and Sylvia was experiencing her first ever encounter. They started to exit the door, but Baba Yaga objected.

BABA YAGA: Wait! Don't you want a reading?

SYLVIA: What?

Triglav, nodded knowingly to Sylvia.

TRIGLAV: Yes, yes, she wants a reading . . . to reveal
the location of our intended destination.

Baba Yaga then invited them to sit at the round table
in the center of the room. An old hound dog lay curled
in the corner of the room, under a long wooden table
adorned by many small and odd shaped bottles of
multiple colors. The dog glanced an eye at them. Then
closed it. All now seated at the table, the event
began to unfold.

BABA YAGA: You have dreams, no?

SYLVIA: Yes, yes. I have been tortured by nightmares
for as long as I can remember.

BABA YAGA: Yes, and that is a long time. Longer than
you know.

BABA YAGA: You have two choices, or Tarot?

Triglav seemed excited. Sylvia's eyes rolled upward.

TRIGLAV: Oh, oh . . . pick Tarot . . . I love the
pictures on those cards.

Sylvia looked at Baba Yaga's hands. They looked like
they had bloodworms as veins crawling under the skin,
and the fingernails extended as long and coal black
and pointy.

Baba Yaga looked insulted, and Triglav looked
nervous.

BABA YAGA: You no like my hands, child? These hands
have touched many things . . . Princes, their ladies,
wood folk, their insides . . .

Triglav nervously looked around the room, whispered.

TRIGLAV: She means creatures of the forest. And, uh
. . . their entrails.

SYLVIA: Tarot!

Baba Yaga, startled, beamed a nervous look.

SYLVIA: I mean, Tarot.

BABA YAGA: Good choice.

Baba Yaga spread out five decks of Tarot cards.

BABA YAGA: Hmmm. Which decks. Ah. Destiny . . . and
Redemption.

Baba Yaga began with the two decks in front of her.
She began turning over cards.

BABA YAGA: Quest, Anxiety, Pain; a darkness inhabited
by shadows, moving shadows, tiny shadows, a large
shadow.

She used a gypsy deck: three rows of seven cards each,
card one started at the bottom left. She looked at
the deck, closed her eyes, then opened them again,
started to turn them over to reveal their intentions,
then voiced her interpretation.

She revealed the nightmares of near death and aimless
falling. Sylvia had past experienced two dreams like
this description: one where she was about to be raped;
and another where she was falling into a large black
cavern as a sharp pain at the top of her head screamed
at her.

A wicked wind blew open Baba Yaga's front door. The
Tarot cards went flying like tree leaves. Baba Yaga
managed to hold onto the final card she was about to

place down. After the wind stopped, most of the cards
were blown to the floor. Triglav, Sylvia and Baba
Yaga started picking them up, until they latched onto
the same card and pulled. It tore into three pieces.
Baba Yaga was hot, so she reached over and flicked
on an old black table fan. Some of the cards were
sucked up into the back of the fan but only one of
them sucked through and spliced into three pieces.

BABA YAGA: Wait!

Triglav and Sylvia, in tandem looked at her and
shouted.

TRIGLAV/SYLVIA: What!

BABA YAGA: The reading is not over.

She feverishly looked around at the placement of the
cards. Some turned down, some face up, some piled
onto each other, and the pieces of the card that she,
Sylvia and Triglav ripped apart, and the pieces of
the card the fan blades ripped, six pieces in all.

Baba Yaga began carefully walking over to the second
ripped card pieces, bent down, and picked them up,
then spoke in an astonished tone.

BABA YAGA: No. It can't be. I've never seen this
combination before.

SYLVIA: We didn't mean it.

BABA YAGA: You didn't mean it, but someone did.

TRIGLAV: Is it bad?

They all got up off the floor and sat back down. There
were four cards left on the table and a large empty
space left in the middle. Baba Yaga took the six
pieces of cards and lay them out, face up.

BABA YAGA: It is not possible.

SYLVIA: What? What isn't possible?

BABA YAGA: Watch!

The two cards that were ripped apart started to move in different directions, and after moving, seemingly by an unseen hand, came together, into one card.

BABA YAGA: You must cross a great river . . . but not of water . . . which only can be found by those not looking for it.

TRIGLAV: Piece of cake. Let's go.

Baba Yaga was still transfixed by the card.

BABA YAGA: When you cross, everything will change.

SYLVIA: How do we find it?

BABA YAGA: There will be signs. This land you are in has many signs, some placed hundreds, thousands of years ago.

TRIGLAV: Don't worry. I have seen many of the signs.

They must give something up to get the Key, which isn't an object but a concept: get lost to find The Murk.

BABA YAGA: Now payment is due.

Sylvia showed her the Aardvark necklace. Baba Yaga was happy because her dog ate the last one. She can now walk through walls.

BABA YAGA (sniffed the air): Time for you to go. A storm is coming.

Triglav and Sylvia again attempted to leave. Baba

Yaga offered a warning.

BABA YAGA: Unfortunately, truth is seen as a rattlesnake amidst a desert of deceits. I would rather be slain by the cut cf one swift truth than courted by a vase of a dozen lies.

Sylvia looked back at Baba Yaga. Triglav realized this goodbye as helpful advice.

As they left, Baba Yaga walked over to the opened front door to assure they were leaving. Piqued by something on the floor behird the front door, the hound dog ambled over. It was another tarot card flopping like a wounded bird. Baba Yaga looked down at the tattered card and shouted out to them.

BABA YAGA: Four Sticks! Beware the river!

SYLVIA: Another puzzle.

TRIGLAV: This land is full of them.

SYLVIA: But we are running out of time.

TRIGLAV: Don't worry. She can't see the future; only what can be possible.

Baba Yaga looked long at the card.

BABA YAGA: At least they have a chance.

11

The village Murk loomed as the destination. Her anticipation of the experience played in Sylvia's head as "Black Dog," by Led Zeppelin.

The creatures of The Murk woods are described below:

Jaculus--winged serpent, launched itself from trees, usually from behind, bites the neck of the victim.

Barguest--black mastiff-like dogs with fangs, horns and fiery eyes, wrapped in chains, drags chains along.

Rusalki--water nymphs in human woman form posed as innocent, pleasant, obliging maidens when not hiding in streams and lakes. When water bound, they appeared translucent in skin, displayed long fish-like tails, Like Sirens, they called to men or small children when no men were available, to coax them into the water where they were pulled down; power to transform into water creatures and horses.

Triglav and Sylvia were seated on an old, ancient oak log in front of another campfire. Their canopy was skyward, the universe, stars and all of cosmology peeked in at their scene. The only sounds were distant howling werewolves, the crackle of the fire from time to time, and a sudden sound from Triglav.

TRIGLAV (sighed): Where do I begin. The Murk is a funny place. Not "Ha-Ha" funny, but odd, weird, strange to the living. It's a place inhabited by the spirit of many evil earth beings. The wild animals that inhabit the surrounding forests are unusual in that they all thirst for blood. There is no fruitful vegetation, only dying and decay.

Sylvia was somewhat concerned.

SYLVIA: Why must we go there? Doesn't sound very

hospitable or helpful a trip if you ask me.

TRIGLAV (not really answering, just continued the story): Some of your earth history's most vile, evil, insane citizens were interred there as punishment, rejected by the seers of varied dimensions in the afterlife. Others visited and never returned. A soul's prison sentence to The Murk is a one-way ticket.

SYLVIA: And why are we going there, again?

TRIGLAV (still deep into the story thought): Visitors become prisoners or at least are never seen nor heard from again, perhaps because there is only one way in and no known way out.

SYLVIA: Great, sounds like a dead end. So why?

TRIGLAV (getting more serious in demeanor): The Murk entrance was supposed to be the sight of a Pillar which imprisoned an ancient god who spread one of the Eight Deadly Sins. Seven out of the Eight gods were sealed into a parallel Realn. One still walks the Earth unseen.

SYLVIA (looked around into the dark surroundings of their camp): Sounds like we don't want to meet that one.

TRIGLAV: Too late.

SYLIA (became scared, stood and looked around feverishly): Where?!

TRIGLAV (points to his massive chest): Here.

The Murk was inhabited by evil men and women, tyrants, the undead, vampires, werewolves, mass murderers, child molesters, the vilest lost spirits of the dead. The village no longer existed, or no one could find it, except perhaps Triglav, since it used to be his

Earth Realm for a time, long ago, before it became The Murk, before he abandoned it. The means to find it was to look for the path of proper signs. Triglav could recognize the signs through sight, smell, sounds. It was the place of the lost penny. When looking for it, could not be found, but when not looking, appeared.

TRIGLAV: Promise me you won't be surprised by anything or anyone we encounter.

SYLVIA: How can I promise that? Surprise is an involuntary reaction.

TRIGLAV: What is an "involuntary reaction"?

SYLVIA: You're kidding.

Snap!

TRIGLAV: Get down!

Sylvia hunched down.

TRIGLAV (sniffed the air, relieved): Oh crap. It's just him.

SYLVIA: Who?

TRIGLAV: My worst nightmare. At least, yours, for now.

Murker stepped from the distant brush.

MURKER: Hey, old man! Thought I'd never see you again.

TRIGLAV: Hoping?

MURKER: Ha, ha! Good one.

Sylvia wondered. As Murker drew closer, she began to stand up.

SYLVIA: So, what's wrong with him?

TRIGLAV: Trust me, you'll see.

TRIGLAV (thought): Oh, no. Here it comes.

Still twenty feet away, Murker spotted Sylvia.

MURKER: Oh, my goodness. What have we here? Mine eyes
have seen the glory.

Sylvia began to feel uncomfortable.

SYLVIA: I think I understand already.

TRIGLAV: Oh! I forgot to tell you, figuratively, he
has the ears of a bat, the eyes of an eagle, and the
sniffer of a bloodhound... some of his good traits.

Murker shivered, falsely and in an exaggerated
fashion.

MURKER: Babe! You got me shaking.

Sylvia whispered under her breath.

SYLVIA: Keep dreaming Bub.

TRIGLAV (thought): Stings like a wasp, conversation
wise.

MURKER: Babe! I can hear you.

TRIGLAV: Picture drawn, envelope sealed and stamped.
Ready for mailing.

MURKER: Looks like we got us a threesome.

Sylvia sat down again.

SYLVIA: Hi, I'm Sylvia. You must be in the wrong dark

forest.

MURKER: No, any doubts were erased seconds ago, Babe.

TRIGLAV: Stop calling her Babe already.

MURKER: Sorry. Just a reflex Big Guy.

SYLVIA (thought): Oh brother.

MURKER: What a reunion. And no, I'm not your brother. Sure, would have liked to have been him, watching you grow up.

SYLVIA (thought): EEEWWW!

TRIGLAV: When did you start reading minds?

Rustling sounds filtered out from the deep brush.

TRIGLAV (harsh whisper): Down...

SYLVIA: Christ, I hope there isn't another one.

MURKER: Nope, there's only one like me. If you are asking what is in the bushes, I suspect either Jaculus or Rusalki. Only difference between the two is how they like us dead, either drowning or dismemberment.

SYLVIA: Wait. I'm not finished. Do you have a name?

MURKER: Do I have a name. Murker, and no, I'm not named after the place you are searching for. Oh, and the rustling sound (he sniffed the air) is just a wolf. It won't bother us; the fire will keep it away.

Triglav wanted to change the subject. He stood, stretched a bit.

SYLVIA: So why are you here?

MURKER: My happy hunting grounds. Sent here by the

one and only top guy, The Pope. Assigned to assist each of you, as needed.

SYLVIA (yawning): Need some sleep.

MURKER: Germanic and Slavic.

SYLVIA: Huh?

MURKER: My name origin. I know you are into discovering and analyzing data like that.

SYLVIA: Good night.

Triglav had already disappeared into the woods. Sylvia scrunched into her tent.

MURKER: Don't worry about me, guys. I'll just lay here and guard the fire.

Another too early morning ascended upon them. The moon was still visible as it snuck between the ridges of otherwise significant cloud cover. The Sun was hidden still on the other side of the mountains.

Quickly they gathered themselves, their essentials, and began the trek to The Murk. Not long into the hike, Sylvia became increasingly irritated by Murker's need to spit.

SYLVIA: Will you please stop dumping your DNA around.

When Murker spit one more time, a wind picked up and blew it behind him onto Sylvia's boots. Sylvia raised a fist to punch him in the back, but he anticipated it coming and ducked. Sylvia began to fall after missing the target. She reached out to stop herself and tugged on the nearest thing she could grasp, Triglav's cloak. The cloak hoodie pulled down, revealed another of his faces. Sylvia was stunned.

She had not yet seen the other faces yet. She almost
didn't believe they were real.

TRIGLAV: Thought I told you, already.

Triglav reached down and helped her up. Murker was
uncharacteristically silent. They continued the
walking. Triglav raised his right hand.

TRIGLAV: Wait here.

Murker and Sylvia looked at each other, confused and
concerned. The wind picked up suddenly, high in the
tall, black oaks which rose into the leafy darkness
above them. The large moon was their only light.
Suddenly, a whoosh sounded all around them. Murker
whispered in a fatalistic, high tone.

MURKER: Jaculus.

SYLVIA: Ja-what?

MURKER: Shush!

A six-foot-tall Jaculus floated down from the tree in
front of them, about twenty feet away, as if supported
by a parachute. Its wings puffed up around it, slowed
the descent. Fiery green eyes glowed, the only light
upon it, except the moonlight.

MURKER: Crap, it's the decoy. That means they are
behind us.

Sylvia slowly turned around, and a Jaculus snapped at
her neck. Suddenly, a shot of adrenalin took hold of
her and she ducked.

SYLVIA: What . . . ?

Then "Snap, Snap!" sounded. Murker had one behind him
also. He immediately dropped to the ground, knowing
the Jaculus liked to snap the head off their prey and

pull them back skyward into the high parts of the
trees, where the victim was devoured.   The long
Jaculus jaws clapped together.

MURKER: They are soft under the belly. Hit 'em low,
just below the belly, if you draw blood, they will
fly up and eventually bleed to death.

But it was too late for Sylvia. She started to stand
up, and the Jaculus bear hugged her with broad wings,
then jumped upward, climbing up the tree using the
hind legs. Murker pulled his Ka-Bar knife and
thrusted into the under belly of the Jaculus hunting
him. It immediately squealed and flew straight upward
into the tree. Blood spewed everywhere.

MURKER: Ah! Ow! That crap stings!

He looked over to Sylvia, and she was gone.

MURKER: Sylvia?

But he couldn't look long as another Jaculus
approached him from behind. Murker now had time to
unleash his Rec-7 and shot off a wing at the stem of
the shoulder. As the Jaculus whirled around, Murker
aimed fire at the neck, breaking it apart,
decapitating it in seconds. It flopped to the ground.
All was silent now.

Then, a loud Banshee like screech resonated, then
thrashing sounds like nails scraped a chalkboard,
then silence, then a rain of Jaculus parts, flesh
chunks, bone splinters, blood drops streaked from the
sky. Then silence again. Murker grabbed the back of
his neck and rubbed hard.

MURKER: Darn that crap stings.

Sylvia was nowhere to be seen. Triglav appeared from
the trees and startled Murker.

MURKER: You missed all the fun.

TRIGLAV: Where is she?

MURKER: Beats me. I think a Jaculus just ate her for breakfast.

TRIGLAV: You really need to work on your emotions.

MURKER: Humph.

Triglav solemnly closed his eyes and concentrated.

TRIGLAV: I can hear another human heart beating nearby. But it is beating amazingly fast. Faster than I have ever heard before.

MURKER: Nice trick. Where is it coming from?

Triglav looked up, at the tree behind Murker.

TRIGLAV: Weird.

MURKER: What?

TRIGLAV: I am looking right where she should be, but I can't see her.

Sylvia had blended her body into the tree lines and limbs and leaves. Her skeletal face could slightly be if a fruit of the tree, but her face was black, blended in with the shadows cast by the moon on the tree. It seemed as if she was in a trance.

TRIGLAV: Something isn't right.

MURKER: I'm going up.

TRIGLAV: Wait. Whatever it is, it's gone.

MURKER: We should look for her. I don't see any of her body parts laying around.

TRIGLAV: Nice. Somehow, she got away. Impossible. A
Jaculus will never let go of the prey once they've
wrapped it.

MURKER: What are you saying? She's dead?

TRIGLAV: I don't know. I don't know.

They turn around to search out Sylvia's remains and
found her standing behind them as the Sun's first
rays somersaulted over the peak of the mountains.

SYLVIA: How are you doing, gentlemen?

Triglav and Murker looked at each other, shook their
heads.

MURKER: Nice trick.

TRIGLAV: Let's get on with it.

Triglav trudged off into the deep brush and
undergrowth. Murker followed. Then Sylvia followed
Murker, but not before looking at the remains of her
work above in the trees. Jaculus body parts lined
several tree limbs.

The three adventurers crossed a river that wasn't a
river, just a foggy, low glow, thick soup like water,
just as Baba Yaga predicted.

They arrived at the front door of the Inn. A sign
nailed to the outer wall read "Un-ring the Bell". The
bell above the door looked like a snake woman, head
forward like a candy cane hook, long flowing hair,
and her dress served as the bell from the waist down.

MURKER: Huh? You can't un-ring a bell.

SYLVIA: Sounds like a joke.

She reached her right hand up with an extended index finger to push the black button.

TRIGLAV (shouts): No wait!

Sylvia pushed the button. A bell mounted above their heads began to sway and then spin and looked as if it was about to grind into her. Murker backed off and was about to blast it, when the bell suddenly stopped. It started to ring in a backwards ring sound: gggnnniiirrrr!

The large, arched wooden door slowly opened inward.

TRIGLAV (shocked): Only demons can open that door.

A large creature, barrel-chested and troll-like except very hairy, dressed in raggedy clothes, stared at them. He scratched his head.

CREATURE: Duh...duh...how you do dat?

Triglav reached down and grasped his huge hand around Sylvia's left butt cheek and gently squeezed. Sylvia's eyes suddenly merged into one cyclops eye and burned red. The troll-like creature lowered his head and sniffed at her like a dog, stepped back and allowed their entrance. Sylvia's eyes returned to their normal state, but Triglav now understood she was possessed by Likho.

TRIGLAV: Just as I thought, Sylvia.

SYLVIA: What?

TRIGLAV: You were the Key.

Gesualdo played harpsichord vehemently in the far corner of the room. Triglav glad-handed and commiserated with old demon friends. Sylvia stood at

the bar ledge, tried not to involuntarily react to
the surroundings. Hitler and Stalin were seated at a
round table, arm wrestling, in one dark corner.
Genghis Khan and Tamerlane, in a drunken stupor
seated at another table, compared battle scars. There
were few women to be seen, but the ones available
were ghouls, eerily beautiful, but each projected a
face covered by scarves to hide their decay. They
were just as likely to screw a patron within an inch
of life or, alternatively, rip the patron's face off
and beat the living hell out of him/her/it with it.

Jack the Ripper and Jeffrey Dahmer ate Caesar Salads
drenched in French dressing. Their bodies, so-called,
sucked unknown poison from catheters stuck in each of
their forearms. They were periodically eaten by
roaming room zombies, vomited back up, then sculpted
into their unliving selves again by elegant female
vampires, for the sheer entertainment of deranged
guests and others interred at this prison, which
essentially was the main purpose of the tavern: to
punish the deceased extraordinarily evil souls as
retribution for the inhumane acts of debasement and
horror created by them upon living human souls in
life.

Murker walked up next to Sylvia. She could see him
in the wall mirror located behind the bar. A loud
smack sound exploded into her right ear. She flinched
a bit as the vibration of the sound ran completely
down her spine, almost weakening her legs at the
knees. Her elbows locked against the ledge of the bar
top, which kept her from slumping downward. Murker's
hand pressed hard against the bar top just to Sylvia's
right. Yellowish goo oozed out of the sides. His hand
had just squashed a chunky yet sleek, long-antennae
water-bug which scooted along the bar top.

MURKER: Wet rag!

The barkeep, a very pale, short, bald man, tossed a
white half-towel at Murker, spraying its warm

dampness onto Sylvia's face. Murker raised his right hand up, revealed the yellowish goo and black speckled remains of the water-bug dripping down his palm, as the rag was about to hit into the mess like a flying bird striking a window.

MURKER (smiled proudly): Bullseye!

SYLVIA: I guess you are the Hollywood idle, bad-ass I have been looking for all my life?

MURKER (demonstrated once again an economy of words could bely a cheap existence): Bingo! We have a Bingo!

SYLVIA: I only need you to do two things if you are in on this thing: Kill and Survive.

MURKER: You love me, I knew it.

SYLVIA: Flatter yourself now while you still can.

MURKER: Ding ding ding ding ding!

TRIGLAV (barges over): We done?

SYLVIA (looked sarcastically over at Murker): I don't know, are we done?

MURKER: I'm thinking.

SYLVIA: I can hear. Need some oil to grease those parts?

MURKER (a teenaged boy grin shined upon his face): I wish you hadn't said oil.

SYLVIA (eyes rolled up): We're done!

Sylvia reached down for a Camel cigarette from her left thigh pouch. A tiny Bic lighter she also pulled out from the pouch. She was about to light it.

TRIGLAV: Uh-oh . . .

BARTENDER: What do you think you are doing?

SYLVIA: Having a smoke.

There are others smoking in the room. Columns of grayish-white smoke float up towards the ceiling in many parts of the room.

BARTENDER (sarcastically): Only the dead, or dying, can smoke in here.

MURKER: Could have fooled me.

BARTENDER: What! Smart ass!

The Bartender breathed in deep, then exhaled a pall of greenish smoke, covering the faces of Murker and Sylvia. Their upper bodies and head sagged down onto the bar top.

When Sylvia and Murker awoke, they found themselves seated against the outside wall at the front of the bar entrance.

SYLVIA: What just happened?

MURKER: I think we were just tossed out. That's funny, he let me smoke in there before.

SYLVIA: Before?

MURKER: Sure. I'm no novice tc this place. It's been a stopping point for me on some of my jobs.

SYLVIA: So, I guess he thought you weren't coming back from some of them.

MURKER: I guess. Can I have one of those?

Sylvia still clung to the Camel cigarette box and Bic

lighter in her left hand. She lit her cigarette, then passed the box and lighter to Murker. She wondered how Murker could become a regular at a place only inhabitable by the dead, dying, or demons.

Close up of the cigarette in Murker's mouth, inhaling, the tip of the cigarette turned bright red.

MURKER: See. I knew you cared.

SYLVIA: We just need each other for now. Don't get used to it.

The Inn door opened inward. Triglav came out.

MURKER: Find what you were looking for?

TRIGLAV: No.

SYLVIA: A waste of time.

TRIGLAV (thought): A good waste of time. If I'd found what I was looking for, we'd already be doomed.

Sylvia checked her text messages as her phone didn't work in The Murk Inn. One requested her presence in Rome immediately.

SYLVIA: Looks like I must temporarily part company with you two.

TRIGLAV: Oh, wait.

He scrounged a hand around in his cloak, then handed an Ankh to Sylvia and an Ankh to Murker.

MURKER: Don't need it. Already have a can opener.

TRIGLAV: Souvenir. It was free Ankh night. Some Egyptian Pharaoh was in the back room gorging on ladies of the night when one of them flipped a few to me.

SYLVIA: Three-thousand-year-old souvenir. Nice.

Sylvia slipped the Ankh into one of her side pockets.

MURKER: Missing you already, Babe.

TRIGLAV: Now to find a way out of this place where there is no means of escape.

MURKER: Piece of cake.

They proceeded to walk a direction towards the unknown to search for an exit that didn't exist. A rumbling growl emanated from outside The Murk Inn. They stopped walking. Triglav turned around to the sight of a Barguest barreling down upon them. Murker raised his weapon.

TRIGLAV: No wait!

Triglav squatted. The wild beast jumped on him; they gave each other a hug.

TRIGLAV: Missed me, buddy, I see.

MURKER: Lunch?

SYLVIA: No, you idiot. Friend.

TRIGLAV: Problem solved. He will help us find the way, but we will have to scrounge up some food for him along the path.

MURKER: Plenty of that out there.

The Pope had returned to Rome to take a break from his Pillar maintenance endeavors. His Eminence stood on his private balcony, exhaled the smoke from a lit cigarette.

THE POPE (thought): Time is running short.

12

The Pope had learned of some very unsettling things
about Sylvia and about her Poland dig trip. He
recalled her to Rome during his break. An assistant
to The Pope invited Sylvia into the room and directed
her to be seated in a white wing chair. The Pope was
seated, across from Sylvia, in his traditional red
wing chair as he perused the handwritten words in a
tattered manuscript.

THE POPE: Sylvia, thanks for coming.

Sylvia nodded. The dimly lit room only heightened her
curiosity about this meeting. The Pope explained the
Seals on the Realm binder stone pillars needed repair
and reinforcement.

THE POPE: The Seals are more than stone. They emit
an energy field, created by the work of Triglav and
his friend whom he calls Willow. The field emanates
from the stone pillar, then encircles the mountain
from top to bottom to prevent penetration into the
human domain. The technology from Triglav's world
saved us. Failure to complete service repairs would
be catastrophic for humanity. Unfortunately, when
Triglav's friend was killed, the knowledge to
maintain the pillar energy emitter died with her.

SYLVIA (thought): Odd. Romanus sealed his own fate
when he killed Willow. At least until now.

THE POPE: Our scientists in Rome believe some of the
Ohdows trapped behind the Seal with Romanus may know
how to better maintain it, possibly even break it.
Our temporary fix would be to use the Solomon's ring,
a sliver which you have in your broach, combined with
Triglav's power of lightening, to re-meld the pillar
coating and strengthen it.

Sylvia explained the side trips to Baba Yaga and The

Murk. Her next destination would be the Holy Cross
Monastery.

THE POPE: There is a complication. For centuries,
small groups of Romanus' forces have appeared on
earth. We think he can communicate with these other
world entities, once independent demons not aligned
by any particular leader, yet called forth by the
misdeeds of humans, for instance, a demon like Likho,
the demon who has cursed your family and who is
trapped, even now, inside you.

Sylvia looked concerned.

THE POPE: There is a tragedy. Your father has been
captured by the forces of Romanus and transferred to
the same prison Realm as Romanus. Your father's
ability to transform, physically blend into elements,
materials, structures, allowed him to be pulled
through into Romanus' prison Realm. It is a case of
curiosity killed the cat.

Sylvia's stoic look concerned The Pope. He masked a
frown, then proceeded to tell Sylvia a story about
Saint Faustina, a Polish Nun who died in 1938. In one
of Faustina's dreams, an Angel had appeared to
Faustina and took her through the Seven levels of
hell. After the event, Faustina wrote notes about the
experience. The Pope read from the manuscript.

"The Seraph was in the sky, but the sky was dark,
except for a large, golden moon. The large rock below
which bordered the forest and savanna, bathed in moon
glow, started to grow and transformed into what
became a 16th Century Roman Catholic Monastery. A
candle glowed in a window of the Monastery on the
second floor.

Outside, at the front of the Monastery, turmoil
ensued, as the rival Nobles tried to break in and
take over and forcibly convert all inside to their
rule or suffer death. Inside, some of the religious

held wooden poles, sharpened at the tip. Nobles loyal
to the Monastery were armed by sword and body armor.

Dressed in black, in the cloth of a peasant dress, I
remained locked in a room. Soon I would know why. I
became overcome by grief. I found a mirror hung on a
wall in the room and looked at myself. I still looked
like me but sensed those on the floor below viewed
me as someone else of some mystericus value. I turned
and peered at the candle on an old wooden desk. I
could hear the muffled conversations of the many
Nobles. They loudly debated my value as if they had
wanted me for their own, for my physical appearance
and my unusual foresight ability. The room desk was
perched under a window which opened to the fields
below. The night was dark, except for the large moon
which spotlighted all. I wondered how this fighting
could end. Perhaps I should give myself up.

Next, I am a mouse in a different room along the
hallway. The scene's view became from that of a mouse.
A high arched ceiling showed the light flickering. I
had sneaked into the room from a hole in the wall at
the baseboard, which revealed the table edge, three
Elders, and the high arched ceiling. Elder Two was
somewhat portly. A basket of blessed bread rested at
the center of the table. The Monastery Elders thought
I was special, a gift from God. They saw me as a
potential savior in this hour of need, but for what
need I was uncertain. They debated how to proceed
around the small, thick table. Tall candles glowed on
taller metal stands stationed intermittently along
the walls. The Elders didn't want to lose their own
power.

Elder One stated 'She is a mystic. We are lost without
her powers.'

Elder Two added 'The Nobles want too much.'

Elder Three chimed in 'A sword in her hand may save

us.'

I climbed one of the metal candle holder standards while I instinctively and brazenly coveted the blessed bread in the basket on the table.

Elder One: 'Her beauty may save us.'

Elder Two: 'Yes, perhaps we can promise her to the highest bidder.'

Elder Three: 'There is simply no more time.'

I crawled from the room and once again found myself in human form. I moved down a long hallway as if floating. The walls of the hallway had sconce-like holes carved into them which held candles every several feet to light the hallway. I could hear the shouts of many men. I wanted to see them to assess the degree of danger. At the end of the hallway was a large common room. A man in the crowd held a staff from which flowed a flag embroidered of a symbol I didn't recognize. I continued, upward this time along a spiral stairway to a second floor. I followed the sound of men shouting in the courtyard outside. I moved to a window and looked down. The rebel Nobles were in the courtyard, about to launch an assault, led by their mysterious man adorned in a glorious red robe which dropped to just above the knees and became the boundary for high-topped black boots. I sensed a Demon possessed him. The humans couldn't see his Demon persona, but I could see it in his red eyes.

The amount of people outside frightened me. They were shouting, but not in unison. I could not understand their demands. Then I heard shouts of 'The Maiden! The Maiden!' The leader in the crowd looked up at the window behind which I was standing. I saw again the fiery red eyes. This Demon seemed to possess the group as he approached the front door. The eyes tried to penetrate my mind into my very soul. There seemed to be a reddish glow visible around his head.

As I turned away from the window, I could hear the
Monastery door opened. I could hear a Friar beckon
the Demon possessed leader to come inside. I rushed
down the long hallway and passed the spiral stairs
as the light in the sconces blew back towards the
room of my prior imprisonment.

Then, I turned down another long hallway, but as I
approached my room, I saw The Elders were waiting for
me, standing outside the door. A tall dark-haired
man, the Demon leader who was in the courtyard, came
walking towards The Elders from the other end of the
hallway. Elder One held a white blanket which encased
a long, narrow object. I believed the blanket was for
secrecy of the object inside. My desire to know of
the object was immediately satisfied. The Elders
showed a sign of hope on their faces.

Elder One: 'We ask you to return this sword to the
place of where it was forged.'

Elder Two: 'We will give you time to find the origin.'

Elder Three: 'The Demon leader wants our answer by
morning.'

The Elders knew the leader was Demon possessed. In
the presence of the Demon, I felt uncomfortable, as
if his vision was physically touching me in many base
manners. It became apparent The Elders were trying to
make a bargain with him. As if he could read my mind,

Elder One intoned: '...and possessed of an extreme
fondness for you.'

Elder Two: 'He will believe when you tell him the
sword has been returned to its origin.'

Elder Three: 'Then this war will be finished.'

I took the sword wrapped in the blanket. I then gave

them a compelled promise, 'I will do my best to accomplish this task.'

I was allowed to enter my room. I seated myself at the desk and prayed on a solution as the blanketed sword sat on the desktop. I looked into the light of the desk candle for inspiration. I then stood and walked to the window. Still standing near the desk, I viewed the scene outside the window for some answer. Apparently, the crowd from outside the Monastery was dispersing and moving away into the night. I noticed the Demon Leader of the crowd was walking away also. I saw the glow from his eyes beam red from the sides of his head. The Demon Leader stopped walking as the others passed by him. His head, but not his body, started to slowly turn around like an Owl's head, until it looked straight at me. The body then turned also towards me. The Leader reached out his left hand. His mind called me to follow. I guessed he could show me where I was to bring the sword. As I walked back to the desk and clutched the blanketed sword, I began to lose consciousness. The dream transported me to another place.

Seated on a rock, in a dark cave, I clutched the stiff blanket to my breast. A long tunnel, bored out of brown rock, lay ahead of me. Fire burned at random parts of the cave walls and floor. I had been transported in a dream to the levels of hell previously, so I recognized this Fifth Level. A voice whose body was not visible said 'Welcome to the weapons sector,' as if I was an expected visitor. I walked down the tunnel. Despite the burning fire at the walls, it was still a dark place which emanated a foul aroma. As I continued down the tunnel, I noticed rooms on each side. I knew the Fifth level forged into one's soul not only evil temptations but also the implements needed to accomplish goals of the same.

Finally, the tunnel expanded into a larger area. An

opening in the rock wall greeted me but the size of the opening was very wide and remarkably high.

Nephilim were the makers of the weapons. They were giants, like a Goliath. The Nephilim workers noticed me as I passed by various working sub-chambers where high arched entranceways glimmered the fires of hell and shadows of large bodies, forge tools, and visible waves of heat. The arches and sub-chambers were carved like tentacles from the main chamber I approached.

The Nephilim seemed to know why I was there. Cantankerous in nature, they encouraged me to open the blanket away from the object I carried. I opened it. Next, they coaxed me to try the sword in my hand, perhaps thinking an innocent virgin Nun couldn't wield a sword or become a warrior. 'Give it a hold. It won't bite ... much.'

They next crowded together and stood at the tall archways lining the main walkway. They spit on me as I crouched over to protect my face. The spit looked like large balls of human sputum. It stuck to wherever it struck me. It stung like an icy, compacted snowball upon impact, except burn marks were gouged into my gown. One of them shouted 'Come on! What are you waiting for virgin!'

Perhaps unwisely, in response I mocked them, 'ugh, eek, demons!' The Nephilim musically responded 'You ain't seen nothin' yet!'

The sword started to sway and fling in my right hand, despite my wishes. Perhaps it was the weight of it. My right arm felt like it spasmed not under my control. The Nephilim workers projected more spittle at me. I turned and walked past the last row of wall arches. The spit struck my back and burned hot through my gown. I stood in front of a larger opening which glowed orange red. The opening was difficult to see into due to a grayish darkness. I heard a voice whisper 'Help me', but it too could have been the sounds of random hissing from the forging hearths in the sub-chambers. I became more determined than ever to find my destination in this desolate place to relieve myself of the sword's burden.

The spittle balls were now burned completely through my gown and into my flesh. Red marks appeared, and parts of my legs and my arms emanated a gurgled steam. I was certain my hips and buttocks were flayed and charred at the flesh as I fell to my knees from the pain. Again, a whisper sounded 'You must reach out to me or nothing can be done.' I looked around and noticed Nephilim in the archways, staring at me, taking in deep breaths as if they enjoyed the smell of my burnt flesh. Their harsh verbalization echoed as 'Ah! Roasted human virgin. It has been a long time.'

A large, winged figure became visible at the hazy, gray smoke curtain of the last archway. Burning spittle still rained down upon my back. Since I was familiar with the specters of the underworld, I was not quite surprised to see Archangel Metatron appear from behind the gray smoke curtain. 'I said there would be hell to pay. Time to pay up.' I raised up my bloody arms while blood streamed from the edge of my sleeves and I tried to unlock my hands to release the sword to Metatron who had cupped his hand below my hands, but a sudden hot wind blew the blanket over top the sword as the sword snapped into the grasp of my right hand. Instead the blanket fell over top of Metatron's hands. Angry, he shouted 'No!'

I stood up, energized by the sword's strength. The sword provided a burst of energy to me as my right arm veins rippled mysteriously. My wounds healed instantly as a shield of light surrounded my body. In shock, Metatron bellowed 'No, it can't BE.' My wounds were healed, although my clothes still tattered from the Nephilim spit bombardment. The mocking gazes of the Nephilim sub-caverns audience changed to amazement. I heard whispers of 'A virgin warrior Nun?' Then sounded a swift attitude change of 'Let's test her mettle.'

Metatron swung a bucket-sized fist at me, but the sword pulled me downward and back just in time to avoid his strike. His swing swished the hot air and wall flames wildly. The Nephilim poured like tea from the pots tip to rush at me. They looked like large, oak trees falling upon me.

The sword turned me with speed. As it extended its reach from my body it extended from my hand, yet the handle remained as the sword acted like axe and maul, spasming swings and slashes into the Nephilim horde, as a storm of blood, guts, flayed body parts formed a grisly mass. As Metatron rushed towards me the sword pulled me as a mule pulled, down to the other end of the cavern. I stopped, looked at Metatron's charge, and prayed. My body began to fade from Metatron's view as he slipped and fell to his knees among the mass of flowed blood and oozed guts and Nephilim shrapnel, stunned. A shuddered whisper tore at my ears in Metatron's wounded voice, 'Oh well...there's still one more chance.'

I awakened in the Monastery room of my initial internment; my hope dashed in the realization I remained an inhabitant of the dream. Bright light grazed through the window. It was apparently morning. A white night gown pressed against my skin. I checked for physical wounds and found none. The black gown, still torn and tattered from the night before, hung draped from a wall hook near my bed. A too fleshy knock vibration shook the room door from the hallway.

I heard scratches of a metal key inside the door, then the doorknob rattled. The door opened inward partway. The sconce candlelight of the hallway betrayed a wide shadow. Elder Two's voice advised 'We have brought someone to protect you.' Another voice I recognized as Elder One intoned 'He is skilled in the art of warfare.' From a bit more of a distance, Elder Three added 'He comes from a wealthy family, a descendant of a Romanian Prince. He gave up his wealth to serve God.' Their efforts to impress were not lost on me. Elder Two noted 'His name is Igor...' The last name sounded from an unfamiliar voice '... Rogescu.' The door then opened wide to reveal a Noble. This Noble's face was the same face from the night previous, of the man with the red eyes. 'Pleased to be at your service, Sister.' As I realized Metatron had sent a spy, the dream faded back into my reality."

The Pope looked up at Sylvia.

THE POPE: I suspect you have many questions.

Sylvia nodded in the affirmative.

Gregorio offered coffee to each. They accepted. A center table was placed in between Sylvia and The Pope. A saucer and cup were placed on each side of the table. Another assistant brought in a silver pot from which the coffee was poured. Sylvia and The Pope declined sugar and cream. They each raised a cup to their lips, took a light sip, then clicked the cup onto the respective saucer.

THE POPE: You see, there have been other warriors of hope in the earth battle of demons against humans, good against evil, right against wrong.

Sylvia remained silent as The Pope continued.

THE POPE: First, your anthropologist friend is safe. The Gargoyle rescued him. They are both at the Holy Cross Monastery.

Sylvia remained silent still.

THE POPE: Your father . . . we know a lot about him. We discovered him, or should I say, one of our Parish Priests discovered him, not long after you were born. Brother Henry referred your father to us for help, rehabilitation, as it were. Your father's nature tempted him to explore, to his detriment, the demon world. We have not been contacted by him for many years.

A light began to shine in Sylvia's eyes at the prospect of learning more about her father.

THE POPE: Your father was near death. We helped him. We learned he had a child. You.

SYLVIA (encouraged): Please tell me more.

THE POPE: We helped raise you.

SYLVIA: Brother Henry.

THE POPE: You showed an intense interest in the physical world around you. We made sure you had all the materials you needed to learn.

SYLVIA: The Study.

THE POPE: We arranged for a scholarship, so you could attend St. Mary's, and learn the craft of the Anthropologist.

Sylvia appeared uncomfortable, squirmed a bit in the white chair.

THE POPE: We set up a foundation and watched as you discovered the entrances to the Pillars which mark the Seven Seals.

SYLVIA: What? You used me to rationalize your fairy tale about the end of the world?

The Pope firmed his lower jaw.

THE POPE: We protected you from those who would see you fail.

SYLVIA: Has my whole life been a lie?

THE POPE: On the contrary. Your society's leaders, by and large, expect the poor to remain poor, especially in spirit and knowledge, although the leaders spout otherwise. It keeps the politicians in power and controls the population.

SYLVIA: I don't know who I am anymore.

THE POPE: Then let me help you.

SYLVIA: You think I could not have made it this far without your help? You pompous . . .

GREGORIO: Child . . . Listen!

THE POPE: No Gregorio. We must let Sylvia choose for herself. It has always been her choice alone. Just as it was her father's. Yet still, his tragedy unfolded by an accident of fate. You primarily control your destiny, aided by an accidental biological anatomy passed on to you through no doing of your own, in a future that remains unknown. Your complete story has not yet been designed.

SYLVIA: What the heck are you talking about? I found the things you wanted me to find. I found six of the seven Pillars for you. I am done!

Sylvia stood up and stormed out of the room.

THE POPE (raised in tone voice): Sylvia, you are a new species; a Trinity of human, demon, and technology. A crucible, as it were, for the beginnings of a new age of life.

The Pope and Gregorio remained in the room.

GREGORIO: There are many places, within these walls,
she could roam, for the purpose of reflection.

THE POPE: Yes, it is all up to her reflection now.

Sylvia was a doubter, hearing what was too incredible
to hear, yet, she sensed The Pope was right. Moments
of her life flashed before her. As she walked the
long halls, she extended a sharp rat nail from her
right-hand index finger, then dug a small scratch
every so often, as a trail marker. The rumination
time ended quickly. She had nowhere else to go;
nothing else to do; a duty of concern for her father.
She returned to the room, but didn't seat herself,
she used the white chair as a crutch, leaned onto it.
She continued her part in the conversation.

SYLVIA: I didn't ask for this. I have tried to avoid
this thing all my life.

THE POPE: And yet it still found you. You are the
product of your genes, your family curse, and
scientific experimentation.

Gregorio could see she was greatly troubled. He drew
closer to her to comfort her. He touched her right
arm, and she drew back, rubbing it. The Pope noticed
her forearm had a scar line in it, however faint.

THE POPE: Please, may I see?

Sylvia reached out her arm which she was rubbing and
turned it upward.

THE POPE: You had a fracture here, a compound one.

SYLVIA: Yes . . . no. I mean, yes, I fell from a tree,
I was hurt, and then just as quick, I was fine.

THE POPE: Your great grandmother, she had the He-La virus. No one knows where it came from, or when it started in humans. The virus grants tremendous healing powers. But not this quick.

SYLVIA: So why did I heal so fast, like, in an instant.

THE POPE: Your father, he was in an unfortunate accident. He was infected by military grade, experimental enzymes. A freak accident. None of the military test subjects reacted as expected. Most died quickly or went insane, their cells overcome and ravished by the enzymes.

SYLVIA: How? How was he infected?

THE POPE: The how is not important. He survived the accidental contact, although he too seemingly went insane over time.

SYLVIA: What did you mean by demon?

The Pope turned to Gregorio, who took up the story.

GREGORIO: The Goralski family has been cursed for over 500 years. Every first-born, at the moment of puberty, became subjected to the ravages of the demon Likho. The demon tempted the cursed one to engage in acts that could ruin the happiness of others and eventually the happiness of the cursed one. The cursed victim rarely survived beyond an age of the mid-thirties.

THE POPE: When a Goralski felt that they had finally made it in this world, everything was taken from them, making the fall harder and longer for the family.

GREGORIO: And now, Sylvia Magnon, you are the first-born. The only female first-born of the Goralski's in over 400 years. The cursed demon has been inside you

since puberty. And it is eating at your soul, slowly,
like a spider sucking the life out of its paralyzed,
trapped prey.

THE POPE: Only now, the tide has turned. The demon
has inhabited your superhuman body. Your cells and
tissue are immune to illness and disease. Your body
houses enzymes which instinctively defend you against
any attempted invasion of your mind and physicality.
Perhaps even protects your soul.

GREGORIO: The demon will only leave you after it has
consumed your soul. Your soul will be strongest at
the moment of your greatest triumph, at which time
the demon will gorge on its irresistible succulence.

THE POPE: But there is hope. The demon has never faced
such a formidable foe. You are a new species.

SYLVIA: My dreams, my nightmares, are they the work
of the demon.

GREGORIO: Sometimes. But sometimes, they are moments
of your life which may be foreshadowed.

SYLVIA: You can't be serious.

THE POPE: Our experience with exorcism has taught us
that the subject human who is possessed has a sense
of being outside their own body, watching it do
things, not realizing that the moments seen are a
possible reality.

GREGORIO: After an exorcism of a normal . . . excuse
me, I mean conventional human, there is no memory of
the reality events experienced.

THE POPE: We think the enzymes have repaired your
memory; the same way they help you physically heal
incredibly fast.

SYLVIA: How did my father handle these things.

GREGORIO: He . . .

The Pope waved him off. Gregorio bowed his head and clasped his own hands in prayer fashion.

THE POPE: Your father, the only one of his kind who survived long enough to confront these events, had great difficulty, and failed many times in his efforts to understand and control his new self.

THE POPE: One of our Parish clergyman in Balmoral tried to help him.

SYLVIA: Brother Henry!

THE POPE: Yes, your mentor for many years as you grew to learn and experience your gifts. Your father never got over the death of his own father. Your father was not open to assistance. His rage overtook him. He sought out revenge and left much devastation in his wake. Then he disappeared.

SYLVIA: Gifts? You mean my curses, don't you?

THE POPE: There is a subtle difference between a blessing and a curse. We all possess gifts of talent and curses of temptation.

SYLVIA (thought): Tell me about it.

THE POPE: For example, some are called to lead. Such a call requires a desire to acquire power. Think of politicians.

SYLVIA: I try not to.

THE POPE: Just for this instance, then. Which is the blessing, and which is the curse?

SYLVIA: Enlighten me?

THE POPE: Leadership is the blessing. The skills required can be honed to match the potential talent, the blessing.

SYLVIA: Go ahead.

THE POPE: A leader needs to feed, on those willing. When there are those not willing, yearning for leadership, the leader may be tempted to acquire dominion, at any cost, the curse. Your father's genetic alteration, an unfortunate accident, caused him the need to make choices that hurt some who caused him incredible pain, and yet some others suffered collateral damage because of your father's actions.

Gregorio stepped in to offer each a cigarette. They each accepted. He lit each cigarette. They each inhaled, then exhaled.

THE POPE: The Beasts, from a distant part of the Universe, are interested in Earth as a Realm of their own dominion, the very reason they were expelled from their own world. The Scarlet Beast, Romanus, wants to exercise his domain over Earth. He has calculated that now is the most opportune time to acquire it. The Beasts have flooded our magnetic field with telepathic thoughts, throughout our history, which have been recorded in the myth, lore, and religious documents of all human cultures. Romanus has tried to take over Earth on various occasions, most recently World War I, World War II, in our historical timeline. Humans now believe that a new Reign is imminent on this planet. Little do they know it is a Reign of Terror.

SYLVIA: Surely the major governments of the world have figured this plot out and are taking steps to undermine it.

THE POPE: This conclusion you posit is true, however, they have no idea how to stop it; and some relish to co-opt it for personal gain. In their quests for power and knowledge, they have become unwitting accomplices in the ultimate destruction of humanity. They have kicked the can down the road, so to speak, in the belief the worst that is yet to come they will not live long enough to see. Enterprising young politicians have campaigned on the idea that they are the Saviors of this world. From the Beasts, Demons, whatever you want to call them, humans have acquired Fire, the knowledge to forge Steel, the formula for making explosive devices, and the ingenuity to explode cataclysmic nuclear weapons. So, you see, all Romanus must do is tip the scales of human consciousness just enough to bring all of humanity to an end. What the Beasts have not anticipated is the human ability to adapt. The latest adaptation, Nanotechnology, is a knowledge they have not anticipated capable of our races on Earth. You are the embodiment of the human spirit, adaptability, hybrid strength, once your father and mother passed their genes onto you. You are the key which unlocks the door to Romanus' re-entry into the earth Realm. We would like to warn them of their imminent failure, but they would not believe us. Our experience tells us they would only exploit the knowledge to entrench their power and further persecute the Religions of this world. Belief in the Truth can engender painful, fatal consequences for the believer. We have warriors who operate against their efforts. Vampyr, Neuri, human spirits, spirited humans, gypsies, the undead persecuted, the Slavic tribes who defend against the physical assaults generated by the demon telepathic energy. We have weapons against their telepathic invasions such as music, art, religious beliefs, nuclear technology, internet technology, and we have helped develop a moral code for the individual and the greater good, which when applied practically through generosity and good works tends to resist their temptations.

SYLIA: I am not a warrior.

THE POPE: This sentiment is true, Sylvia Magnon. But

you are the Ultimate Weapon. If you decide to join us, willingly, in our imperfect union, a new world may be created, a better world, more resistant to the diabolical strains of demon temptations.

THE POPE (speaking to Gregoric): Sometimes imperfect pieces make one perfect puzzle.

GREGORIO: I hope you are right, Your Eminence.

13

Sylvia agreed to rejoin her new friends, Triglav and Murker, at the entrance to the Holy Cross Monastery. She requested another Jeep from The Holy See. The request was granted.

She arrived outside the Monastery, but there was no sign yet of her friends. She set up camp and waited. She had enough supplies and food for about five days. The weather was becoming cooler as it was just past mid-autumn. In anticipation of early arrival, she brought much reading material from the Vatican Library to prep for what was to come.

She first reviewed a book about curses, the elements, purposes and cures. Next, she reviewed a book about Gypsy tribes in the area, their culture, purpose, genealogy, lifestyle. She learned, to support themselves, the tribes specialized in various skill sets such as curse creation and mitigation and know-how to caste the spells respective to each, the ingredients and words, if needed; forging knives and using them; basic survival skills and mobility.

The Pope recommended and provided to Sylvia a book about an artist named Dina, her relation to the Gypsies and the influence of her paintings created while she was interred at the World War II prison camp Auschwitz. The Nazi's praised, yet also feared some of her works, so some of the paintings were locked away, to prevent the presence of a Gypsy spell cast upon them creating an influence on the officers and guards at the prison. Her paintings hinted at the end of days. The Pope also noted Dina's whereabouts are unknown. She was listed on the records at the prison camp, but her fate wasn't indicated.

Sylvia listened on an MP3 Player to "Painted Black", by The Rolling Stones, then Beethoven's "Symphony No. 7 / Allegretto", as she further reviewed the story about Dina's paintings. The paintings amazingly were various shades of black. They looked like solid black to the casual observer, but when Dina painted, it was as if she was possessed by something.

A closer and studious look at some history books revealed moments of Earth history which had been influenced by the Demons—
   --the initial landing/entry into the Earth Realm;
   --the development of humanoids, abused by the demons;
   --the great flood, which was meant to wipe out the humanoids, but didn't;
   --the battles between Bahamut and Leviathan, mainly due to Leviathan's jealous rages; she loved Bahamut.

Another book from the Vatican Library recounted Vivaldi's moments in hell; how he tricked The Scarlett Demon (aka Romanus) to allow him in; how he Vivaldi, too was racked by the Onionhead curse. How the Gypsies developed into specialized clans after the Scarlett Demon destroyed the Indus Valley civilization, because he did not want its purity and knowledge to be transferred to the rest of humanity. The surviving Indus groups moved towards Europe, settled in various Slavic countries, and individually preserved the knowledge of metal working, magic, and warrior/survivor skills.

A manuscript was also included to recount how the last great battle for humanity, when the Seals to the parallel realm were being forged, stranded Triglav and his true love (now The Willow) and led to the great battle on the Holy Cross Mountain plain. Another manuscript revealed discovery of where the Pillars are located which mark the location of the Seven Seals around the world (information updated and confirmed by Sylvia's previous missions work); and how the Scarlett Demon could be defeated.

The Pope referenced, in the event Sylvia's reading was somehow sidetracked by events on the ground, the

Gypsy curses were born of human or animal blood, earthen dirt, and interaction either spiritually or telekinetically or physically with hell-zombies who transmitted the evils of the Seven Deadly sins.

The Pope also referenced a theory, which she should ask further detail about from the Monastery Monk Hugo Grotius, that posited the collective consciousness on earth had long ago been invaded by The Beasts (demons) from the parallel Earth Realm, causing mankind to enter hyper-intense states of chaos, paranoia, jealousy and greed, stoked by modern communication technology.

On the third day of Sylvia's encampment, Triglav and Murker arrived, apparently no worse for the wear.

SYLVIA: Where's your doggy friend?

TRIGLAV: Oh, we found him some food after he led us out of The Murk zone. Then he went home, I guess.

Sylvia commenced packing up her gear.

MURKER: Got another Jeep, I see.

He helped her load the gear. Then off they went as Triglav clung to the back of the Jeep.

MURKER: You sure this thing can hold him?

SYLVIA: It's a Jeep, isn't it?

When they arrived at the Holy Cross Monastery, they followed a dirt road up to the ancient site. The Monastery was hewn into a small mountain-sized stone. The road led all the way around the stone, but there was no entrance visible. Small tunnel openings and pipelines pocked the exterior. A larger mountain was a few hundred yards away. One spot, high up the side of the larger mountain, emanated a dim glow.

SYVLIA (shouted back towards Triglav): The Seventh
Pillar?

Triglav nodded in the affirmative. He stepped off the
back of the Jeep and started stalking an access to
the Monastery. A voice from remarkably high up
shouted, from the plump round head of a man, Brother
Hugo Grotius.

HUGO: Hold on! I will send transport!

Two gargoyles then swiftly descended from the
Monastery roof area, softly landed on the ground in
front of them.

TRITSCH / TRATSCH (in unison): At your service. Just
hang on.

Music from the pipes sounded "Tritsch Tratsch Polka"
by Strauss.

Tritsch picked up Sylvia, then Tratsch picked up
Murker.

TRIGLAV: No problem. I'll just wait here.

Tritsch and Tratsch returned to lift Triglav.

Once inside Hugo's study, they each exchanged cursory
greetings, which is all Hugo would have allowed
anyway. His work was his life, his only means of
stimulation. In other words, the sum of his small
talk vernacular was in the negative. He explained
that Revelations forecasted the end of one age of
civilization and the beginning of another. The end
meant the purge of all unclean spirits. Since the
beginning of human-time on Earth, over 20 billion
humans have existed. Many of them still had spirits
clinging to the Earth realm. The Revelations Demons
would attempt to unleash the unclean spirits upon the
current living humans, as they had tried to do 100,000
years ago, and more recently in the World Wars, so

the Demons could once again reign over the planet.

SYLVIA: What about my gear, still outside.

HUGO: The gargoyles are already taking care of it.

Triglav, Sylvia and Murker all looked at each other.
Hugo continued.

HUGO: There is one flaw with the collective
consciousness theory. Everything isn't written down.
For instance, the curse inflicted upon your family.
It was an accident. The curse was not supposed to
last this long. When it was cast, a demon was nearby,
and was included in the casting of it. The End of
this World myth that is prevalent in many cultures
cannot be predicted, because a key ingredient is
missing.

SYLVIA: What key ingredient?

HUGO: You.

Sylvia sighed. Hugo continued.

HUGO: In each myth, the Earth has no chance. Humans
are considered ultimately doomed. It is like in
baseball. When the pitcher throws the ball, he can
throw a pitch that results in an out, or in a hit.
The current End of the World myth predicts a homerun
for evil, but the thrown pitch could also result in
a strikeout. Evil can be struck out. Soviet Union era
and US underground testing of atomic weapons have
damaged and cracked the Pillar's seals, allowing the
inevitable escape of the demons which previously
controlled human and humanoid destiny.

MURKER: What's with all the pipes and holes poking
outside the walls.

HUGO: The Monastery serves many purposes. One purpose
is a weapons capacity. There is a musical weapon of

ghostly Symphony players housed underground. There are similar arrangements at the other Pillars. The music is carried by magnetic fields.

MURKER: That must cost a lot.

HUGO: To the contrary. The spirits eat, sleep and drink musical performance.

SYLVIA: What musical arrangements do they play?

HUGO: Here, only those composed by The Red Priest, Vivaldi.

SYLVIA: And the Polka?

HUGO: That was a recording. The gargoyles love it.

TRIGLAV (rubs his stomach): Okay then. When do we eat?

MURKER (silly grin): And drink?

SYLVIA (voice dripping of a pungent taste of sarcasm): I'm sorry Hugo. The boys have worked up an appetite, saving the world and all, you know.

HUGO (raised eyebrows): This way please.

Hugo led the motley crew to a large dining hall in the lower level of the Monastery, after trudging down several circular stone staircases. Hugo showed them to a table, then he moved to a side of the room where he started to play an arrangement of folk music from the area on a CD player. Sylvia seated herself at a long and wide wooden picnic styled table and Triglav and Murker just across from her on the other side of the table. Some spirits dressed like World War II officers of the Polish military, Hussars, spirits of Russian officers and soldiers, more formally dressed Vampyr, and living Gypsies were seated at other tables scattered around the room. Much ale had been placed out, in bottles, on the table. Large plates of red and gray kielbasa tempted their appetites from the middle of the table. Murker wasted no time in cutting off pieces of the kielbasa sausages and passed them around using the porcelain plates stacked at the end of the table. The eat and drink commenced in earnest. No bottle of ale or plate of kielbasa was discriminated against. All was welcomed, soaked into the senses, then consumed. Triglav and Sylvia started drinking their cohorts under the table.

The Hussars and Polish Officers, the Russian Officers and warriors commenced a Cossack dance on one of the tables, kicked over some of the horde of empty ale bottles. The toast "na zdrowie" was variously shouted around the room, many times, before a chorus of ale chugging commenced in unison. Some participants started to keel over, vomit, fart tremendously, pass out. A heap of food and drink victims piled around or on each table. A food and drink lust overtook the room, and continued, and continued beyond the point of continuing. The brasher members of the crowd started throwing boasts around like darts at each other. Chest pounding, upward hand thrusting blew the room's plague of dust in mini tornado swirls about the room and up into the ceiling rafters. Then Murker stepped up onto the table.

MURKER (dribbling vowels): Now it's time for a pro.

He thrust forward a bottle of ale attached to his left hand, into the air, shouted an unintelligible drivel of words for a toast attempt, then crumbled down upon the table. The ale bottle rolled along the edge of the table, the remaining fluid dripped off the edges onto the drunken pile of men, women, spirits which now appeared as a dense carpet upon the floor.

Sylvia had to top that event. She turned her head 180 degrees, vomited out kielbasa muck and thrusted her hands behind her to catch it, then tossed it in the air, then spun her head to each side to catch it. Her strain to perform the stunt ignited the rat and roach instincts inside her. Her face started to mutate into a rat face, roach antennae popped from the sides of her forehead. The crowd went silent, shocked at the spectacle.

But not silent for long. Rousing cheers from the crowd erupted like the sound of a waterfall crashing into an innocent pond below. Now the two gargoyles had come down, and the spirit Nuns had come up from their familiar locations to join the mob of excesses, but not Vivaldi. Vivaldi never showed for these events. At this point, Triglav vomited onto and into his bottle and onto the table. He studied the mess. Then he quickly downed the glass contents, slurped up the vomit from the table as his mouth worked like a vacuum. Triglav started to make his way over to Hugo.

Sylvia farted, audibly. All around her became dizzy, started waving their hands, went cross-eyed.

SYLVIA: Whoops? A kfart.

MURKER (popped his head up, eyes still closed): Dang! That's a potent weapon (as his voice trailed off weakly).

HUGO: Well, this event was a bad idea.

TRIGLAV: No, perhaps not. They needed to blow off some steam after all they have been through.

HUGO: And in anticipation of what they will go through.

Triglav nervously laughed.

HUGO (raises mug): I'll drink to that! (Whereupon he downed a whole mug of ale, then vomited it up in a matter of seconds onto the CD player.)

The music stopped and that was that. No more excess

could be managed.

14

Next morning the group of Hugo, Sylvia, Triglav, and Murker gathered in Hugo's Study for a briefing of plans to consider, knowledge to be digested, to prepare for the events to come. Hugo explained his interpretation, from his readings, of the final confrontation battle configurations.

He had found a previously undiscovered Nostradamus Quatrain:

> When weeds grow high on the edge of Polan,
> The Muse of Death, revealed in the martyred plain,
> Hordes rain down as ash from the mountain,
> The Scarlet one breaks the Seal in Revelations.

SYLVIA: What does it mean?

HUGO: I think it means many Nations have been neglected or abused, Poland indicated as an example. Death will occur here, but not by the hands and weapons of humans, but by another world's doing. On the edge of the Polan Nation, inside and outside the border areas, exists a peripheral culture, an ignored or forgotten troupe of creatures and beings relegated to myth, who are finally exposed as necessary to survival: Neuri, Vampyr, Revenants, spirits of the dishonored dead that protect and carry messages to the humans. The hoards are other Realm demons that enter the human world, right outside this window perhaps, and at the other Pillar locations you have discovered, to destroy the human and mythical beings in this world who would help keep the Demons from exercising total domination over all. In other words, a battle of all battles is in the offing.

SYLVIA: When does this happen?

HUGO: It is hard to say. Nostradamus' Quatrains tend

to be reinterpreted after the events predicted do not come to pass. Some thought in 2012, but there are several Quatrains after that date which seemingly predict not a rebirth of human culture, but the end of it. Sir Isaac Newton estimated at about the year 2060. What we don't know is when the event will start. It could take several decades, where humans are slowly exterminated, or one great event. The one great event has never successfully been consummated, or we wouldn't be gathered here discussing the possibility.

Hugo explained, even now, here, the Neuri, Vampyr, Revenants (some in the form of Winged Hussars and Russian soldiers) are massing, moving towards one point where they are prepared to make a last stand, outside, at the base of the mountains, at the edge of the plain. We suspect a similar preparation unfolds at Megiddo; and at the other known Pillar locations.

HUGO: Brother Henry's research work discovered the potential other Keys to the destruction of Romanus have not been born as they should have been. There were supposed to be Seven, one for each Pillar, but all have died before birth, except for you, Sylvia. Sylvia felt a prick on top of her head and rubbed it.

HUGO: Earth started as a penal colony. It was first inhabited by demons and served as a punishment for crossing the Supreme Being of that demon world, or simply, another galaxy world. Then the Supreme Being of that other galaxy world began creating humanoids on another planet, but a meteorite brought the microscopic beginnings of those beings, by chance or choice is unknown, to earth. After they developed, over the course of eons, into humanoid life forms, the demons ignored them as a nuisance, then enslaved them, then began hunting them out for sport.

Hugo mentioned there are many gaps in the known historical records as many of these events happened in the time before humanoids and humans created written records. Most history up to then was passed on by word of mouth or scratched into or painted onto cave walls and cliff or mountain sides.

HUGO: Some of the pre-history is in artwork, so-called, hidden in many places around the earth world, away from the demon visage, as a means for the humanoids and humans to remember, pass on the knowledge. Some of the pre-history referred to sounds, we believe music, used to assuage the demon propensities of violence and subjugation.

TRIGLAV (interrupts): Tell her please, more about the importance of the sound of music.

HUGO: Yes, yes. I was getting there. Vivaldi was able to create the most beautiful music. It could soothe the human soul, but at the same time could destroy the demon soul, make it bleed.

The atmosphere of the room became infected by disbelief of Murker.

MURKER: Nothing like a Rec-7 to clear, ahem, settle a room.

HUGO (frowned, then continued): Yes, demons have souls.

Hugo proceeded to relate the story. Vivaldi had to make a deal with a demon to spare the Holy See from attack and domination, but as part of the bargain, he had to earn his way to Hell, or the dimension residing in the sentient mind conceived to be such. Vivaldi's music was performed by women, Nuns, whom he himself trained. To earn his admission to Hell, he had to do the thing most evil for a priest, most evil for a man, most evil for humanity: sexual intercourse forced upon a virgin, and not just any virgin, a Nun. Vivaldi was rumored to have nurtured an interest in one of the Nuns for some time, but rumors are only as credible as those who spin the tale. Apparently, the deed was completed, as Vivaldi was granted a temporary admission to Hell, from where he learned, through trial and error, the sounds that grated and irritated most on the souls of the demons and their minions.

To communicate this knowledge to the Holy See, Vivaldi was given a vial of blood to drink, believed to have been taken from the cloth that washed Christ's face at the crucifixion. This blood, immortal, could survive Hell's atmosphere. Vivaldi then could write the music, and subsequently transport it back to Earth via Gargoyles. Gargoyles were demons who had repented and fled to Earth, not being quite fit for Heaven. When they arrived upon Earth, the Gargoyles took pity upon the humanoid race entities after witnessing first-hand the searing trials of human existence.

MURKER: And where is the confirmation for these deeds?

HUGO: Dina, or her paintings, per se.

MURKER: Dina? Dina who?

HUGO: Sir. My research is detailed and impeccable. The Holy See had recognized it as reliable.

MURKER: Sure, sure. Tell us another story then. How about the Ark of The Covenant?

HUGO: Sorry. That history and knowledge I am not authorized to comment upon.

SYLVIA: Please let him continue.

HUGO: Thank you. Yes. Where was I? Dina was a prisoner at Auschwitz during World War II. The Nazi's allowed her to paint pictures, once it was determined her work could provide pleasure for the Officers there, and perhaps wealth from future provenance of the paintings in the Art world at large. The paintings, as it turned out, contained more than the potential for future provenance. They contained warnings, foreshadowing's, as if inspired by a voice outside of the artist.

MURKER: So, what was found in the "foreshadows"?

Hugo continued, as if not fazed by Murker's doubts.

HUGO: Secrets the Holy See didn't want revealed. After the war ended, the Roman Catholic Church acquired the paintings through the works and funds of Bishops and Archbishops. It is said some of the German Officers, and later, Allied troops who discovered a few of the paintings left by the Nazi's, were hypnotized or entranced physically, if they viewed the paintings for too long a time, as if they were watching a movie. We have been investigating ever since at The Vatican to read or interpret the visions generated by the paintings. The common wisdom developed was Vivaldi, The Red Priest, was inadvertently captured in the mind of Dina, which allowed her to paint The Red Priests escapades in Hell. Dina also painted the Eight Pillars in scenes that helped us discover their locations. Sylvia's work has confirmed the locations. Dina even painted a scene which illustrated a huge mushroom, perhaps a cloud, a moving entity, that rose and rose into the sky as high as a mountain. We think she was depicting an atomic bomb explosion, yet the painting pre-dates that explosion by a few years. By the way, Vivaldi's sexual liaison with a Nun was learned to be a consensual affair initiated at the opportune time.

MURKER: Right.

HUGO: Time for each of you to take a break. Tritsch
and Tratsch will take you down to ground level for a
stretch. Take as much time as you need, or even use
it for your own desires. Try to make it back before
evening falls. Your stomach will let you know.

15

"Tchaikovsky - Waltz of the Flcwers" played in Sylvia's ears, plugged by the earphones of her MP3. She, Triglav and Murker are walking for a while, not far from each other.

Battle 1

They reached a clearing. It opened to a wide expanse of plain. From the ground, a mist like a shroud slowly boiled over top of it.

TRIGLAV: Ahhh. I remember this place.

SYLVIA: Strange.

TRIGLAV: Not strange.

MURKER: Surreal. Cool.

Sylvia dropped her phone as she took it out of her side pocket to take a photograph. She reached down to pick it up, looked close at it and pointed out towards the mist, then half dropped, and half flung it down.

SYLVIA: Damn!

MURKER: What?

TRIGLAV: What did you see?

SYVLIA: The mist, there is something in it.

MURKER (raising his Rec-7): Where?

Triglav reached his index finger over to Murker's arm, pushed the Rec-7 downward.

Sylvia, now down on her haunches, intently stared at

the phone screen after picking it up and putting it in front of her eyes.

SYLVIA (frantic whisper): My God!

Murker rapidly approached. He reached over and pulled the phone from her grasp and pointed it at the mist, moving it around.

MURKER: Cool!

SYLVIA: What on earth are they doing?

TRIGLAV: Waiting. Preparing. Judging. By their condition, I would say they are anticipating something to happen very soon.

MURKER: Something?

SYLVIA: Can't we go anywhere in this country without some oddball something or other happening?

A windy whoosh sounded behind them, from atop the trees. The gargoyle Tratsch approached from the wind.

TRATSCH: I trust you require an explanation?

SYLVIA: Go on.

TRIGLAV: He has been following us.

MURKER: A spy?

TRATSCH: Guardian.

SYLVIA: The Pope's idea?

TRATSCH: But of course. You can't be too careful now. Everything rides on your mission.

MURKER: I like to hear that. We are important huh?

TRATSCH: Let us just say failure is an option not tenable in the maintenance of our future existence.

SYLVIA: Okay, okay. What's in the mist.

TRIGLAV: Winged Hussars. Hundreds. Thousands.

MURKER: They helped Poland rule this area for 150 years. Long ago of course. Probably some Hungarians in the group too.

TRIGLAV: I suspect, when their time to leave this earth came, they were given a choice.

SYLVIA: Okay, that's enough myth.

TRIGLAV: I kid you not. They chose to stay, waiting.

TRATSCH: As a scientist, Sylvia, I suppose you require evidence.

Tratsch looked deeply at Sylvia's phone. He fiddled with the connected wire to her earphone buds.

TRATSCH: Don't worry. We are merely spectators to this event. Sylvia, may I see that object?

She handed the phone to him, wondered what event was about to unfold. Tratsch touched the edge of the phone to the Polish soil. The phone he propped up against a series of small stones, so the camera lens pointed to the mist.

TRATSCH: Watch. There is still magic in this world.

They sat around the propped-up phone in a circle. Tratsch sat in the middle, in a relaxed manner, hands turned up on his thighs. He chanted in a tongue unfamiliar to all except Triglav. He then turned up the phone volume, possibly inadvertently after the earphone plug popped loose, but the music had changed to Brahms "Hungarian Dance No. 4".

Pencil thin rays of light crossed the center of the phone screen. The light beamed across at right angles, east-west and north-south, seemingly for infinity. The view of the Hussars becomes clearer and larger as Tratsch's words enhanced the phone screen size and depth. The Hussar's were assembled in a long row. The focus of the distance showed a huge army of demons of all imaginable shapes, size and contour. The Hussars suddenly begin moving forward on their horses. Faster, faster, faster. Then the Hussars, winged helmets searing brutal cries of the wind, hit the wall of demons with a loud clap and clang. The demons were annihilated, strewn and splayed, dismembered across the plain. The Hussars turned around and came toward the seated audience of Sylvia, Triglav, Murker, and Tratsch, who were transfixed. The Hussars dripped of blood, body organs, ears, eyes, limbs, fingers, toes, tails, horns all dangled from the Hussar horses, armor, and 10-foot-long spears which appeared like a shish-kabob of body parts and organs. The Hussars came ever closer, but they faded out and turned back into mist.

TRATSCH: Battle One. Won and done.

If there was such a thing as "rest" in this woeful place, the group returned to the Monastery to seek and find it. They were feeling good and light-hearted, having witnessed a victory in the first battle. Sylvia was concerned of the term "first" as she wondered how many more were to come. In Hugo's study, they intended to report the findings.

Hugo had apparently used the time to become idle and recruited a bottle of vodka to keep him company. His courage empowered by the bottle's liquid contents, he felt no regret in his use of the words his mouth paraded forward, loudly, to reveal his most recent and deepest wish and wonder.

HUGO: I know I am a mere Friar, Monk, Brother as it were, but I have always wondered what it would be like to lay down next to a woman, and . . . you know?

Sylvia was intrigued. Triglav, Tratsch, and Murker were somewhat shocked to hear such talk from a Friar. Each of the males managed to grin as they peered at Sylvia. Sylvia's hair, in the back, began to stand on end.

MURKER: Time to put the cork back in that bottle.

SYLVIA: Okay guys, I get your drift.

HUGO (addressing Sylvia, asked): Do you know where I can find a woman?

The guys, standing behind Sylvia, put their hands to their mouths in unison, trying to muffle their near guffaws. Tritsch was stationed on the ledge outside a window of the study, on watch, when she coyly responded.

TRITSCH: Here I am, you little chubby chub man.

Murker and Tratsch looked at each other; glanced a knowing expression.

TRATSCH: Rusalka bait.

MURKER (nods): Rusalka bait.

TRIGLAV (heading for the door): Time for my nap. See all of you later, I hope.

SYLVIA (exaggerated tone): Besides these three behind me . . . yes.

The guys glared at her while their smirks faded. Tritsch giggled.

SYLVIA: Out of the room!

"Black Dog", Led Zeppelin, played in Sylvia's mind.

The gentlemen skirted out of the room and pulled on the large, roundish, oaken door. It swished closed behind them. Hugo blushed, then went pale in the face.

HUGO (blurts out): What?

Sylvia cleared the Friar's worktable with one two-handed swoosh as Hugo backed away in surprise. She grabbed and spun him onto his back upon the tabletop. She straddled him, knees on each side of his waist, as the guys and Tratsch pressed their ears to the door in wonder. They heard male screams. Enough audible evidence having been obtained, they scattered to their respective evening quarters of the Monastery.

Later, Murker passed by Sylvia's room, heard strange sounds, and concerned burst in, to find a demon hovering over Sylvia, feeling her up (by Murker's crude ability to make such determination).

MURKER: So, that is it.

SYLVIA (surprised, but relieved that the demon had evaporated): What is it?

MURKER: Humans aren't good enough for you.

SYLVIA: Are you checking up on me?

MURKER: I heard a strange noise. I feared for you.

SYLVIA: What? Did you think I was involved in something? Not able to take care of myself? Now I must lock the door?

MURKER: Well . . .

SYLVIA: Is that all you think about?

MURKER: Well . . . I . . .

SYLVIA: What!

MURKER: I thought we were developing something.

SYLVIA: In your dreams.

MURKER: Don't you ever think of men?

SYLVIA: I was just thinking of you, as a matter of
fact, as you made disgusting sounds in the bathroom
down the hall. You think if you kill enough demons,
I will run to you, as if . . .

MURKER: No! That's not it.

SYLVIA: I think it is.

MURKER: Wait a minute.

SYLVIA (sarcastically): You were just trying to help,
right?

MURKER: Is this your moment? With a guy?

SYLVIA: Get out.

MURKER: You've never had this conversation before,
with a guy.

SYLVIA: What do you know? So, what?

MURKER: Nothing. Nothing.

SYLVIA: That's right. I have a life, it is seeking
knowledge, about certain things.

MURKER (whispers): Right. What was I thinking?

SYLVIA: Keep asking yourself that if you must.

MURKER (he bows): What? You can read minds? Good night, Milady.

SYLVIA: Whatever.

16

Hugo recommended to Triglav and Murker to take Sylvia down to a little river a few miles from the Monastery. He told them the walk would do them good, and especially, it was time for Sylvia to confront the demon inside her.

TRIGLAV (thought): I have a bad feeling about this trip.

Murker did his usual best effort to attract, in his view, Sylvia's affectations but just further succeeded in pissing her off and alienating her. Triglav stayed out of the mix; tried to play the diplomat. Baba Yaga had told them to cross a great river but provided no knowledge of a map.

Sylvia heard a song in the wind, a haunting sound. She recognized the music as "Stairway to Heaven", by Led Zeppelin. In this instance, Romanus' voice did the singing, audibled from an unknown source, and other demons made up the band (according to Brother Hugo's account in the journal he had created, after all was said and done).

Unfortunately, the minions of Romanus had staked out the river. Sylvia tried to cross the river as it appeared low in depth. Her feet were tired. She removed her shoes and socks and started to wade into the gentle waves rolling into the shore. When the water reached up to her knees, Murker and Triglav joined her, walked into the water, but a red sludge took over the waves. Murker and Triglav were strong enough to escape the river before the red sludge completely invaded. But Sylvia was caught in the pull, the tug, of invisible hands in the low tide.

Murker and Triglav were forced to witness the Baptism of Sylvia, now named "Sophia" by these earth-bound demon brethren of Romanus, into full demon status. Minions of Romanus and Rusalki ascended from the water to prevent Triglav and Murker from passing through a wall of wind that swirled in front of them, as they witnessed three dunks of Sylvia's head into the water.

A serpent-like beast, wearing priestly garb, arose from the water, performed the faux Baptism. Archons and demon minions encircled Sylvia.

MURKER: They are killing her.

TRIGLAV: No. They are Baptizing her . . . converting her into one of their own. They hope she will join them once they invade from the Pillar near the Monastery.

Dark and light clouds, claps of thunder, streaks of lightening were all around them, a strobe-light effect. St. Michael and other Archangels emerged from the light, attacked the Archons and the minions of Romanus. St. Michael forced the overhead clouds to become like rocks. The clouds started falling into the water to disturb the ceremony. The serpent priest snapped at the Archangels, kept them at bay. During the baptism, the water curled up, like musical Harps, and strings of water strummed into musical sounds by invisible hands as Sylvia's true hybrid self was revealed. She morphed into crow, rat, roach, and then the final combination, a Cratch, like her father Tihomir. To the demons, Sylvia now became known as Sophia.

TRIGLAV: She has now been given the full knowledge of their evil ways, so she may be tempted by it.

MURKER: Of course, they are using her human free will against her. What is she?

TRIGLAV: Be careful around her. Don't pluck any emotional strings, or she may involuntarily transform from human to creature, at least until she learns how to control the urges.

MURKER: I think St. Michael is talking to me. My mind is flooded with thoughts of protector. He is trying to convince me to be her brother, not a lover.

TRIGLAV: Free your mind. Accept the counsel.

MURKER (dazed): Yes, yes. It is working. My mind has accepted the new purpose. Such a relief. Honestly can't say I don't like it.

TRIGLAV: Perhaps this moment is your Baptism, too. St. Michael has gone. Sometimes he goes rogue but looks like he was called back. Fairly sure we are on our own for the rest of the way.

Triglav added that Murker should never try to call Sylvia by the name "Sophia", if he knew what was good for him.

MURKER (solemnly): Got it, big guy.

17

Romanus' Lair, mountain near Holy Cross Monastery

ROMANUS: So Cratch, how are you today?

Cratch, Tihomir Goralski, is chained to a cave-like
wall, stuck in his morphing state.

ROMANUS: Time to tell all.

CRATCH: Never.

ROMANUS: Oh, come on. We have been at this game for
25 years now. Surely you must be tired of it?

CRATCH: I told you a thousand times. I didn't get
there in time. She was aborted. You can have one of
your minions or human traitors check the FBI records.

ROMANUS: We did! FBI guy is a vegetable, or near so,
I'm afraid. Dementia. We worked on him hard. He
finally hid inside his innermost cellular place.

CRATCH: And now he is trapped.

ROMANUS: Your daughter, Sylvia, we call her Sophia
now, is indeed alive. And we WILL find her. Or maybe
we should just let her find us.

CRATCH: No!

ROMANUS: I hear some earth demons baptized her into
our culture. She is hard to find though. Hides like
a possum.

Romanus waved to one of the Ohdows. The Ohdow pulled
a lever and a sharp, thick sword blade popped out of
the cave wall in a long slit behind Cratch's neck,
sliced off Cratch's head and the head rolled halfway
across the cave floor. The enzymes in Cratch's blood
extended like taffy a thread trail to retract the

head. Another Ohdow pulled a different lever and it loosened the lead-lined chains from the wall, like a leash, allowed Cratch to meander around, search for his head.

He was on all fours, waving his arms around, then stopped, and closed his eyes, used his telepathy from the enzymes which long ago infected his body and put him in this state, to send out a signal to his severed head. Parts of his body, from the severed neck area, gushed out slowly, snake-like, searching for the head, until they had it, and slowly reeled it in like a fish on a hook, until it attached back to his body. Then the Ohdow pushed the lever back up, and the chains violently pulled Cratch back hard against the cave wall.

A long vein-like tube appeared above Romanus' head. He listened to vibration sounds emanated from it.

ROMANUS: Something is brewing. It is all over the collective consciousness.

A Cheshire cat grin crowded his jaws.

ROMANUS: It won't be long now.

18

Hugo assigned the crew to another mission. They were tasked to make a trip to Auschwitz to attempt recruitment of lost souls who may remain. No instructions were given for the undertaking, other than "if you can find them, help them". Find "who" and "how to help" wasn't accompanied by any measure of advice. They loaded up the Jeep, attached to which was a small-windowed trailer for Triglav to occupy and remain out of sight, and started the mid-December 300 plus miles trip. They arrived about 8 hours later, in the evening. Hugo had given each of them entry passes, but Triglav indicated they weren't necessary, yet didn't explain himself. Sylvia pocketed them anyway, just in case.

On a crystal-clear night, Triglav, Sylvia and Murker hunkered down, close circled around a small but blazing orange-red fire. All were cloaked for warmth. Triglav suddenly stood up. He spied the Christmas Star. He started singing "O Holy Night". Sylvia and Murker reacted, stunned, not knowing of this talent from the big guy. The winds started blowing lightly in the greater camp environment. A pleasant chill massaged Sylvia's spine.

SYLVIA: That was beautiful.

Triglav bowed. Sylvia wiped a tear from her eye.

MURKER: You sounded like Josh Groban. Hey, still not sure how we got into here.

TRIGLAV: If we were not welcome, the souls here would not have allowed it.

MURKER (sniffs): Smell that?

They looked around, Triglav still standing. Thin reams of phantasmal smoke emanated from one of the building towers in the distance.

Intrigued yet perplexed, they all made their way over to the building. After some time, they heard dancing and singing of songs in the building. The smoke stopped rising from the roof top as they moved closer.

TRIGLAV: Spirits of the dead, at Block 15. If I am not mistaken, smoke will rise from Blocks 14 and 16 too.

MURKER: Weird.

SYLVIA (whispered): Hush. Please show respect.

Triglav suggested they wait outside. He will encounter the spirits, if they so allow.

TRIGLAV: They know we are here. The ghost smoke, the sounds, were a means of communicating to us.

Triglav entered Block 15. Sylvia felt the presence, along the outside wall, of some adult female spirits. Her demon blood allowed her access to such an inclination. Murker could only see flashes of light and dust moving, as if he had cataracts blocking his vision. Quite a bit of time had passed. Murker's silence started to concern Sylvia. They each sat down and leaned back against the outer wall.

SYLVIA: You okay?

MURKER: Sure, sure.

She wasn't convinced. Then Murker felt a warmth on his left cheek, near his ear lobe. He reached up to rub it. Sylvia could see the spirit of a middle-aged woman as she attempted to unriddle his aroma.

SYLVIA: I think she likes you.

Murker looked to his left.

MURKER: I see nothing, but it is warmer to my left.

Triglav then appeared from around the far corner of the building. He explained his encounter. He said he convinced some of the spirits he could help them ascend to their next domain, if they helped in the coming cataclysm. They at first expressed reluctance, but when he explained a current evil may be extinguished, some agreed. They promised to spread the word to some of the other Blocks.

TRIGLAV: Some are not ready. Some are still in mourning. Perhaps they know something we don't.

MURKER: Like, even if we should be so lucky as to eke out a victory in the coming mess, we may still need their help in the future, when they're ready.

TRIGLAV: Yes . . .

19

Dvorak's "Slavonic Dance, Op. 46, No. 6 in D Major", sounded from overhead loudspeakers, courtesy of a CD Sylvia borrowed from Hugo.

Battle 2

The Demon minions' Captain sat around a table also inhabited by Sylvia, Triglav and Murker. Captain, whose face displayed a partially fuzzy and obscured definition as if maimed during some catastrophic event, was dressed in World War I officer's garb, including a Prussian Pickelhaube helmet adorned by brass accents and an Imperial Officer's Spike on top. Captain's personal minion poured vodka into shot glasses arranged around the table for each being seated. Captain stood and turned and looked outward and below him. Then he raised his glass of vodka to his Lieutenants, who stood taut all around a solid floor of red sludge that almost looked like an ice hockey rink. Then Captain turned to his guests and raised his glass to Triglav, Sylvia, and Murker at the immediate table. His toast rang out as, "To innocence". All raised glasses. Some sipped, some guzzled, some inhaled. They turned and looked out to the red sludge occupants.

A crystal chandelier hovered high above the sludge surface, emulated the appearance found in a large ballroom. The chandelier began a light sway, then swirl, after which a white haze the length and width of the rink surface, slowly descended. As the mist faded and disappeared, the presence of beautiful women, of varied ages and dressed in flowing soft gowns, stood next to each of the Officers around the rink. Others of the women hovered above on the edges of the rink, as if on a balcony. Triglav, Sylvia and Murker looked at each other in shock. The Demon Captain, unaware of the plot, clapped loudly at the beauty and glory of the scene below. Dvorak's "Slavonic Dance, Op. 46, no. 8 in G Minor" boomed in earnest, at which point the women grasped the outstretched hands of their selected Officers' hands (some hands were more like claws) and engaged in an enchanting dance upon the red sludge surface.

Captain seemed content in the quality production of this prelude to a war gathering. What the Captain didn't understand was "Battle 2" had commenced and proceeded like clockwork before his sullied vision.

CAPTAIN: So glad I suggested you provide the entertainment.

TRIGLAV (smiled, bowed head): Don't mention it.

As the dance ended, the women from the balcony switched out with the women on the red sludge surface. The Lieutenants who danced were looking a bit weary, as if their "energies" had been drained, which was exactly what happened. The next group of women would finish off the production. As the chandelier lights went dimmer in shine, Khachaturian's "Waltz" from "The Masquerade Suite", thundered into action. The earlier mist returned, from above and below, but left only doorways of clearness as the couples danced in and out of misty folds along the sludge surface. The red sludge began to undulate and melt. The dancers slowly modulated up and down along the less solid surface as the previous women spirit dancers descended again and matched two each to one Lieutenant. The entire scene now looked like the finest wedding cake ever created, as the dancers visibly vibrated, rose and fell in intensity. The mist gave peeks of the scene every so often, enough to trick the mind from moments of suspense to explosions of grandeur.

SYLVIA: Why don't you join them, Captain?

CAPTAIN: Join me, my dear. You look divine in that Peasant dress.

They each ascended, arm in arm, to the mist above the dance floor, stopped just below the dimmest glow of the chandelier and floated downward amidst the chaos of the mist, undulating red sludge and intensity of the Waltz musical chords. Triglav could see the faces of the undead and demon Lieutenants and Captain, the faces of the Auschwitz spirits, and Sylvia's face, which transformed into the face of a Cratch as she rested her chin on the left shoulder of the Captain's service coat. During varied views of the rink below, Triglav noticed the Captain's head missing, then on another pass of the mist, his lower body had disappeared, then finally, Sylvia standing, or rather floating on what was now complete liquid form on the rink surface. Sylvia had entered complete Cratch transformation. Murker didn't notice as he took care of the minion table server, not in a nice way, until its earthly existence was extinguished. Sylvia's vengeance had reached exhausting proportion. She was about to collapse, but Triglav jumped down to prevent her from being sucked into the sludge. The spirit dancers raced to Triglav, held him up on his way down, steadied him, so he could cradle Sylvia in his arms. Then Triglav, clutching Sylvia, was carried back to the Captain's table above. Triglav, kneeling, still holding Sylvia, looked up at the Auschwitz spirits.

TRIGLAV (slowly voiced, holding back a tear drop): Thank you, thank you.

The music stopped. The spirits then ascended along a vertical tunnel of mist, skyward. Murker returned to the table, swishing demon detritus from his hands. He approached Triglav who was still kneeling. Triglav cradled Sylvia to his chest as she transformed back to human form.

MURKER: Is it over?

TRIGLAV: Almost, my friend; at least, for this evening.

20

On a foggy morning, a hard, flat ground, bordered in a horseshoe shape by a tree line of oaks, just outside of Holy Cross Monastery, served as a stage for the chirps, tweets and whistles of local avian life. Gradually, the bird sounds slowed, dissipated, stopped as sounds of movement in the brush and surrounding forest area increased. The sounds were footsteps of bodies sweeping along the vegetation of the forest interior. At first, no order to the sounds could be characterized as measured. Human voices, low growls, muffled howls floated into the fog. Talk of the events at Megiddo pervaded. "No word yet" was the rumor. A Pillar known to be in that region likely engaged troops amassed from many nations. Hugo had not been updated by The Holy See regarding efforts initiated by The Pope during his in-person, world-wide visits to repair the seals of the known Pillars. Normal communications via mobile or electronic means had become spotty and now were non-existent for days. Even second protocol communication efforts, using winged messengers (vampires in this case) had ceased. Nevertheless, efforts at the plain adjoined to Holy Cross Monastery churned to completion and readiness. Triglav suspected The Pope didn't make it out of Megiddo, as Hugo had been incessantly playing the sounds of Vivaldi's "Filiae maestae Jerusalem" in the Study.

Battle 3

The troops milled around fringes of the plain, wearied, ragged looking. For many, a long arduous trek preceded the brief respite before war. Living, dead, undead, mythical beings and creatures had united, for this time, perhaps only time in earth history to help repel Romanus The Scarlet Beast from gaining dominion over the planet, or at least this part of it in the Slavic lands. Another rumor floated into the minds of the warriors: The Pope died trying to repair the Pillar seal in Mount Tabor at Megiddo which subsequently unleashed the escape of Bahamut and Leviathan to roam as they pleased. Of the varied conclusions roaming about the warrior groups, one involved Bahamut and Leviathan joining up with Romanus. Triglav, out on reconnaissance, encountered the whispers of this morale deflating consciousness.

Triglav tried to give an inspirational speech. It didn't strum the strings of hope he had hoped to engender among the groups. Finally, in desperation, he stated loudly: "Vodka for everyone!" A rousing cheer rippled through the motley fighter crews. "Turn on the music" someone in the crowd shouted.

Trans-Siberian Orchestra's "Christmas Eve/Sarajevo" magically blared among the black oaks. Crates of vodka, shipped from the finest distilleries in Poland and Russia, were virulently cracked open like gunshots. Speakers mounted in the high oaks (by Hugo's doing, aided by Tritsch and Tratsch, under the theory, if there was music to alter the plots of the demon hoard, there must be music utilized to inspire the protectors of earth plain) blared the music sound into the forest and across the plain. Then the festivities really started as Savatage's "This is the Time" resoundingly blasted into the plain, cleared the fog. The Pillar seemed to shake in the distant mountain. Clouds of black emanated from varied parts of the mountain terrain and buzzed towards the still rigid grounds.

Triglav tried to bring into the real earth world the spirits of the Hussars. The call to war had begun. He used his lightening energy to send the signal but at first succeeded in only frying some oak trees, and unfortunately some of the ghostly Hussars. A few of them, their spirits turned to glistening puffs of light, then floated upward. One audibly rang out a curse, in Polish tongue, "O, kurwa". Triglav's saddened face slipped out the words, "Damn, no vodka for him now. I hope there's vodka in heaven."

Polish guerilla warfare tactics and Russian ingenuity were inherited traits. The Russian human and undead, seasoned on the Battle of Stalingrad, and the Vampyr, the Neuri werewolves, and the undead from centuries of Polish and Russian military exploits, hid themselves amidst and among the trees. Some of the Hindu Vampyr had already pledged to shout, "Long Live Apu!" when the fighting started. The spirits of Katyn Forest Officers had been offered and readily accepted the task to lead the respected troop units.

"Les Indes Galantes" by Rameau, mysteriously from the heavens, peeled across the plain. Triglav started to wonder if not Angels on high were using music to attack the airborne demon hoard expected to soon approach towards the plain. Hugo could see everything transpiring below and around him from his Monastery window. He penned his observations like a spider spinning the web necessary for the feast to come.

Pre-planned depiction of this battle would involve explaining Slavic battle tactics, such as the peasant pawns in the front, in old history, using pitchforks and wooden pikes, a first row of short mesomorph types, almost dwarfish in appearance, who dropped and thrusted upward, then rows of jumpers, who leaped over the front rows like chess Knights, using the dead or dropped bodies as leverage, then a cavalry attack from the Winged Hussars, which eventually sandwiched the enemy for a final rear guard assault. Such tactics were not the case, because the demon hoard leaders would anticipate it. Tratsch had planted the idea among some of the demons hovering near the mountain, well in advance. The demon hoards were locked into, convinced of what they expected to see when the battle commenced.

Vivaldi's, "La Follia", played in Hugo's head greeted by the emanated sound from the basement and filtered through the walled pipes. Then Hugo heard the musical sounds filter through and about the exterior rim of the mountain, the interior halls and towers of the Monastery, which meant it was also transmitted to Romanus's lair deep in the mountain, and all throughout the mountain interior. Hopefully, the sound was wearing all the interred demons and exterior stationed demons down into a mucky mist of hopelessness.

The demons were well attuned to the musical tastes of the Slavs, so when Hugo beamed Tchaikovsky's "March Slav" through the mounted oak tree speakers, the demon leaders expected a grand march onto the battlefield. The demons sent out a first wave of smallish blob-like balls of multiple extended limbs, larger type octopi, and winged medium-sized serpents. They descended upon and just over the field. The solid ground of the field started to bubble and ooze red slime which served as an energy source for the demon horde.

Yet, no Slav warriors or allies appeared upon the field. The first of three Demon troop leaders then directed a march into the woods which surrounded the plain. The demon soldiers entered the central woods in columns. Still there was silence. The wind took a rest. Even the music had stopped. The sun became covered by dark clouds. A light rain began to fall. The two other troop columns fanned out to the left and right but did not yet enter.

The second Demon commander had halted his group to await the outcome of the first group's entry into the now darkening wood. Many grunts and groans could be heard, intertwined by silence as raindrops began to pelt into the oak leaves of the tall oaks. After many minutes, the first demon group didn't emerge. The second group entered; a bit wary. The same condition resulted.

By now, the red slime on the plain, combined with the rain from the heavens, coagulated into a mucky mess of mud and sludge-like material. Navigating the plain became difficult by foot.

Some winged demons flew to the forest and dropped lighted torches and balls of fire, but they were extinguished upon striking the soaked trees and mushy ground therein.

The tactical point of this first level of the Holy Cross defense was based on Tratsch's findings at the Megiddo battle. Many demon troops had survived. A significant number of Megiddo demon warriors followed Bahamut and Leviathan, each of whom wanted to control the Pillar at Megiddo but could not agree who would stay at Megiddo and who would travel to Holy Cross Mountains to assist Romanus, in the covetous hope of gaining more Pillar control for each of themselves. The Pope had survived long enough to give Tratsch a message about such intrigues, so Brother Hugo could be warned.

On the Polish plain at the Holy Cross Monastery, Bahamut and Leviathan now appeared, each leading demon warrior troops. The third Demon leader of the remaining troop force declined to enter the forest as the first two groups had not returned. The music started blaring again across the plain, just after the rainfall concluded.

Orff's "O Fortuna, Carmina Burana" played in Triglav's head. Triglav knew all the demons couldn't be killed, only contained or controlled, because the minds of humans were potential transmitters of their evil; and if those minds functioned, the battle would continue, just not on such a grand scale, but by small leaps and bounds, over and over, until another Megiddo day, another Holy Cross Mountain day. Human frailty and Demon evil had become a patchwork quilt, inseparable. The goal was to once again entrap as many of them as possible behind the binding Seal of the Pillars, for as long as possible. Triglav hoped Sir Newton was wrong about 2060.

Amidst the concerns of the battle plain, Sylvia had embarked on her mission, which was to neutralize Romanus.

Romanus The Scarlet Demon, seated on his throne in the bowels of the mountain, looked upon his prisoner, Tihomir, in disdain.

Romanus The Scarlet Demon feared the menses of human women. He coveted the control of evil in humans. He had imprisoned Cratch, and another weapon that could kill him: the souls of the unborn dead and aborted. Their cries created a sound that was more powerful than energy of an atomic bomb when focused properly. Their voices, in the dead world, were legion. They could ring a devastating barrage of sound and fury through the giant mountain core, more searing than the blast of the shofar. The sound could disintegrate evil of the Demon nations; splay their bodies; splinter their souls like fine glass; annihilate any possibility or hope of resolution or restoration.

Romanus The Scarlet Demon made way along a tunnel and escaped from the ever-failing Pillar Seal; stood at the edge of the Seal doorway; looked at the valley plain. Then, his voice, to his credit boomed forth.

ROMANUS: Here and at Megiddo, humans will perish, have perished! The Armies of humans, humanoids are fated to their last stand.

TRIGLAV (wondered): He's getting a little bit ahead of himself.

Bahamut and Leviathan struggled, and their grudge match spilled out onto the plain. Many demons perished, crushed during the confrontation, as the Winged Hussars charged in, a solid ground unnecessary to transport the spirits of their noble steeds. The Hussars' feathered wings screeched a hostile sting of sound as they plowed across the red sludge plain from the unguarded side of the battlefield. Their steeds puffed steam from nostrils like the smokestack of a locomotive. Hooves pounded into the solid ground before entering the red ooze, spraying grass and mud balls everywhere. The first long and wide grouping lowered lances and glided over the red sludge, impaling every living, undead and demon thing along their path. The next wave did the same, and the next, and the next. All that was left in the way of a battle on the field was for the remainder of the ground forces to emerge from the forest for cleanup, feast on the detritus of meat, bone, flesh of the plain. The detritus feeders, including the efficient Revenants of the Allied Holy Cross forces, were unleashed in a fury upon the red sludge field and finished the deed like clockwork.

Each unwilling to bear the burden of a defeat, Bahamut and Leviathan retreated, perhaps to continue a long-standing appetite for blood and lust into eternity. If that meant ignoring the machinations of the human earth world, so be it. Their concern wasn't whether the earth world would be better off, for now.

The haunting sounds of "Smoke on the Water", Deep Purple (Bahamut) vs. "Unbreak My Heart", Toni Braxton (Leviathan) music trailed off in the distance. (Note from Brother Henry: I told Brother Hugo I didn't want to use this excerpt from his war journal, but he insisted. Apologies.)

Sylvia had transformed into her Cratch II state and waited for Romanus to step out of the Pillar opening. Triglav had climbed to just below the Pillar step. He reached up to grab The Scarlet Demon's leg, but he slipped and fell along jagged rocks as he is tried to push the Demon completely into the opening of the Pillar. Sylvia spied the action, pulled the Ankh from her side pocket, jumped down onto Romanus' head and shoulders from behind, plunged the Ankh into the spine of Romanus, and her weight pulled him backwards into the long, wide tunnel connected to the Pillar doorway. Triglav climbed back up to the Pillar ledge, looked at the darkness, but could see nothing. He was unable to squeeze far into the tunnel due to his extreme size, yet he saw a spatter of blood along the tunnel wall. Triglav remained half conscious and became weaker, bled profusely from his left side, at the Pillar entrance.

Vivaldi's "Summer Presto" started from the horns of the Holy Cross Monastery, played faster than ever heard, by the Holy Spirit Nuns. Their violins stroked impeccably the instruments as the sound poured into the Romanus cavern along timeless pathways and ancient boreholes. On the way down, along the rounded tunnel walls, Sylvia lost a grasp of Romanus. He disappeared fast into the tunnel depths of which he was familiar, and she was not. Sylvia used her long rat nails to grip along the sides of the tunnel, until she was stopped by the dirt floor which opened into a small hallway. She then retracted the nails from one hand and pulled from her pocket the broach case, held it in front of her to help clear the way of debris as it emitted a beam, like a laser, and shaved off some of the tunnel walls in order to fit her body inside as the circumference closed in at certain portions. Her sense of smell was heightened by the Cratch II transformation. She could follow Romanus like a predator sniffed out prey. She entered the parallel Realm of Romanus and his minions, into a large, high ceilinged hall. It was a place where humans couldn't survive unless cursed by possession of a demon spirit.

The Ohdows quickly overtook her during the time she adjusted to the underground atmosphere, as she had lost some of her Cratch II anatomy and retracted to human form due to her weakened state. She saw to her left, chained to a wall, what appeared to be an undead, a zombie, of scaly skin, yet hairy. Sylvia squinted a closer look. Use of her enhanced senses revealed the creature as her father. He did not die at age 35. Perhaps the enzymes protected his human body beyond the timed limit of the curse abomination. Sylvia knew the Onionhead spirit still inhabited her at the time of the Demon baptism. Some of the Onionhead spirit may still possess her father, too, clamped inside by the experimental enzymes.

The Onionhead curse of her father, at this point in her young life, had become a blessing. She could only survive the atmosphere of the parallel Pillar Realm because of the curse. She still clasped the broach, as she had retracted it into the body of her hand while the Ohdows chained her. She used the broach beam to break the chains on each wrist. The Realm atmosphere overtook her again until she almost lost consciousness.

A piece of debris from the ceiling hit Sylvia in the head, and she started to resuscitate. She sensed another being above her. Romanus, about to seat himself on his underground throne, looked back, shocked and peeved off to see her, while the Ohdows congregated at his back to remove the Ankh. And at that moment, he noticed the broach case open and the head of the Solomon's pin aimed at him. The pin seemed to know when and how to react to a target. A gold beam from the pin pierced Romanus' chest and struck the spinal cord as partially paralyzed he became. From above, Dina's spirit stirred Sylvia forward. Imbued by an adrenalin rush, Sylvia moved faster and stronger. She fully transformed into Cratch II again, flew forward at incredible speed and jumped upon a weakened Romanus, vengefully tore him apart with her claws and bites, then gave him a direct shot of the broach pin laser until he passed out.

Sylvia continued her attack right into Romanus' chest as her father's own rage began to take over. The broach beam glowed brighter and wider, cut through and across the Scarlet Demon's body, like a Hari Kari cut, until a quarter of the torso was lopped off, and the Demon became disabled. Sylvia, energy and inspiration spent, collapsed to the floor.

Triglav, able to hear the goings on from far above, barely breathing, intoned softly "It is done."

Bach, "Toccata and Fugue in D Minor" played in Hugo's Study, but Vivaldi's "Winter" portion of the Four Seasons filtered into the Pillar Realm and across the plain of war.

Alternative perspective of battle (according to Tihomir / Cratch I, yet he admitted he was in and out of a state of consciousness at the time, chained to a wall in the Demon's Hall, like a mounted trophy; in hindsight, these accounts are like the New Testament gospels as each recounts an event some of the others do not):

Romanus and Sylvia fell to the end of the tunnel as she pierced the Demon's spine with the Ankh. The round end of the bracelet Tihomir had long ago provided to Sylvia's grandmother, Nana, surrounded Sylvia's hand. The long end extended from her palm.

As the two hit the ground, Sylvia's head became severed by a swipe of the Demon's sharp, talon-pointed paw, but because she was part roach, and she inherited Tihomir's enzymes into her biology upon inception, she didn't die. Her brain still functioned. Tihomir, chained to the far wall, used the energy he had left and shouted, "All hope is lost, long live all hope!" He shook and pulled the chains that bound his limbs until they started to crack and crumble. He transformed into mostly rat and leapt toward Sylvia, stabilized her, and carried her over to a side tunnel, yet her head remained in the Hall.

Romanus commanded the Ohdows to put Sylvia's head on a pike. He mocked Sylvia, called her "Sophia", while the Ohdows helped Romanus sit on his throne which had been brought in from the main chamber. Romanus' body had been torn apart at the midsection during the fight and he bled profusely from the back of his thoracic spine region where the Ankh protruded. Romanus concentrated on the repair of his body, used his mind as a surgeon would use a hand upon scalpel. An Ohdow hopped onto Romanus' lap to help guide the ghost-like scalpel. More Ohdows appeared and feverishly worked to repair Romanus' body as he spouted insults at Sylvia's head. Sylvia's head murmured, "The Ankh, need the Ankh". Romanus reached to his back and pulled the excised Ankh from the Ohdows, then flung it into the outer corridor in disgust.

Tihomir held Sylvia's body, in the more roach-like phase, as he slowly moved towards a side tunnel that housed a cloudy pane of glass-like seal over it. He didn't know what an Ankh was and how it could be useful, but he had heard Sylvia's whisper. Suddenly the Ankh came scrapping across the corridor floor. He lowered Sylvia far enough for her hand to grab the Ankh, then lifted Sylvia up to the cloudy pane of glass. Tihomir had grown to know about the inhabitants on the other side of the glass from the Ohdows over the many years of his imprisonment. Sylvia's right arm struck the Ankh into the glass seal, turned the Ankh until the seal was pierced enough to allow a larger hole to grow, and out poured winged, tiny pairs of eyes. The eyes screeched cries and giggled laugh sounds, like the sounds of young babies.

Sylvia's head asked out loud "What is this?" from the main Hall, as the winged cherub-like creatures flew wildly into the room around her impaled head and among the room's dark parts. Romanus nervously bellowed "The millions of souls of unborn humans extinguished since the beginning of time. They are part of my collection, among other souls and spirits." The lost souls' eyes fluttered about, in the unison of hordes of bats, banged into everything in their path. Their eyelashes acted like whips, and their clicking movement slashed and gashed everything touched; tore skin from the panicked Ohdows. Then the lost souls horded themselves into a large, spear-like form.

Romanus' shuddered. His concentration was broken
which stemmed the effort to repair his trunk. The
Ohdows fell like mush piles of flesh and bone and
blood and organs as separate hordes of the lost souls
descended upon them like wolfen packs. Romanus' fate
was then sealed in the same manner, as the spear of
lost souls extended into a multi-pronged trident,
penetrated his flesh and tore it apart. The lighted
essence of Romanus The Scarlet Beast escaped to the
main chamber where it entered a liquid pool,
reanimated as only a stew of the bacteria and slime
of pre-history, biological and chemical life. His
being remained, but only in the form of a primordial
state: still living, yet subject to the eons of
evolution's rules. Only the passage of time could
bake him into the Demon who could resume a reign of
terror upon humankind.

The baby-eyed, winged souls swarmed Sylvia's head,
pulled it off the pike and carried it to her body,
still cradled in Tihomir's arms, where they placed
her head upon the eager tendrils of holy flesh, blood,
sinew, bone. Sympathetic Ohdows then assisted in
sculpting her head back to her body, where the enzymes
in her body helped reanimate her entirely. Tihomir
had run out of energy and collapsed right after Sylvia
was completely restored. Sylvia had to transform into
Cratch II form to obtain the strength to carry him
up the tunnel and out to the Pillar step.

Triglav, seated on the edge of the Pillar ledge,
almost recovered from his wounds, helped them both
down a bit, until Sylvia felt comfortable enough to
fly as a fully transformed crow and carried her father
up to the Study window of the Monastery, where Tritsch
let her in so Tihomir's wounds and mental state could
be addressed. Sylvia returned to the battlefield to
check on Triglav . . . and to search for Murker.

Triglav had one more task: to Seal the Pillar. A
massive white stream of flashing wings attached to
beautiful, innocent eyes ascended from the Pillar

doorway and up into the heavens. Laughs and squeals
of joy echoed all around, into the trees, into the
distant mountains. Triglav's remaining strength was
enough to call forth a large, javelin like bolt of
lightning. He then hurled it at the Pillar which
electrified, re-energized and sealed the Pillar once
more. The energy stream was enough to restore the
seal breadth all around the mountain.

SYLVIA (scratched her head): I have often wondered
why we just didn't try that when we first arrived
here.

TRIGLAV: The Holy See and Brother Hugo knew your
father was trapped inside and would continue to be
so, for as long as the Seal lasted on the Pillar.

SYLVIA (not satisfied, as usual): But what about...

TRIGLAV (interrupted): Also, only you and your father
together offered the hope that the imprisoned unborn
could be released to the "next" plain of existence.

SYLVIA (thought): They saved us.

At battle's end, "The Battle of Evermore", by Led
Zeppelin, blasted from the speakers at Holy Cross
Monastery. Casualties were assessed, and Murker
couldn't be found. After many demons and other being
body parts were sifted through, a shout came that
Murker had been found, but his health state remained
uncertain. He was barely conscious. Blood stained his
left arm, which was half severed, and puncture marks
pocked his chest. Murker was dragged to safety.
Sylvia and Triglav came around to see him. They tried
to make him comfortable, seeing he had mortal wounds
to his chest.

SYLVIA: Wait . . . I haven't tried this before.

She grabbed Murker's knife. Cleaned it on her pants;
cut a slit in the fat pad on her hand and made a fist.

The blood dripped, and she held the fleshy spout over
his chest and the severed portion of his arm. Murker
saw what was happening.

MURKER: No . . . I saw what you are . . . at the
River. I don't want to become that.

SYLVIA: Are you ready to check out then?

TRIGLAV: It works for Vampires.

MURKER: That's what I'm afraid of.

While Murker was saying this, Sylvia squeezed the
blood into his wounds. Murker didn't realize it
because he faded into a daze.

TRIGLAV: Nothing is happening.

MURKER: I said no. I don't want what you have.

SYLIVA: Are you sure?

TRIGLAV: Maybe needed isn't the Cratch blood, maybe
it is the saliva.

SYLVIA: Saliva? Yes, maybe.

Murker was losing consciousness.

TRIGLAV: Kiss him, on the lips.

SYLVIA: Yes . . .

Sylvia leaned down, kissed the almost unconscious
Murker on the lips. Murker started to have a seizure
like tightness in his face as his teeth clenched.

TRIGLAV: Spit in his wounds.

Sylvia complied.

SYLVIA: Sphht.

Murker's body started to heave, his arms and legs
began to jiggle. Sylvia and Triglav backed off. Then
Murker's seizure suddenly stopped. A tear began to
fall down Sylvia's cheek while her eyes were closed.
Triglav's eyes were also closed and his head tilted
to the ground. Murker's eyes slightly opened.

MURKER: I saw that.

They helped him to his feet. Two Yeti blooded
bodyguards, who hailed from a village in Siberia,
assisted.

Triglav walked among the dead, undead, shattered
spirits who littered the plain. He kneeled before an
old near branchless Willow.

TRIGLAV: I miss you, hon. The world has changed so
much, things have gone strange.

He touched the round middle of her trunk.

21

A smoky haze began to cover Tihomir's eyes, as he lay on the body-loaded and blood-stained Polish plain. The nations of the world had already met their partial demise on the Jewish plain of Megiddo, according to Romanus' proclamation during Tihomir's imprisonment. Tihomir wondered whether boasting or wishful thinking had triggered The Scarlet Beast's proclamation. Tihomir remained uncertain of the fate of the events at the other Pillars. He squinted to try to peer through the haze. He couldn't tell, in the distance, whether Sylvia had accomplished her mission. The Pillar appeared as a pin in the distance. A dark blob rested on top of it, thrashing about. The plain had the appearance of a Hieronymus Bosch level of hell. His vision faded out. He awoke from the dream.

A bright light poured upon him, after a cold wetness pressed as a blanket across his face and partially blotted out his vision. An elderly looking woman, dressed like a nurse volunteer, wearing a black wool-knit sweater, gold buttons lining one side of the sweater, seated to his right, smiled at him. She held a cup of water but didn't sip from it. A small, rather thick book occupied her hands which were placed on her lap, as he rested on his back in a hospital bed, hooked to an I V tube, his face gaunt, his limbs thin and unmuscular, atrophied from non-use.

Tihomir asked, "Am I dead?" The nurse responded, "You're back", as her voice bathed over him. Tihomir, still in a daze, asked in a confused look "Where am I? What happened?" The sun started to rise, tried to shine through the cracks of the dark brown Roman shade. The nurse's voice said, as she stood and walked towards the eager glare of the window, "What WILL happen is your concern." Tihomir thought she would lift the shade, but she didn't. "Is Sylvia okay?" he asked. Silence.

He could no longer see the nurse. He blinked a few

times to adjust his sight. The light continued to attempt penetration into the room from the shade, but it was held back, remained truncated and could not find his body where he lay in the shadows. The woman's voice uttered one more tidbit of counsel, "There is much more work to do . . . I think you may understand now". Draped over the back of the empty chair to his right, as the nurse's body faded into the thin lines of light from the window shade, he noticed a black wool knit sweater. Pinned to one side of the sweater was a name tag which read "Dina".

Pachelbel's "Canon in D Major", transformed to "Christmas Canon" performed by Trans-Siberian Orchestra, flowed into the room from a ceiling mounted speaker.

His rat sense then kicked him. The aroma of fresh and recently baked kruschiki's, Angel Wings, bow ties, coated in powdered sugar, lit a spark of temptation in him. His roach sense detected, outside in the hallway, about 100 feet away, on a desk at the Nurse's station, a bounty of culinary bliss. Another mission loomed in the offing. He almost moved, almost transformed, almost accepted the mission. Instead, he accepted a sensation of the kruschiki aroma as the means to please him. He imagined he was flying.

Demons to some may be Angels to others. In the shadows, he still lived, for now, in the shadows.

End Ave Megiddo

If you enjoyed this book, don't forget to leave a
review on Amazon!
I highly appreciate your reviews, and it only takes
a minute to do.